No More Tears

Eva Abbo

No More Tears

Copyright 2014 Eva Abbo

No reproduction without permission

I dedicate this book to:

Freddy Abbo, my soul mate, my life companion and the happiness we've shared.

To my beloved:

Ileana, Eran, Larry, Susy, Edward, Karen, Jonathan, Michael, Daniella, Daniel, Alexandra, Michael, Ariella, and Gabriel, the lights that illuminate my path.

... and to all my loved ones and dear friends.

Acknowledgments:

To Freddy Abbo for his invaluable computer tutorials, technical assistance and overall support.

To Stefanie Resciniti for the magnificent book cover design.

To Loriannne Weston for her professional translation and dedication.

Chapter 1

One lovely December afternoon, migrating birds from the north crossed the sky in perfect formation, guided by their leader in search of a safe haven to spend the night. The leaves in the grove of trees danced in the wind and from the underbrush, a serenade of chirps and croaks cast a magic spell over the multicolored December sunset, a tonal explosion against the metaphysical blue backdrop of the heavens.

Karen crossed the threshold of the door of the master bedroom and as she continued down the wide hallway, an enormous gilt-framed mirror on the wall reflected her profile: young and slim, with a strong cast to her face, a fair complexion and coltish legs. Her face hinted at her anxiety over the events to take place that night; however, her luminous blue eyes shone with tenderness and tranquility. Her blonde tresses moved freely in the way that Philip preferred. The black Giorgio Armani dress set off her figure. She had on a single strand diamond necklace, set with exquisite artistic taste in white gold. Earrings and a bracelet completed the picture – gifts from her husband for their anniversary. She descended the broad staircase with a slow but determined step. Her heart beat anxiously. So many thoughts crowded her mind. Can this be real or is it just a fantasy, she wondered. She continued to the main floor and began to look around at the familiar surroundings with a loving gaze. She was the owner of a stately mansion, that reflected her personality by its elegance and simplicity. It was completely modern, but warm and cozy at the same time. The entrance, in Carrara marble, was partially covered by a scarlet Persian carpet woven with exquisite designs, typical of the oriental style. A Henry Moore sculpture was the centerpiece in the left wing of the entrance, leading to a spacious living room, furnished with soft furniture, refined paintings and decorations, and many expensive and unusual curios, all aesthetically placed on the various end tables and consoles. A quick glance at the elegant dining room, in cream lacquer, also showed everything to be in order. She and the servants had all worked hard, to make tonight especially successful.

A few minutes later, the waiters began to move like clockwork to be ready for the guests. Exotic tropical blooms of varied colors in fine crystal vases, placed at strategic points, gave off a subtle fragrance that complemented the aristocratic setting. The musicians had not yet arrived, but the hostess was not worried since they were known for their punctuality. Her husband was not yet home from the office, either. Glancing at her tiny, jeweled wristwatch, she saw it was still early, and feeling calm and happy, she went to the study to enjoy a few minutes of solitary meditation. She made herself comfortable on the sofa, and with a deep sigh closed her eyes, and went over in her mind, to the momentous milestones leading up to this most important moment in her life. She clearly remembered everything. Her mother had told the story so many times...

Poland, late 1919

The Belgian stallion trotted quickly through the sandy, snaking pathways of the *Shtetl*, leaving in his wake a cloud of dust. His panting breath kept time with the constant opening and closing of his thick, black lips and sweat from his efforts glistened on his long mane muscular body, and full tail. A carriage full of luggage hooked on behind prevented the horse from moving more quickly, but it was still early and Joseph Kupperman, who confidently held the reins in his hands, had enough time to deliver the luggage to its destination.

Theresa fixed her gaze on her brand-new husband: young, twenty-four years old, six foot four, virile and handsome, with a straight nose and light brown hair. As she relaxed with the pleasant view and the constant rocking of the horse-drawn carriage over the dips and rises in the road, she became infused with a deep feeling of peace and weariness. Turning to the right, she admired the profuse wheat fields extending for acres into the distance, their tall stalks dancing in time to the wind, presenting the traveler with a view of endlessly swaying, magical, golden rays. Further ahead, a group of horsemen galloped across the pathway, and on the other side of the road, she could make out several straw-thatched huts and some peasants gathered in a lively discussion.

"I feel so sorry for those people!" she exclaimed aloud. "Their work is terribly hard. They get up at dawn, till the fields, care for the animals, sell their produce to the highest bidder, and at the end of it all, their hard-earned wages are barely enough to ensure their precarious subsistence".

"How do they trade their products?" Joseph asked her curiously, startled by her sudden outburst.

Surprised by the question, she thought for a few seconds and then answered:

"There is trade between Polish and Jewish farmers, which doesn't only include buying and selling goods, but also a kind of barter based on each one's needs. Unfortunately, there is a lot of suspicion and tension between them because of their religious and cultural differences."

Joseph turned his head, impressed by her thoughtful answer. He realized in that instant how intelligent she was. That she was beautiful, he already knew. She was young like him, graceful, with a slim figure, and firm breasts that were concealed under her white cotton blouse which was buttoned up to her neck, and long, slim legs peeking out from the swirling green and gray checkered skirt. Her thick mane of hair, the color of the setting sun, was held loosely by a gray headscarf, in a fetching tangle that fluttered in the wind. Her fine features and cheekbones, and the curvaceous outline of her full lips, were what first attracted him to her, when he arrived in the village. He rejoiced silently in the abundance of her intellectual and physical qualities, and he felt renewed admiration for his beloved wife. He clicked the reins and urged the horse on to Warsaw.

The time passed as his gaze shifted from the skyline to the broad, ancient trunks of the leafy trees, to the wonderful wide green fields where wire fences divided each lot and farm, some with chickens and geese running, filling the air with strident cackles and honks, and the occasional pig snuffling in his constant search for food.

Conversation between the newlyweds was sparse, except for the odd question or to point out an exceptional view along the road. Each was deep in thought, replaying the many events of the past few days. Joseph was a recently graduated civil engineer from Warsaw University, and his parents, who were childhood friends of Theresa's parents, agreed upon a *Shidduch*[1], because they were confident of the family's moral and religious background. When Joseph obtained employment with a construction company, and considered himself financially ready, he asked his parents to present the formal request for marriage to the Sprintis family through the matchmaker. The answer was affirmative, and from that moment on, both in the village of Jalowiec, where Theresa lived, and in Warsaw, preparations began for the couple's marriage.

Marcos and Anita Kupperman's arrival with their children in Jalowiec, was a happy event. The families had not seen each other for many years, and the occasional bit of news sent by a visiting traveler could not compare with the years of growing up together, when Joseph's and Theresa's parents had lived in the same neighborhood. In accordance with Jewish tradition, the groom was called to read the *Torah*[2] on the Saturday preceding the wedding. Family members and guests joined in the prayers sung for the occasion. The rabbi, in his speech, interpreted the prayers as symbolic of entering a new stage of life. At the end of the ceremony, those present threw candies, raisins and nuts in Joseph's direction, to wish him a sweet and fruitful future. Later, Theresa gave him a silk *tallit*[3] that she had made, with a decorated neckband and the four corners reinforced with squares of cloth perforated in the middle for the fringes, in accordance with biblical law, to remind the wearer of the divine commandments.

---

[1] *Shidduch*. Hebrew name for the marriage arrangements and negotiations that take place between the parents of the bride and bridegroom. (Author's note)

[2] *Torah*. Hebrew term meaning doctrine or teaching. (Author's note) Books of the Torah. Manuscript or scroll that contains the Pentateuch and is read during a synagogue service. (Author's note)

[3] *Tallit*. Prayer shawl used by Jewish men during religious ceremonies. (Author's note)

On Tuesday, the wedding day, the couple fasted and prayed, according to custom, to ask God's forgiveness for past sins committed so they could begin a new life together. Before the marriage, the *kinyan sudor*[1] ceremony was held: The rabbi gave the groom a handkerchief, to seal the engagement. He blessed a cup of wine and toasted for their happiness.

Finally the time for the solemn celebration of the marriage had arrived. Theresa, dressed all in white, with her lovely face covered by the traditional veil, was a vision of loveliness. Abraham and Sylvia Sprintis, impeccably attired for the occasion, led her by the arm down the aisle, one on each side, between the rows of chairs where the guests were sitting. The bridesmaids, each holding a burning candle, lit the way for the bride toward the *chuppah*[2], where Joseph, accompanied by his parents, was waiting for her.

Romantic strains of music filled the hall and Theresa, radiant in her pure-white gown and with a pounding heart, moved forward with firm, graceful steps, prepared to embrace this most important event that her destiny held for her.

Once the couple and their parents were gathered under the canopy, Rabbi David Morawski began to read the *ketubah*[3]:

"On the second day of the week, fifteenth day of the month of Adar of the year 5679 according to the Jewish

---

[1] *Kinyan sudor.* Means handkerchief agreement. Under Jewish law, exchanging handkerchiefs in this way confirms a purchase or transaction. (Author's note)

[2] *Chuppah.* Nuptial canopy formed by a silk cloth or other material set on four rods. The bride and groom stand under this canopy while the marital blessings are pronounced in symbolic representation of the couple's future home. (Author's note)

[3] *Ketuba.* Written marriage contract. (Author's note.)

calendar, corresponding to March 17, 1919 of the era in which we now reckon, in the village of Jalowiec, in Poland, the sacred bond of marriage was celebrated between the groom, Joseph Kupperman, son of Marcus Kupperman and Anita Kupperman, and the bride, Theresa Sprintis, daughter of Abraham Sprintis and Sylvia Sprintis. Said groom made the following declaration to his bride: Be my wife according to the Law of Moses and Israel. I promise with all my heart to be a faithful husband to you. I will honor and cherish you eternally, keep you and protect you. I will give you shelter and all that is necessary to sustain you properly, in accordance with the duty of a Jewish husband. In addition, I assume all my relevant obligations for your maintenance during your whole life, in accordance with our Holy Law. In the same fashion, in compliance with the precepts of Jewish tradition, the bride accepted her respective duties and solemnly swears to be eternally faithful to him, agreeing to fulfill all the duties of a Jewish wife in accordance with the religion. This marriage union has been duly carried out and witnessed on this day, in accordance with the custom and Law of Moses and Israel."

The couple and the witnesses all signed the documents. Then the couple drank wine from the same cup that was given to them by the rabbi, symbolizing the joy and sadness that they would have to face together as a couple. Joseph, with deep solemnity, took Theresa's hand and slipped a simple gold ring on the index finger, and she, gazing into his eyes, repeated the gesture with a similar ring. Finally, the rabbi placed a wineglass on the floor in front of the groom, who, upon the rabbi's signal, smashed it with his foot[1].

---

[1] The breaking of a glass represents an expression of mourning for the destruction of the temple in Jerusalem (Author's note)

"*Mazal tov!*"[1] the guests shouted and began to wish each other well, while the newlyweds exchanged a kiss to seal the signed agreement. "*Mazal tov!*" was heard again and again. The bride and groom started down from the *chuppah* holding hands, under a storm of rice and nuts thrown in their path to wish them a fruitful and prolific life, and went to a nearby room where they were finally alone for the first time.

How restrained Joseph was, out of consideration for his wife's youth and inexperience. He did not wish to do anything that would frighten her in any way at their first meeting, even though, in accordance with Jewish custom of the time, they were supposed to consummate the marriage. This went by quickly in a happy blur. Everything that happen on that night, seemed like a dream.

Unfortunately, happiness is never complete unless it is accompanied by a moment of sadness, in this case, having to say goodbye.

Sylvia hugged her, reminding her of her duties as a Jewish wife. Abraham kissed her gently on the cheek.

"I will miss you, my darling girl", he said, fighting to hold back a choked breath.

"So will I, father. Please promise you will visit me in Warsaw as soon as you can", she begged, as a tear slid down her cheek.

"I give you my word " he answered.

"I will hold onto that". "Until we meet again, dear brothers and sisters. I will write you often. Please write back quickly."

Sarah squeezed her in a strong hug, trying to make the moment last, with a sudden premonition that she wouldn't see her sister again for a very long time. Max

---

[1] *Mazel tov.* Good luck, happiness. (Author's note)

came forward to join the family group. Joseph, moved by this scene, invited them all to come and visit in their new home.

"Thank you, answered Abraham", pulling his other children away from Theresa.

The newlyweds got into the carriage and taking the reins in his hand, Joseph gave them a snap to get the horses going.

"Theresa, my heart goes with you!" yelled Max, crying.

But she didn't hear him anymore, choked by her own sobs.

"Please don't suffer", her husband begged, moved by her sadness." My family will be your family. My parents, brothers and sisters will return home next week. They are warm, caring people and you will get along with them easily. They will help, in part, to fill the great emptiness you feel being so far from home".

"I hope so", she answered, catching her breath, still recovering from the separation from her family.

Night fell, and the faithful horse continued at a steady clip, when suddenly the sound of its hooves hitting pavement startled them.

"We are getting close to Warsaw!" exclaimed Joseph excitedly, shaking off his thoughts.

They began to see rows of houses lining the road. She observed everything with interest, since this was her first time out of the village. As they passed a street of shops, by the light of the streetlamps, Theresa admired the variety of shops, shoe stores, hat shops, clothing stores with mannequins modeling the latest fashions, fabrics and gabardines.

"There is too much traffic", he commented with fatigue, wrinkling his brow.

Theresa gazed speechless at the intersection filled with

streetcars, droshkies, buses, cargo wagons and bicycles.

"Oh, Joseph, the city is marvelous! I never imagined there could be so much life, so much action and light. It is incredible".

"Yes, it is", he answered, understanding her excitement. "My wife is enchanting", he thought to himself, with satisfaction and pride.

The carriage continued forward, moving away from the downtown area of the capital. The streets became darker; still, one could make out the outlines of buildings and flat areas that were the parks and plazas. Joseph turned the horse, to the left, onto Franciskanska Street, went a few more blocks, and then he pulled up on the reins to come to a stop.

"Finally, we have reached the end of our journey. We are home".

As she stepped down from the carriage, Theresa could just make out the building: four floors, with wide balconies, of a vague, dark color.

Arriving at the main entrance door, they rang the bell and a doorman came out quickly to help them unload the luggage. Climbing up to the third floor was difficult, but as she went through the door, Theresa became aware of the luxury throughout the apartment. The cushiony golden carpet stretched out as far as the eye could see. Hand-carved, dark wood furniture filled the living and dining rooms. A case with beveled crystal glass stood in the most visible corner of the room and she could see that it held a *Hanukkah*[1] candelabra, a silver cup for the blessing over the

---

[1] *Hannukah.* (in Hebrew, dedication) or the festival of lights. It commemorates the victory of Judah Maccabee over the Syrians in 165 B.C.E., which led to national independence and the dedication of the Temple that had been profaned by pagans. (Author's note)

wine, a *siddur*[1] of the same material carved with colored symbols for the Twelve Tribes, a breadboard with a mother-of-pearl knife for the blessing over the bread, and a Passover bowl. Paintings by famous Jewish artists covered the walls: Rybak, Barlevi and Glicenstein.

"Come, Theresa", Joseph urged, taking her by the hand. I want to show you the rest. "Do you like the bedroom?", he asked her in fluent Yiddish, showing her a large room with a double bed decorated in pastel colors. Night tables in natural polished wood stood by each side of the headboard, and the goose down comforters on the bed were covered in white scalloped material, with Joseph's initials embroidered in the center.

"My grandmother, may she rest in peace, embroidered these. She was a very special woman".

A desk was visible in the corner of the room, and sitting on it, was a bookshelf holding leather-bound volumes, somewhat worn by use, by such authors as Dostoyevsky, Tolstoy, the brothers Grimm, Strindberg, Heine and various specialized engineering books.

They went down the hall, where a bathroom with blue and white tiles could be glimpsed.

"The second bedroom will be for our children, and you shall decorate it as you like", he said, while noticing a deep blush creep over Theresa's face.

"Now, let us go to the dining room and have something to eat. The maid is a Polish peasant girl. You should speak to her in her native language, since she doesn't understand Yiddish".

The table was set impeccably, in honor of the new mis-

---

[1] *Siddur*. Prayer book for the synagogue that contains the order of the religious service, adapted from the ancient rituals of Temple sacrifices. (Author's note)

tress of the house. The silver candlesticks belonging to his grandmother had been set out. Telsa served an exquisite meal. Quick by nature, she bustled around trying to please them. She was a pretty woman, of medium height, with large, dark eyes and a full mane of taffy-colored hair pulled back with a ribbon, distinguished in her dark blue uniform with the white apron and cap.

"My darling, is our new home to your liking?" he asked her anxiously.

"I love it! It feels so cozy and comfortable. It has a real feeling of home".

"The tea service is ready in the next room *proszepana*[1]", they heard Telsa say. He took his wife by the arm and led her to an aquamarine loveseat where they both sat down, in front of a glass-topped table edged in gold metal and adorned by several Lalique crystal pieces and a vase of the same material holding a bouquet of flowering buds and baby's breath.

"The swan is beautiful", she exclaimed, touching it gently.

"Theresa, now that I have a moment alone with you, I want to tell you about my family".

He paused briefly, then continued.

"Papa is sixty-two years old, from a pious and orthodox Jewish family; he is a self-made man, very cultured, who is also both intellectual and spiritual. He struggled until he became the owner of the best jewelry shop in the country, located in the city center, and his ability as a diamond cutter and connoisseur is renowned. His wealth now allows him to enjoy the rest of his life comfortably, yet he still continues to be a tireless worker, demanding the same dedication from himself and from his employees. On the other hand, my

---

[1] *Proszepana*. Polish, sir. (Author's note)

mama is the typical *Yiddishe mama*[1], faithful to the Jewish traditions. Her home runs like clockwork. She has the unconditional support of the three maids and Gerardo, the gardener, who has worked for us many years. With an expert eye, she watches over everything that goes on in her home. She is completely in charge and yet, very loving. "What a matriarch!" – he exclaimed with a smile. "Rivka is a typical older sister of twenty-five – very serious and responsible. She got married at a young age to Ariel, a doctor in the capital, and they are an exemplary couple. As parents of Halinka and David, they are demanding but fair, and are very loving. Shoshana is fifteen years old, my favorite, and extremely funny. She is sometimes crazy, and gives my father big headaches, but her explanations are convincing and usually papa and mama put up with her stunts. Finally, Golda, little Goldaleh, as we lovingly call her. She had her eleventh birthday recently, and is always the center of attention because of her sweet and compliant character. Once in a while this is a sore point with Shosana and she gets jealous and furious, but they do love each other sincerely and always make up in the end".

"You have a wonderful family!", said Theresa with feeling.

"With time, you will grow to love them as much as I do. Now, let's go to sleep. I can see you are tired from the long trip".

Holding hands, they made their way to the bedroom and began to undress. Theresa finished buttoning up her white cotton nightgown, slipped into the bed and covered herself with the down comforter, enjoying the feel of the clean, starched sheets. Almost immediately, Joseph turned off the light and lay down beside her. After a brief moment,

---

[1] *Yiddishe mama*. Jewish mother. (Author's note)

the yearning newlywed bride felt his hands slip softly over her body. Slowly and sweetly he began to kiss and caress her. He didn't show his passion at the start for fear of startling her, given her youth and inexperience, but their closeness fired the desire in their young bodies. She tensed up instinctively, not knowing how to react as he took her lovingly in his arms, hugging her and seeking out her lips. He dominated her gently and his caresses became gradually more urgent until he could no longer contain himself. He pressed his fevered body against hers, and with rhythmic movements, he took her.

The lovers moved slowly apart and absolute silence reigned in the room. Theresa remained motionless in the dense darkness with her eyes open, trying to come to terms with the experience she had just had. "He is my husband", she mused with acceptance after a few minutes," and our marriage has been consummated."

The construction company where Joseph worked had given him a few days off for his wedding and he decided to organize a tour of Warsaw to familiarize his wife with the city. They left early the next day, after a breakfast of exquisite rolls, eggs, and café-au-lait prepared by Telsa, and went to Warsaw University, where Joseph had completed his engineering studies.

"My university", he said proudly, showing her the enormous columns of carved, gray stone at the entrance. "It is one of the largest in Europe, with ten thousand students here currently. The main building, built on the spot where the Kazimierzowski palace stood, was originally built by King Ladislaus IV in 1653, and was destroyed by a fire. Further ahead you can see the Faculty of Medicine, Engineering, and Architecture..."

He pointed out the various faculties and they came out again onto the main road. Continuing down the street, they moved on to the Warsaw Grand Theater, built in 1825 in the classic style favored by Corazzi, and bedecked with ornate decorations, tapestries, and paintings. They passed by the Warsaw Philharmonic concert hall, the Bank of Poland building, and the Blue Palace, a classic structure holding the Zamoyski Museum and famous library of the same name. They stopped at the monuments to Joseph Poniatowski, the immortal military hero, and at the bottom visited the Tomb of the Unknown Soldier. Finally, they gazed in awe at the Royal Castle, with its majestic salons and drawing rooms, and a gothic wing dating back to the thirteen and fourteenth centuries, from the days of the Mazovian Dukes.

"The castle is wonderful!", exclaimed Theresa.

Every citizen of Poland has a special place in his heart for this fortress. For several centuries it was witness to important historical events and the scene for both triumphs and defeats. The invading Swiss vandalized it, but in the early eighteenth century, King Augustus III rebuilt it, raising a new wing on the side overlooking the waters of the Vistula and the picturesque countryside. The interior renovation of the castle cost millions of zlotys for the fees of artists, painters, and sculptors, among them such names as Fontana, Merlini, Kamsetzer and Bacciarelli, who restored it to its former splendor. They walked through the throne room, the reception hall and the marble salon. As they left the castle, thrilled by the beauty of the historic architectural monument, Joseph suggested they finish off the delightful and unforgettable tour by stopping for lunch in a restaurant.

"I am starving"! he said playfully. "Let's go now."

"What can I get for you?", the waiter asked, as they sat down.

"For me, borscht[1] with potatoes", answered Joseph immediately, "and for dessert, a piece of apple strudel[2]".

"The same for me", added Theresa, "but I prefer cold borscht with yogurt, and water to drink".

"Madame, would you like some wine?".

"No, thank you".

After the waiter left to place the order, Theresa said happily:

"Oh, Joseph, Warsaw fascinates me. I am so excited that I will be living here. I know I will be happy with you".

"I am glad to hear you say that, my darling. All new beginnings are difficult, but a positive attitude like yours will help to overcome any problems that may occur in the future".

After a few minutes had passed, she asked about two people who had come into the restaurant.

"They are *Chasidim*[3]," he answered, taking in their beards, side curls, long coats and hats. "They study the Torah, wear ritual fringes and use phylacteries at their morning prayer".

"My father also studies the Torah and Talmud", she said. "At night, he and several others who are also dedicated students, go to the synagogue near our house and spend hours learning there. I admire them deeply. The Torah is written in ancient Hebrew, which makes it very difficult to understand".

---

[1] *Borscht*. Traditional Eastern European beet soup. (Author's note)

[2] *Apple strudel*. Pastry prepared with apple and phyllo dough. (Author's note)

[3] *Chasidim*. (From the Hebrew word, Chasid, meaning in Biblical literature: benevolent, charitable, and in rabbinical literature: pious, scrupulously religious, or holy). The Chasidim or pious ones is the name given to a specific Jewish group in the Hellenist era, characterized by their strict religious beliefs. (Author's note)

"I share your admiration, Theresa. After so many years of persecution, Poland has given the Jews the chance to practice our religion and enjoy a rich, flourishing culture. To have *kosher*[1] homes and food, synagogues, study halls, Chasidic prayer centers, libraries, newspapers and Yiddish theater. The authors, poets, literati, journalists, musicians, and painters have the opportunity to exhibit and publish their work without having to suffer persecution, thanks to the Minorities Treaty[2]. Marshal Pilsudski's military coup in May, 1926, eliminated the parliamentary regime and opened the doors to antidemocratic, nationalistic, and reactionary aspirations. But there is an ironic twist to this story. Pilsudski, in order to preserve his dictatorship, was obliged to reject his anti-Semitic principles and ally himself with business magnates, powerful landowners, and representatives of political and social ideals that were opposed to the interests of the workers and peasants, and the Jews had been integrated into the middle class for centuries, being pillars of the economy in the areas of business and industry".

"How interesting. I would love to hear about it in more detail", she commented animatedly.

The waiter brought them the check and they paid and left the restaurant without lingering. They took in the warm

---

[1] *Kosher.* (in Hebrew, clean, acceptable) In general it is used to denote ritually pure foods and the dietary rules followed at home. For example, a Jew may only eat certain animals as defined in the Bible or according to rabbinical interpretation considered not to be impure. Kosher may also refer to a Torah scroll free from blemishes, a child born of permitted marital relations, etc. The observation of the whole set of rules is known as Kashrut. (Author's note)

[2] Minorities Treaty. The Minorities Treaty of June 28, 1919, was signed in Versailles between the allies and Poland, and guaranteed full equality of rights to minority groups, whether religious, linguistic, or ethnic (Author's note)

breeze from the Prague Forest, a suburb of Warsaw, joined to the city by the bridges crossing the Vistula River. They were young and carefree. The world was theirs. Joseph took Theresa's hand and pulling her along, exclaimed:

"Let's go to the bazaar. I want you to see a typical market".

They crossed the narrow streets, bordered by endless rows of unpainted houses with smudges of dust and smoke coming from the chimneys, and wet clothing hanging from pegs on long lines, flapping in the wind, all of it permeated by a penetrating smell of garbage. Along the way they were startled from their reverie by the sight of barefoot, dirty children crying from neglect. Finally, they arrived at the square.

"You can find anything here", said Joseph, leading the way.

They wound their way between stands and baskets belonging to sellers of fruit, vegetables, meat, chickens, ducks, and many different kinds of fish. The cheese, milk, and yogurt looked fresh and appetizing.

"Step up! My prices are cheap", they heard a lady call out in Polish. "Butter for 65 zlotys a kilo, bread for 20, potatoes for 6.50, milk for 3.50". Joseph stopped and bought a bouquet of flowers for his wife.

"Theresa, where are you?", she heard him calling once when he lost sight of her.

"Looking at these fabrics. Here to your right."

"For you", he said, giving her the flowers.

"Oh, thank you, they are lovely".

"Do you like this cloth? "she nodded, smiling.

"It is yours".

They paid for the purchase, and bought several other items that Telsa had asked for, and finally, they wearily headed for home.

The days passed and the Kupperman family returned

from their trip to Jalowiec. On Friday night they all walked to the synagogue, a wondrous place. The wooden building had magnificent coffered walls and pagoda roof indentations. The central structure rested on four columns in the middle of the main hall, and the walls and crowns of the columns displayed Jewish motifs, such as a *menorah*[1], a *shofar*[2], flowers and pentagrams. The red pile carpet stretched out from the main entrance door, which was made of solid wood, and ended at the foot of the sacred ark on the eastern wall, which was covered by an embroidered, velvet curtain held up by a thick golden bar with two impressive-looking lions on the cornice. Eight small lamps were placed in front of the ark, symbolizing eternal light, and a huge Star of David and stone tablets of the Law were displayed on the upper section. The bimah, or table for reading the Torah scroll, was placed on a platform in the middle of the room, and the officiant's pulpit next to the ark, set into the floor, to show the humility inherent in prayer.

The rows of benches were facing the ark, and Marcos Kupperman sat in the second row next to Joseph, looking proudly at him. He was his only son, and had fulfilled his father's highest hopes. The prayer service had not yet started, and the congregation kept coming up to congratulate them on the recent marriage. From time to time, he

---

[1] *Menora.* In the bible, a candelabra. Religious symbol used since ancient times. Since the inception of the modern State of Israel, it is the official emblem of the Israeli government. (Author's note)

[2] *Shofarr.* One of the most ancient wind instruments, made from a ram's horn, wich produces a sharp, penetrating sound. It has played an important role in Jewish life, since ancient times, and is still used today during the services for Rosh Hashanah (New Year) and Yom Kippur (Day of Atonement). (Author's note)

would point to the place on the upper balcony level[1], where Theresa, sitting beside her mother-in-law and sisters-in-law, was being introduced to the other ladies, who were wishing her happiness in her new married life and welcoming her to the community. She greeted them warmly, favorably impressed by their refined manners, elegant clothing, and their unusual, fair beauty.

Suddenly, the room fell silent. The officiating rabbi opened the sacred book and began to pray, followed by his faithful congregation. Their voices resonated throughout the hall, deeply concentrated on the service. The intense illumination in the hall reflected off the glass walls, breaking into hundreds of rays of light, giving the synagogue an air of mysticism and majesty. The service ended with the singing of Adon Olam[2], and Joseph, adjusting his tallit, which was about to slide off his shoulders, stood up to shake the hand offered by his father with a greeting of "*Shabbat shalom*[3]."

"*Shabbat shalom*", he answered, giving him a warm hug. "Come, father, let's find the ladies. It is time to go home."

The table looked splendid set with a traditional white tablecloth, a four-armed candelabra with burning candles that had been blessed by Anita before leaving for the synagogue, the two challah[4] loaves covered by a cloth embroidered in gold thread and the silver wine goblet full of wine. Marcos Kupperman got up from his chair and looking over

---

[1] In orthodox and conservative synagogue congregations, the seating is not mixed between genders. A special area is reserved for women, usually the balcony. (Author's note)

[2] *Adon Olam*. Special prayer praising God. (Author's note)

[3] *Shabbat shalom*. In Hebrew, peace be with you for the Sabbath. (Author's note)

[4] *Challah*. Offering of bread dedicated to God. (Author's note)

the table, began to recite the *kiddush*[1]. Theresa watched the family with respect and reverence. The scene was familiar to her. A feeling of warmth and devotion was palpable in the room; it was the same feeling she had on Friday nights around the table with her parents and family, praying the same prayers, and singing the same songs. The meal was served expertly by the three maids, looking clean and elegant in their black uniforms with white aprons and caps. The conversation was pleasant and Theresa felt warmly received. At the end of the evening, the whole family, holding hands, danced to the rhythm of *horas*[2] until fatigue overcame them.

---

[1] *Kiddush*. (In Hebrew, blessing). Ritual to proclaim the sanctity of the Sabbath. (Author's note)

[2] *Horas*. Typical Jewish dances. (Author's note)

Chapter 2

One warm May morning, the sky rejoiced as a flock of jubilant larks soared and dipped with giddy spins and loops, in delighted enjoyment of their endless freedom in the infinite space. Rachel trekked through the countryside, bedecked in spring blossoms, deeply inhaling the fresh, delicate perfume of the wild flowers. She was on her way to school. When she was about a hundred yards away, she spied a group of people gathered behind the classrooms, and heard a confused murmur of voices. Spurred on by curiousity, she quickened her step. Students were not usually in the yard at this time. As she arrived, she noticed them staring at her, strangely silent, and they made way to let her pass.

"What is the matter?," she asked anxiously.

No one answered. Suddenly, in the midst of the group of young people, she made out the figure of a boy lying on the ground. He was lying on his stomach, his head turned to the side, as if asleep, with his eyes half-open. A thread of blood seeped from the corner of his mouth. His skin was pale, except for a bruise on his forehead. Suddenly she recognized him.

"Mendel! It can't be. What is the matter?. What has happened to him?" she questioned in a tremulous voice, her wide eyes reflecting her increasing fear.

Immediately, with an impulsive movement, she leaned toward her brother, almost touching him, and cried out in a voice choked by fear:

"Mendel, tell me what is wrong! Why did this happen? Please, answer me!"

Receiving no answer, she knelt down and began to touch his body, looking for some sign of life, but the boy remained motionless and cold.

"Mendel, Mendel, answer me, please!" Rachel insisted, sobbing.

The school's principal, Mrs. Popovich, who was watching the scene and seemed to be quite upset, moved closer to Rachel and looking at her with a distressed expression, bent toward her with her hands on her knees and said quietly:

"Your brother was just hit by another boy, and we didn't think he should be moved. We have called the doctor and he is on his way. Please, try not to worry!"

"But, Mrs. Popovich, why isn't anyone helping him? Look at him! He is so pale. It looks like he isn't even breathing."

Mrs. Popovich shuddered inwardly as she heard Rachel's questions. Could the child have died while she was phoning the doctor? she thought anxiously, and kneeling down beside Mendel, with a shaking hand, she felt for his pulse.

"No, Rachel! Thank God, he is alive and breathing. The doctor should be arriving any minute now."

Rachel continued to try to wake her brother, pleading and patting his cheek, but seeing no reaction, she stood up crying and suddenly noticed Esther, a friend from school.

"Esther, were you here when this happened to my brother?"

"Yes, Rachel. When we were crossing the yard to go into the classrooms, a Polish boy with a threatening expression yelled at us, "Go away, Jews, we don't want you here." Mendel was with us when the fellow began to yell and he continued to stare at him without saying a word. Then he started insulting us with nasty, rude words, trying to start a fight, but when no one answered his insults, he got even more angry and picked up a rock from the ground and threw it hard at Mendel. There was no time for him to dodge the rock, and when he was hit, he fell down flat on his face. He hasn't moved since. The Polish boy, after this, ran away as fast as he could."

"No one tried to stop him or talk to him to try to prevent the attack?," Rachel asked, nervous and confused.

"I'm sorry. We were all paralyzed by shock."

Rachel shook with anguish and suddenly ran away from the scene. She needed to get away. She couldn't believe what had happened to her brother. Mendel was a quiet, kind boy who didn't like to fight. Rachel ran and ran. She had to tell her mother what had happened.

"Mama, mama," she screamed as she arrived at the main door of her house. "Open the door, please."

Sarah was in the kitchen. She was hurriedly preparing dinner, since she had to leave soon to go work at the store with her parents. Hearing her daughter's voice calling, she ran down the stairs.

"Rachel, what are you doing back so early? What is the matter? Are you all right, child?"

"It's Mendel, mama!. He doesn't answer me. He's lying on the ground in the schoolyard, unconscious. A boy hit him very hard and the doctor is coming."

Sarah stared at her daughter, horrified, and without

stopping to think, began to run. Tears blurred her vision. The long kitchen apron tangled between her legs, preventing her from going more quickly. Yet, she could not stop.

"Mama, mama, wait for me," called Rachel.

But Sarah didn't hear her. She sobbed and thought of Mendel. What could have happened? Why had they hit him? My dear son hurt – Oh!, please God, don't let it be. Help me, make it be all right, please let it be nothing.

Sarah continued running, until she made out the group gathered in the distance. Anxiety tore at her. She wished she could run faster. She had to find out what had happened.

Rachel had fallen behind. Although she was running as fast as she could, she couldn't keep up with her mother and her mind was full of tortured thoughts. Poor mama! She is always so worried about us and now I have to be the one to bring her bad news. She has enough problems already with seven children to feed and clothe...on top of her work, tiring her out day after day. She continued in this way, running and fretting, arriving at the scene a few moments later.

Sarah drew close to the group, just in time to see several nurses placing her son into an ambulance on a stretcher. The doctor was supervising the attendants, making sure they followed his orders. Mrs. Popovich, seeing Mendel's mother coming toward them, stepped aside to speak to her.

"Mrs. Ratovich, I'm glad you are here, I am very sorry about what has happened. Come this way, please. The doctor can explain more about your son's condition. As you may have heard by now, he was attacked by a boy who is not from our school. This way, please, follow me. Doctor Wasserman, this is Mrs. Ratovich. She is the mother of the injured boy. "

"Pleased to meet you," said Doctor Wasserman holding

out his hand, and seeing the mother's expectant expression, silent and suffering, added:

"I have just examined your boy, as best I could under the circumstances. He appears to have a severe concussion. We must take him immediately to the hospital. If you wish, you can come with us."

Sarah wiped her tears away. She couldn't speak and felt confused. Gathering her wits about her, she nodded mutely. She was shocked by what she had just seen. Nothing could have prepared her to see her son injured and being placed in an ambulance.

A nurse, noticing the urgency on Doctor Wasserman's face, stepped out of the vehicle and came over to Sarah, saying:

"Come this way, Ma'am, let me help you get in. You can sit beside the stretcher. Be careful going up the steps; don't trip. Keep going all the way to the front and you'll find a place to sit. Carefully, please."

Sarah went to the place indicated and sitting down, looked over at Mendel. The boy's eyes were half-open, and he was extremely pale and still. His mother felt her eyes filling up again with tears. With a superhuman effort, she calmed herself down and taking her son's hand between hers, she began to murmur in a choked voice:

"My darling, sweetie, it's mama. How are you feeling? Does your head hurt very much? Please, try to answer!"

She waited for him to answer, but Mendel remained blank and lifeless. In a stronger voice, she continued to urge him:

'Mendel, Mendel, answer me. Tell me that you are all right, please, speak to me."

After a short while, she began to cry again.

"God help me!" she begged, "don't let anything happen to him."

One of the nurses, noticing her desperation, patted her back gently and said:

"Ma'am, have faith. We will be at the hospital soon and your son will be helped by the best doctors. Please, don't worry."

She stared as if not comprehending anything, although at some level she felt grateful to the nurse for her concern. She turned back again to Mendel and began to pray fervently. Seeing her son like this was unbearable. Only a few hours ago, she had been saying good-bye to her sons as she did every day before they left for school and Mendel, her beloved son, was a lively, joyful child. Now, here he was lying on a stretcher and nobody could tell what might happen from the blow to his head. She caressed his face lovingly, as if trying to erase all evidence of harm from him, and thought pensively:

"What will happen to my son? Dear God!..."

The ambulance turned off the main road and slowing, drove up to the side entrance of the hospital where a large sign indicated: "EMERGENCY". Two nurses were already waiting for them, having been alerted by the ambulence siren, and they immediately went toward the vehicle where it was stopped and began to open the rear doors. They rapidly pulled out the guerney where Mendel was lying and transferred it gently to the ground. They moved inside and after entering the building, picked up their pace, rushing down the hall. Sarah followed them closely, with a hurried gait, but as she reached the two large swinging doors leading to the emergency room, a uniformed man stopped her.

"Ma'am, you cannot go in here. Please go to the reception area," he said, pointing out the way. "You need to fill in some forms to admit your son."

Looking back in the direction where Mendel had been taken, she moved silently to the area he indicated and with a shaking voice, identified herself to the attending nurse. She was a pretty girl, with almond-shaped eyes and long, dark brown hair held back by her white cap, wearing the white uniform of a professional nurse. She asked Sarah in a soft voice,

"How can I help you?"

The anguished mother took a few moments to answer, trying to put her thoughts in order.

"My son has had an accident and they just brought him in to the hospital. I understand that I have to fill in some papers for them to admit him."

"Where did they take him?"

"To Ward Nineteen," she answered tearfully.

"Please, try to be calm. Your son will be fine. I'd just like you to fill out these two sheets. As soon as you are done, give them back to me and we can admit him."

Sarah looked at the nurse with a vacant expression.

"Are you all right?"

"Yes, nurse, don't worry." With these words, she moved away from the reception desk. She sat down in a red chair near the window, staring blanking out at the horizon. She couldn't focus on anything in front of her. Her eyes reflected her deep shock and tears spilled down her cheeks. Finally, a familiar voice drew her out of her revery.

"Mama, mama," said Rachel, Uncle Max picked me up at school as soon as he heard what had happened to Mendel and we came to see how he is and be with you.

Shaking herself mentally back into reality, Sarah smiled weakly at her loved ones. Max gave her an emotional hug, drawing it out as if to draw out his sister's pain and anguish, and when they finally pulled apart, he asked anxiously about his nephew's health.

"I really don't know how he is now," answered Sarah in a sad voice. 'They moved him into the hospital ward. The doctor said that he was suffering from a severe contusion from the blow he had received at school. But he looked awful to me. He was unconscious, he wouldn't move, couldn't hear me...Dear God, how horrible!"

"There, there, my dear Sarah. We will find out how he is now. Surely the doctor is completing his examination now."

"Max, they gave me these forms to fill out, but I can't seem to concentrate on them. Please, can you do it for me?"

He took the papers from Sarah's hands and went to the reception desk to fill out the forms. Meanwhile, Rachel tried to console her anguished mother with loving hugs.

Half an hour later, they saw Doctor Wasserman coming toward them.

"Doctor, my name is Max Sprintis. I am Mendel Ratovich's uncle, the injured schooboy who was brought in. Please tell us how he is doing."

"The patient is in grave condition," answered the doctor with worried frown. "The blow he received to his head was quite serious, and he is in a coma now. The only thing we can do now is to wait for him to gain strength and see if he can recover from the coma. We will keep him under strict and constant observation to see if there is any change in his condition."

Sarah watched him, her face contorted with worry.

"But, doctor, is he going to die?"

"I don't know, Mrs. Ratovich. It all depends on how he reacts over the next few hours. If you would like to see him, come with me."

She followed in silence. Behind her Max and Rachel walked along, looking down at the floor and lost in thought. There was nothing more to be said. Sarah trembled with fear and concern. Her heart was heavy in her chest. How she needed her husband Nathan at a time like this, but he was so far away, without any idea of the mortal danger facing his beloved son!

As they entered the small room assigned to Mendel, they all looked toward the boy. His waxy face was an expressionless mask. A nurse was sitting beside his bed, waiting for any sign of change. His mother could no longer control herself and began to sob wretchedly. Mendel was only twelve years old. How could he be on the brink of death, when he had always been such a healthy boy, so full of life? Rachel stroked Sarah's hair as she sat on the edge of her son's bed, and wiped away the tears that continued to roll down her cheeks. Max gazed with emotion at the tableau formed by his sister, nephew and niece.

"Rachel," said Sarah, "you have to go home. I need you to help your brothers and sisters while I stay at the hospital. Tell them to behave while I am gone."

"Max, please, take her home. The children will be getting back from school soon and dinner isn't finished. She will have to take care of things until I come back. And please, don't tell grandmother anything until Mendel gets better. She will only worry herself."

Rachel, listening to her mother, came over and kissed her good-bye.

Suddenly, on impulse, Max pulled his sister into his arms as if trying to infuse her with strength and courage, and then without a word, they moved to take their leave. Sarah watched them leave the room and then went over beside Mendel's bed. Seeing him continue to lie in the same position, she thought anxiously that this was not a good sign. Without her faith to support her, she would have thought her son was dying. But she held on to her faith at all costs. Perhaps God would hear her and give her the miracle of seeing her son walk out of the hospital healthy and whole to rejoin the rest of the family.

Meanwhile, Rachel arrived home with Max. After thanking him for bringing her and saying good-bye, she carefully opened the front door to the house, for fear that her grandmother, who lived on the lower floor of the building, would come out and ask where she had been. She began to climb slowly up the stairs to the second floor. Once in the door, she breathed a sigh of relief at the thought that she had avoided having to tell her grandmother about what had happened to Mendel. She still had twenty minutes before her brothers and sisters came back from school and besides finishing dinner, she had to clean the house and put everything away.

After several hours, Doctor Wasserman came to look in on Mendel. He couldn't see any improvement, and despite his professional demeanor, he felt sorry for Sarah as he realized that there was very little that could be done for the child. His knowledge and experience in similar cases told him that his patient wouldn't survive the night, and he felt impotent and useless in the face of the cruel evidence that medicine had still not evolved sufficiently to save the poor child from death. He looked over at the unfortunate woman, who had been sitting there for so many hours with her son's hand held in her own, with the distressing knowledge that he might not survive, praying to the all-powerful Lord of the universe. But in this case, there was almost no hope. The boy's life was hanging by a thread. He came over to Sarah and asked her kindly:

"Madame, would you like to rest for awhile? You have been sitting here for so many hours. I can ask the nurse to set up a sofa for you, and you could rest and get back your strength."

"No, thank you. I want to stay here with my son as long as I can. Tell me the truth, doctor, do you think he will get better?"

"I honestly don't know, dear lady. I would be lying if I said otherwise. For now, I cannot see any change in the child's condition. His pulse is still weak and he hasn't responded to treatment. It is all in God's hands now."

As he left, the kindly doctor thought how he would have liked to have been able to tell the good woman that her son would get better. But he could not. He didn't believe it would happen.

Sarah gazed after him. He had given her no hope, but she still had her faith and continued to believe a miracle could happen.

"My child, you will get better. I know that you will open your eyes soon and speak to me again."

But even she did not believe this, and she suddenly shivered with a terrible premonition that he would soon be dead.

Mendel survived for a few more hours, but never regained consciousness. Max came back at dawn to sit with his sister and nephew, but when he arrived, the boy had just perished and his sister was crying inconsolably.

They buried him the next day. The morning was wet and foggy. Their families and friends followed in a procession behind the coffin containing Mendel's body until they reached the cemetary. The whole village had liked the family and the boy for his easy-going and loving character.

His grandmother cried silently as she watched her daughter. How different everything would have been if Nathan, Sarah's husband, could be by her side! But he had gone to South America six years before, following the path of so many other thousands of European immigrants, seeking their fortune in the New World, perhaps not so new anymore hundreds of years after the first explorers, but bright with a cornucopia of opportunities for economic betterment for those bold enough to try. The years preceding the departure by the head of the household had been difficult ones, mostly because their income was insufficient to cover basic household expenses. Sarah had been forced to help her husband by taking on odd jobs outside the home to help boost the family income, to keep up with the every-increasing cost of living. But it still wasn't enough to cover their modest needs. Sometimes, they even had to skip meals so that their children would have the food they needed to keep growing properly. With such terrible economic hardships, Nathan, following a friend's advice, decided to try his luck in abroad, and to save enough money to send for his family. After more than five years, his dreams were still very, very far from becoming a reality, and now tragedy had struck the family...

"It is all over", thought Sarah as she finished praying the *kaddish*[1].

The pine coffin had already been placed in the grave and the mourners were overcome with the painful emotions of any human faced with the final departure of a loved one, made even more difficult in this case by the realization that this was a young life that would now never have the chance to blossom into fullness. Max threw a handful of earth on the coffin, and several family members and friends followed him in the ritual. The rabbi, with grave solemnity, gave a short, heartfelt speech. But Sarah's mind wandered back over the whole chain of events. It seemed like a nightmare. Only yesterday Mendel had left home for school and today, his life was over. It didn't matter to her the identity of the child who had hit him, who had no doubt been inspired by unhealthy ideas inculcated by fanatic and irresponsible adults. Every human being, she thought in her grief, has a

---

[1] *Kaddish*. (Aramaic: Holy) Aramaic hymn of praise to God that has become the principal prayer to commemorate the dead. (Author's note)

right to his identity, religion and life. But her poor Mendel had been denied his right to all of this when he was merely twelve years old. Dear God, look down on your child who can no longer remain with us, and take him to Your side; please don't leave him alone! She began to cry silently, large tears that sprung from the depths of her soul.

Rachel came close to her and holding her arm gently, said:

"Mama, it is time to go home. Let us leave."

She allowed herself to be led, glancing back one last time and taking her leave of her little one. As she made her way back home, surrounded by her family, she murmured:

"Good-bye Mendel, I will always carry you in my heart. No one can take that from me."

Returning home, the family began to prepare for the *shiva*[1]. According to Jewish tradition, they had to sit on low chairs for seven days as an outward sign of mourning, giving them a chance to think back over what had happened, and even if they could not accept it, at least to take the time to resign themselves to the inevitable.

Rachel moved quickly, trying to help the others. She had to take care of her brothers and sisters, being the oldest girl, and at the same time, tried to comfort the adults in their time of deepest suffering. Sarah seemed tranquil, although the occasional tear rolled down her cheeks. Doctor Wasserman had given her medication to deal with the depression, which kept her in a slightly groggy state. Max watched her intently, thinking that she did not deserve what she was going throught. She had always been a strong woman, fully dedicated to her responsibilities.

A few months passed after the burial. Sarah was hav-

---

[1] *Shiva*. (Hebrew: seven) This is the first and most intensive period of mourning. (Author's note)

ing terrible times facing reality. The continued nightmares and the feeling of guilt that maybe she could have done something to save her child's life, didn't allow her to live. So in view of the circunstances, Max decided to take her to a "Rest House" were she stayed for three months.

When she went back home to her children she felt calmer, but the scar in her soul remain forever.

Chapter 3

Max, Sarah and Teresa, on whom nature had bestowed a valuable gift, that of physical beauty, had been raised in a comfortable middle-class home and had received the best education that their family's favorable economic position could provide. Max, the eldest, had graduated from high school with top grades and had decided to work in the prospering family business, a fruit and vegetable shop, with the hope of acquiring the experience he would need to set up his own shop at some point in the future. At twenty-one, he was a very handsome fellow: average height, elegant, with dark brown hair and lively eyes that were always noticing an attractive girl. It was a point of adolescent pride in his mind, the fact that he was known as a ladies' man.

Sarah was slender, willowy, and curvaceous. Her creamy white skin was a perfect canvas for her light brown hair and piercing green eyes, and the graceful harmony of her features combined in an indefinable distinctive air. When she was just past her sixteenth birthday, and already of marriageable age, a shadow of concern crossed her young existence, as she listened one night to her parents

having a quiet discussion about her future marriage pro-
spects. She had been anxiously waiting for this moment to
come. Obedient and respectful of the longstanding traditions and customs, she was also very aware that once her
parents had chosen her husband, she could not object.
However, she also resented this strict rule, since it dashed
the secretly dreamed illusions nourished in her young girl's
heart. These fantasies arose unbidden whenever a handsome, young man appeared at school with the characteris-
tics of her mystical dream prince. Her imagination would fly
away with her, and she would daydream that the one chosen by her parents to be her life companion would precisely
be this wonderful knight in shining armor. The chance of
this happening was quite slim, as the romantic Sarah was
to discover with a thud of reality in a very short time.

Abraham and Sylvia Sprintis were a conservative couple, holding orthodox ideas. They believed that their daughter's happiness depended on a marriage to an upstanding
and moral gentleman, one who would support his home,
and be a model to his family. This led them to seek the
candidate for their daughter's hand in a *yeshiva*[1]. These
educational institutions, taught their students strict behavior
based on ethics and a deep love for their religion. After
some time asking among various people in the community,
they met Nathan Ratovich's parents. He was a student of a
yeshiva in Krakow. After the parents reunion, they arrive at
the conclusion that their children were both ready to marry,
and shared in common their religion and an unimpeachable
moral background. Based on these two fundamental values, they would be able to build a stable and fruitful home.
At the beginning, love was not considered absolutely nec-

---

[1] *yeshiva*: Talmudic academic institution or advanced rabbinical school.
(Author's note)

essary for the couple to build a life together. This would come with time, familiarity, and the shared experiences.

Nathan was a fair young man, not very tall, but slim, with small eyes, a straight nose, rather reserved and with a blank expression. He was an avid student and could always be found immersed in his books. Day-to-day life outside the yeshiva held no interest for him and he completely lacked experience when it came to women. He knew that he would have to marry one day, in accordance with religious dictates, but he had never stopped to think much about it. His studies occupied all his time.

One morning, Nathan's parents went to visit him. School rules held that meetings between students and their parents took place in a small, but cozy, room with high walls and antique wooden bookshelves holding hundreds of religious books available for the students to consult. On the only wall bare of these shelves was an enormous painting. It showed, with amazing realism, a young man with a kind expression on his face, absorbed in study or meditation. The furniture in the room also included various gray-upholstered chairs arranged in a semicircle, and a massive, old armchair covered in rather worn ochre leather. Meir Ratovich was the first to arrive, with his delicate bones and fine features, and he came forward to embrace his son warmly, his face reflecting his joy at their meeting. Still embracing his father, the boy asked with a touch of concern:

"And where is mama?"

His question sprung from the fact that his parents usually came to visit him together.

"Don't worry. I was so anxious to see you that I walked on ahead. She will be here soon. And how are you?"

"Very well, papa. I have a lot to study. As you know, this is my last year at the yeshiva and I really have to apply myself to get good grades. Anyway, I love my studies so I don't mind."

"Nathan! Nathan! My dear boy, how are you?" asked Blima Ratovich with excitement as she came in.

A moment later, the two met in a warm embrace and a shower of heartfelt kisses.

"You are as beautiful as ever, mama," he said, looking at her lovingly.

"Thank you, my dear. I know that is how you see me and it makes me happy," she added, aware that she was not a great beauty, being rather short, with a robust complexion and having dark brown hair with reddish highlights. Despite this, she did possess a certain attractiveness due to her luminous countenance, no doubt the reflection of a rich inner life and her excellent qualities as a wife and a mother.

"How happy I am to see you! Come in and sit down. Papa, sit here in the armchair. It is well worn, but it is very comfortable. And, mama, come here and sit beside me."

They followed his invitation and once settled, Mr. Ratovich began to speak slowly and emphatically.

"Nathan, the main reason for our visit is to speak about something of great importance with you."

The young man looked at his father with a surprised expression at the weightiness of these words. Mr. Meir continued:

"In six months you will be finished with your religious education and your mother and I have decided that once you graduate, you should settle down and marry a suitable girl from the community. It is time for you to start to form your own family."

Nathan listened attentively but with a dubious expression on his face. "Me, marry?" he thought. It can't be. "I am only twenty years old, just starting to prepare for life. I pay no attention to what goes on outside the yeshiva. My time has been dedicated to study and I really don't even know what it means to be a good husband. How could I even maintain my family...?"

His father interrupted these thoughts, saying:

"What is the matter, Nathan? Why the doubtful look? You know it is a *mitzvah*[1] to marry. You will carry on our family name through your heirs. Your mother and I have always looked forward with happiness to the wonderful day when we will have grandchildren."

Nathan looked back and forth between his parents. He saw how proud they were at the mention of their future grandchildren. As the only son, he sensed their frustration at not having had more offspring and having to accept their destiny of only one child.

"Nathan, we have been speaking with Abraham and Sylvia Sprintis. Mrs. Avivi, who knows them to be a religious, morally upright family with a good economic background, introduced them to us, and she is willing to help us organize the proposed match.

The young man listened impassively to his father's words, however, inside, he felt his heart sinking. Whatever arguments he might raise, he knew there was no escaping his fate. Young people could not disagree in these cases. Their parents made the decision and they had to obey.

"But, papa, do you think I am ready for marriage? Up to now I have only done one thing – my religious studies. I don't know how to maintain a family, or how to manage in the outside world."

"Don't worry, that is how we were when we first married. At the beginning, we didn't know what we were doing. Experience in marriage comes with time. As a husband and

---

[1] *Mitzvah.* Commandment, precept, good deed. (Author's note)

wife get to know each other, their destinies are linked more and more closely and they become as one, and begin to move in the same direction. When children come along, the union is strengthened and they both work together for the same things. You will see, it is not so complicated. Besides, you will have financial help from your future father-in-law, who will let you live in the upper floor of his home, and will be happy to have you nearby."

Mrs. Ratovich had not yet entered the conversation, in order to allow her husband to explain fully the agreement they had concluded several days earlier. But at that moment, she felt it was the right time to add:

"These are good people and we have heard that their daughter is very beautiful and a wonderful girl. From every point of view, the fact that she has been chosen is a true privilege for you. Once you meet her, you will agree. Moreover, Mr. Sprintis' financial help will allow you to continue your religious studies at home and at the synagogue. Don't worry so much. Trust in God and everything will work out for the best."

Nathan decided to accept his parents' decision. Judging by the turn of the conversation, it seemed that it had all been decided already. After the heads of the families met and shook hands, it was set in stone and there was nothing that could change it. His father had given his word and he, Nathan, had to abide by this.

Several months went by. Nathan graduated and went to live at his parents' home, waiting for the day he would marry Sarah. He still had not met her, and tried to imagine what she was like. According to Blima, she was beautiful, intelligent and kind, but he had no way of judging for himself and this made him anxious. Sarah's parents also told her about her future engagement to Nathan and she felt rather afraid. At her young age, she had much to learn about keeping a home. Although she helped her mother with some of the household duties, she still had so much to learn! She had always been guided by Sylvia and thought of the difficulties that she would have once she was no longer living at home. Of course, she would be in the same building, but as a married woman, her many responsibilities would prevent her from always asking her mother about every little thing. Oh, goodness! What would it be like? she asked herself, wondering if all women felt such fear before their wedding day. Besides, she kept trying to imagine what Nathan was like. Would she be attracted to him? Was he tall and slim, short and plump, or gawky and ungainly? Did he dress well? Poor Sarah! So many questions went through her mind. The information given to her by her parents seemed very meager. She wanted to know more. But, until her wedding day, she would not be able to discover the unknown. Nathan lived in the town of Birkenau and would not be arriving until the evening before the wedding.

"Come, my dear, let's not make your father wait," Sylvia said to her daughter on the night of their engagement. "He must be getting impatient."

Sarah left her room. Her anxious heart beat rapidly. She would finally be meeting Nathan.

"Come over here, Sarah," her father said. "I'd like you to meet the Ratovich family."

"Meir, this is my daughter, Sarah."

"I am very pleased to meet you. *Baruch Hashem*![1] You are very pretty, just as we were told."

She blushed and looked down shyly. Recovering, she offered her hand.

"Pleased to meet you, sir."

---

[1] *Baruch Hashem*: Blessed be God.(Author's note)

"Come, my dear," her father called again. "I want you to meet Mrs. Ratovich."

"It is a pleasure to meet you, ma'am, she said politely."

" The pleasure is mine," answered Blima, who had been watching her since she entered the room and was thus far favorably impressed with her future daughter-in-law.

"And this is Nathan!" her mother happily exclaimed to Sarah.

Suddenly embarrassed, she looked at him for a moment in silence. Then, Nathan said to her:

"Hello, Sarah, I have been so anxious to meet you. My parents have told me so much about you...and I see they have not exaggerated," he added, smiling.

"Hello, Nathan, I have also been waiting to meet you," Sarah answered him timidly.

Immediately, Abraham led the guests to the dining room table. The rabbi had already arrived and was ready to begin the engagement ritual. Two silver candlesticks decorated the center of the table, and Sylvia was lighting the candles. The men, still talking among themselves, came up and took their places. Sarah took advantage of the moment to get a closer look at Nathan. Out of modesty, she had not looked directly at him when her mother had introduced them. "How short he is," thought Sarah. "I am so much taller. But he is charming, seems to have nice manners, and his smile is very winning. When he smiled a moment ago, I felt drawn to him."

"Quiet please," said Rabbi Zohovich. "We have come together today for the happy occasion of the celebration of Nathan and Sarah's engagement. Would the future spouses please come here beside me. I want to explain a few basic concepts for your future life, on this most important day for you both."

The ceremony continued with solemnity, and was followed by a joyous celebration. The future in-laws were euphoric. For both Nathan and Sarah, the clouds of uncertainty and doubt had cleared away. He watched her with adoration as she returned his looks disingenuously, and began to indulge her vivid imagination with visions of the approaching wedding day, when she would walk down the aisle to the strains of the wedding march and be joined with the man who would be her husband for the rest of her life.

Chapter 4

Winter had been mild this year in the region of Poland where Jalowiec was located and was already retreating, with the warm breezes of spring more evident each day.

It was March 10th, the day set for Nathan and Sarah's marriage. She had been up before dawn and had spent part of the morning with her mother, going over all the details for the celebration of the happy event. Now she began to brush her beautiful brown hair before putting on the elegant bridal gown. As she moved through motions of this mundane task, sitting in front of the mirror over the chest of drawers, she began to recall her first meeting with Nathan. She had liked his personality and way of speaking. They had immediately felt an affinity between the two of them. The only note of discord was due to the physical difference between them. She was tall and he was short. When she mentioned this, her mother answered her with a slight reproach:

"My darling, in a relationship between two people there are values more important than mere physical beauty. Your future husband may not be tall and handsome, but he has many positive qualities that influenced us greatly in our decision in his favor. You must also remember that it was a short man, Napoleon, who brought revolution to Europe and is one of the few people who has changed the world in an important way", she added smiling. Sarah did not reply, then stood up and moving away from the chest of drawers she began to admire the bridal gown that had been placed on the bed.

"How lovely it is!" she exclaimed with satisfaction.

Her mother had made her a long gown in white lace set off with iridescent sequins. The headpiece was an exquisite tiara covered in tiny flowers that had been made by a family friend. It was finished in various layers of white tulle, and one layer would be covering Sarah's face as she entered the synagogue.

As soon as the wedding day had been set, Sylvia began to work feverishly on the preparation of her daughter's trousseau, and her first task was to buy all the materials for the various garments and articles that would have to be made: dresses for Sarah and linens for the house; sheets, finished by hand with lace and ribbons decorating the edges, and towels embroidered with the couple's initials. It had all been chosen carefully and in the best taste, just as it had been for Theresa's big day. She also placed two wooden side tables at the entrance to the house on which to set the gifts as they arrived.

Many family members, friends, and neighbors were invited to the reception, which was to take place on the same day, under the noonday sun. First everyone would go to the ceremony at the synagogue. From there, they would proceed to the Sprintis family home, where a party would take place in honor of the new couple.

As the time to leave for the synagogue approached, Sylvia walked hurriedly to her daughter's room, knocked on the door and went in.

"Please, close the door. I am still not dressed," said Sarah.

"Let me help you. It is getting late and your father is about to arrive to pick us up," said Sylvia.

"Yes, mama, I will hurry up." She began to lift the bridal gown and slip it over her head.

"Be careful! You'll mess up your hair. Good. Now, the buttons."

"Thank you, mama. Please pass me the headpiece."

As Sarah turned from the mirror, Sylvia helped her pin several hair clips to hold down the brilliant tiara. She looked wonderful and her eyes shone with excitement.

"Turn around and let me see you," her mother said. "Oh! You look beautiful, a true angel!"

At that moment they heard a knock at the door and Abraham's voice.

"Come in, my dear, and look at Sarah."

"My darling, you look beautiful!" exclaimed Mr. Sprintis as he came in. "With God's help you will be very happy. A daughter as wonderful as you deserves all the good things the world has to offer."

"Thank you, papa, for all the love that you and mama have given to me. You are the best parents."

"God bless you," added Mr. Sprintis.

"Let's go! We must go now as it is getting late," said Sylvia, taking Sarah by the arm and leading her out the door. "Come, Abraham, we must leave."

The ceremony took place at the synagogue near the family's home, where they attended Friday night prayers and the High Holiday services. Nathan and his parents were already waiting under the chuppah.

The anxious guests turned around in their chairs to see the lovely bride come in, flanked by her parents. The first notes of the wedding march began to fill the room and the ceremony began. Sarah did not miss one single instant of the solemn rite. While the rabbi spoke, she looked at Nathan, serious and elegant in his dark blue suit, with his distinguished bearing and an impassive expression on his face. Grandmother was also absorbed in the wedding ceremony, remembering back to when she herself had once been the blushing bride, and she wished happiness for the healthy, virtuous couple. Max watched his beloved sister with enormous pride and his thoughts, somewhat distracted by the familiar ritual, strayed back to memories of times past when he, Theresa, and Sarah used to run happily through the fields playing games and getting into mischief. It seemed that the time had flown by in the blink of an eye and now Sarah was getting married… Suddenly, he heard a loud crack. Nathan had just stepped on the wineglass to break it, and as the rabbi explained, "The tradition commemorates the destruction of the ancient temple in Jerusalem and reminds the newlyweds of the importance of protecting their marriage".

The groom leaned over and kissed Sarah. The ceremony was over and the guests began to move. The couple's parents hugged them, shedding tears of happiness and wishing them happiness always. Theresa and Joseph, who had come all the way from Warsaw for the occasion, joined the happy tumult to congratulate them. The guests kept coming one after another to bestow their best wishes. Finally, the group of newlyweds, parents, and friends left for the Sprintis family home for the festivities. They spent many hours in conversation, over a delicious lunch prepared by Sylvia, raising their glasses to toast the newlyweds. At last, the moment came for Nathan and Sarah, who were somewhat fatigued from the day's celebrations and emotions, to leave the party. They first went to Abraham and Sylvia, with whom they exchanged a few words of mutual consideration and affection. Then, to Nathan's parents, who would be leaving the following day for their home town, and as they bid them an affectionate farewell, both Sarah and her mother-in-law had a hard time hiding their sadness over having the departure.

As the days went by, Nathan and Sarah began to find their grounding in their new life together. Nathan continued his religious studies, while Sarah undertook her domestic tasks with efficiency and dedication. She most enjoyed cleaning the small apartment and its few pieces of furniture until everything was sparkling, and cooking for her husband. She was already getting to know his favorite foods. The rest of the time she helped her parents in the shop, where she would often stop to chat with Max.

From what their parents could see, the marriage seemed to be everything they could have wished for. Naturally, there was the anticipation of the happy day when Sarah would announce her contribution to the family tree. They did not have to wait long. One Friday night when, as usual, Abraham and Sylvia were with their children at the traditional *Shabbat*[1] dinner, Nathan and Sarah took the opportunity to share their news. The first baby was on its way. The family was overjoyed and with hugs and good wishes for the future parents, they all spent the happiest evening they had had in many months in their home, where faith and the Jewish religion was their guiding light. For the expectant mother, the days and hours went slowly, as if crawling along. From time to time she would stop in wonder at her transformation as she observed her pregnant figure growing. Nathan was happy about the idea of having a child. Upon finding out that his wife was to be a mother, he began to show more affec-

---

[1] *Shabbatt.* (Hebrew; Saturday) Celebration of the arrival of the *shabbat.* (Author's note)

tion toward her and often helped out with the household chores. To Sarah's surprise, he limited his study time at the synagogue to be home as much as possible.

One morning, Sarah woke up with back pains. She was already in the ninth month of her pregnancy and any different feelings from the usual ones made her feel nervous, and imagine that the birth might be imminent. When she mentioned the pain to her husband, he became nervous and ran to tell his mother-in-law, who in turn hurried to her daughter's side.

"How do you feel?" asked Sylvia anxiously.

"Mama! How good that you are here. I have started to have contractions and they are getting stronger."

"I think that the baby will be coming soon," said Sylvia. I am going to bring the midwife right away. Meanwhile, just rest in bed and stay calm. Nathan, please, stay with her. Don't leave her side until I return."

He came over beside his beloved wife, looked at her tenderly and taking her hand, sat on the edge of the bed.

"Don't worry, my dear. They will be here soon to help."

But she was not listening to his words. The contractions were getting so strong that each one made her double over. Her face began to contort with pain and she flushed deeply. "Dear Lord, help me!" She prayed silently.

"Sarah, darling, does it hurt very much?," Nathan asked her aloud, interrupting her thoughts.

In answer, she yelled with pain. The contractions, which now were coming stronger than ever almost without a break, were unbearable. Nathan began to fear for his wife. At that moment, he saw his mother-in-law come in with the midwife.

"Thank God you are here now."

The experienced professional came over to examine Sarah. Sylvia asked her son-in-law to leave the room and go advise Abraham. Nathan hurried out.

"Abraham, where are you?" Nathan called out nervously, coming into the fruit and vegetable shop.

"What is the matter?" Max asked, from where he was helping a customer.

"It is Sarah. She is in labor. Your mother and the midwife are with her."

"Papa, papa!" yelled Max, come quickly. "Nathan is here and says that Sarah is having the baby."

Abraham, hearing his son's words, came out immediately. Moments later, the three were on their way to the apartment upstairs.

The midwife checked Sarah again and seemed satisfied. The cervix was almost fully dilated. She could just see the top of the baby's head. Sylvia wiped her daughter's perspiring brow. With gentle words, she tried her best to calm her daughter.

"Mama, mama! I can't do this anymore. Help me, please."

"Be brave, my sweet girl. It will all be over soon."

"Push hard, harder!" yelled the midwife. "The head is almost out."

"Now, now!"

Sarah, hearing these words, gathered up her courage and pushed with all her soul. And with that, the baby's head pushed out. The midwife slowly and skillfully pulled the infant until finally, she was able to bring out the baby, carefully turning the newborn over and spanking the bottom gently. At that, to everyone's delight, a cry rang out that was heard even by the men waiting outside.

"It is your child!" Abraham said excitedly to Nathan. "Your baby has been born."

"God be praised!" exclaimed Nathan, hugging his father-in-law firmly.

Now, Nathan's concern was to find out how his wife was doing and whether he had a newborn baby boy or girl. Overcoming his shyness, he approached the bedroom and knocked on the door. No one answered and so he, Abraham and Max decided to wait another moment, sure that the women were still cleaning up the infant and mother.

"It is a boy, Sarah," said the midwife, bringing the baby to her so she could admire each tiny feature. She looked at every detail, his eyes, fingers, and with a sigh, whispered to him:

"My son, how I have longed for you, how small you are..."

Sylvia looked at them from across the room and felt a wave of tenderness engulf her. My first grandchild, she thought joyfully.

After a few more minutes had passed, Nathan, Abraham and Max, began to get nervous and anxious from all the waiting.

Sylvia finally broke the tension by opening the door and exclaiming:

"Nathan, you have a boy!"

The new father was speechless.

"Mazal tov!" Said Abraham. "May God grant him a long and happy life."

"Amen, added his wife."

They began to hug and congratulate each other, when they were interrupted by Nathan asking:

"And Sarah, how is she?"

"Baruch Hashem, she is well. She had a hard time during labor but it was a normal delivery She is resting now."

"May I see her?"

Nodding her head, she added:

"Go now, while she is still awake."

Nathan went toward the room, and after calling out

twice, opened the door. From the doorway, he could see Sarah, who was waiting for him with a smile on her face. Holding her arms out, she said:

"We have a beautiful, healthy boy and I am so happy!"

"As am I. Darling, let's call him Samuel, as we had discussed."

"Yes, it is a wonderful name for our son."

As Nathan invited his parents-in-law to come into the room, he mentioned the name they had chosen. Abraham looked at them with gratitude. His father, who had passed away two years before was named Samuel, and it was an honor for him that his first grandson should have this name[1]. The circumcision[2] was set to take place at the synagogue on the eighth day following the birth. The appropriate blessings and prayers were offered and the ceremony finished with a festive banquet.

Samuel was growing up in a loving home. As the only child in the family, everyone fussed over him constantly. Nathan continued his religious studies at the synagogue, but Sarah didn't feel lonely anymore when he left for the day. Little Samuel filled her hours with joy. His games and childish mischief made her laugh all day. When she went down to help at the shop, he came along. Abraham, Sylvia and Max took turns watching over him.

Another visit by Sarah to the family doctor, to find out

---

[1] The European Jewish tradition of giving one of the children the name of a paternal or maternal grandparent became common during the middle ages, to honor deceased relatives. Among the Sephardic Jews, the tradition is to give a child the name of a living relative. (Author's note)

[2] *Circumcision*. (Hebrew: milah) This is one of the basic rituals of the Jewish religion and signifies membership or belonging to the faith. It is an operation that consists in removal of part of the foreskin, to allow it to be retracted behind the penis gland. (Author's note)

why she had been feeling poorly, gave them the news that she was expecting once again. This was a reason for rejoicing for the young couple, but also a source of concern since she would have to take care of her very young son, and also do the housework and help out in her parents' shop. But her youthful energy helped her to shed her fears and she said to Nathan:

"I am sure I can do everything. I pray that our second child will be as healthy as Samuel."

The pregnancy was normal. Sarah had a beautiful girl, who they named Rachel. The family continued to grow with the arrival of four more children: Saul, Etty, Hannah, and Mendel.

Chapter 5

Sarah was fulfilled in her life with the seven children. She felt proud watching them grow into a healthy, happy family. She only wished she had more time to be with them, but there didn't seem to be enough hours in the day. Between cleaning the house, cooking for the family, caring for Nathan and the children, and working in her parent's shop, the days would fly by. Sometimes at night, she would be so tired that she thought she would not be able to go on the next day. This was a great source of worry for her. Their financial situation was precarious and her contribution to the household was essential. Her parents helped them out greatly by letting them live for free in the upper floor of the building, but the lack of space was becoming unbearable. With nine mouths to feed, their income could no longer cover the family's expenses. One night in bed as she tossed and turned, Sarah began to ponder various ideas to resolve their economic dilemma. But she soon rejected each idea in turn, one after the other. Nothing seemed to be the answer. "What must I do, Lord?" She thought. "I cannot go on like this. I am exhausted. I feel as if my whole body is aching and I don't know how much longer I can stand this situation. All of the responsibility is on my shoulders." Tears of anguish began to trickle down her cheeks and suddenly, unable to contain herself any longer, deeps sobs of desperation burst from her chest. Sarah's emotional torrent went on for several minutes, until she heard Nathan's voice from the darkness of the bedroom, asking her:

"What is the matter? You have been crying for some time."

She sighed deeply, trying to calm herself and said:

"It is time for us to face reality. We have brought seven children into the world and we have to give them the security that each child deserves from the moment he is born. We have been having some money problems lately. At the end of each week, I count the slots that are left over. Sometimes I tremble at the thought that one of the children may get sick and we would need more money. We would have nowhere to turn. I feel bad that we have to buy most of the food we eat every day on credit from my parents. And, I am exhausted. I am more than willing to continue working. Until now I have been able to keep up with my responsibilities, but every day they grow larger, and I cannot keep fighting so hard..."

As the last words left her mouth, she began to sob again. He moved over in bed, beside her, and caressing her hair, he said sweetly:

"Sarah, please don't cry anymore. I think I have found the answer."

Drying her tears, she listened attentively.

"For the past several weeks, your brother and I have been thinking about going to Warsaw to set up a textile factory. The income from the business would help better our situation. Max is ambitious and wants a better life. I have been thinking of taking a break from my religious studies, despite the fact they are very important to me. I will only spend my free time on them. I want to work hard and learn everything about the textile business. Then, when we are more organized, I will send for you. I wouldn't have mentioned this to you, because nothing is certain yet, but today after dinner, while you were putting the children to bed, Max came to tell me that he had managed to lease the building where he wants to set up the factory. We will be leaving to go there next week."

"So soon!" exclaimed Sarah, who had calmed down somewhat upon hearing her husband's words. "But while you are gone, our financial problems will continue. I can't do this all by myself...please, you must help me!"

"I think you don't understand. Once the factory starts making money, I will send you some to cover the expenses and then when things are set up properly, we will be together in Warsaw."

"Nathan, I think it is an excellent idea. But it makes me sad to think that we will be separated from you and Max. God only knows for how long!"

"Don't worry, my darling. It won't be for so long. Max has a good head for business and if he has decided to go, it is because he has something worthwhile to do there."

The following week, they left for Warsaw, leaving their family behind feeling sad but hopeful at the promise that they would send for them soon. They even discussed the possibility of selling Abraham and Sylvia's fruit and vegetable shop and reopening another one in Warsaw so they could continue to live and work close by their children and grandchildren.

With Max and Nathan's departure, Sarah not only felt a tremendous emptiness but also, her workload doubled because her brother was no longer there to help her parents and she had to spend more time helping out at the shop.

Every week she would get news from her husband. He would tell her how the factory was beginning to take shape, and describe for her his workday. In his letters he praised Max, who had shown himself to be a natural leader. He would soon send for them, to give them the comfortable life of which they had so often dreamed. These words would give her the hope and courage she needed to go on with her heavy burdens.

Eleven months had gone by since the men had left. One morning, Sarah awoke to hear her mother's anguished cries coming from the lower floor apartment. As fast as she could, she wrapped a shawl around her shoulders, stepped into her slippers and ran down the staircase.

"What is the matter, mama, why are you yelling like that?" she asked anxiously.

"It is your father," exclaimed Sylvia in an agitated voice. He has a terrible pain in his chest and he almost can't breathe. Come and see if you can do anything. Sarah followed her mother into the bedroom she shared with Abraham, and quickly made her way over to him.

"Papa, what is the matter?" she asked gently.

"I felt a heavy pressure on my chest and a pain in my left arm, but don't worry, because it is already going away. When it is light, I will go to the doctor. Go back to sleep, you'll catch a cold here. And you know that we can't have that happening."

Sarah heaved a sigh of relief to hear her father joking, and tried to comfort Sylvia.

"Mama, please don't worry. It was only a scare and he is better already. Maybe he ate something too heavy last night before bed. Go and rest and if papa starts to feel poorly again, call me. I will be just upstairs."

Two hours later, Sarah felt her mother sit down on the edge of her bed and let out a heartrending sob. She leaped out of bed to ask what had happened.

"Your father has just passed away. His heart could not hold out any longer."

"What!" cried Sarah. "It can't be true! He was feeling better just a short while ago. Let me see him."

"No, don't go down now. The doctor has just left. The pain that Abraham was feeling before you came down to see him was a heart attack. About an hour ago it began to happen again, so I ran out to fetch the doctor. When we got back, there was nothing to be done. He was dead. He died alone. I wasn't there with him; I left him alone!" Sylvia cried out in anguish.

"But, Mama, why didn't you call me?" sobbed Sarah. I would have helped you. At least, I could have stayed with him until you came back with the doctor and I would have been with him, she continued with a wail. Oh, mama, we have lost him!" she exclaimed and embraced her mother, who was crying inconsolably. Feeling her daughter's embrace, Sylvia caught her breath for a moment and said to her in a voice thick with tears:

"He is gone, my darling, and we cannot do anything more."

As soon as Sylvia sent word to Max of his father's death, he, Nathan, Theresa and Joseph traveled immediately to Jalowiec. The funeral was well attended. It seemed that the whole town had come to accompany Abraham to his final resting place and to console the family in their time of sorrow. He had been a generous man, always willing to help out those in need.

Abraham's sudden death, and his absence as a good husband, good father and exemplary neighbor, was a hard blow for the Sprintis family and cast a pall of mourning over the townspeople of Jalowiec. But life must go on no matter what, just as the bright spring must follow the scorching summer, melancholy autumn, and the cold, hard winter.

For the family, the death of their venerable patriarch meant the closing of a chapter. Another chapter would begin with the sale of the fruit and vegetable shop and the move to Warsaw.

Chapter 6

Adapting to Warsaw was slow and difficult. Theresa, after looking long and hard, managed to rent a place to live on Lezno Street, near the factory. The factory was already beginning to show a profit, but all the money it made had to be reinvested for the purchase of materials to satisfy the coming orders. Sarah was not completely happy about the move, but on the other hand, felt great relief at being able to leave behind the nightmare of her father's death. Each corner of the house in her village reminded her of life with him. Once she had time to think about the move to Warsaw, she was able to realize that, thanks to the help of her sister and the Kupperman family, the transition was less traumatic than it would have been. This was, in no small part, due to the fact that the family was uprooted and forced to adapt to these new surroundings at a time when they lacked sufficient economic stability and feared for their uncertain future. Soon after their arrival, Theresa noticed her sister inspecting the apartment where they had just moved. It was clear that it did not measure up to the comfortable home they had in her parents' building. Everything was worn out and in poor condition. The walls were painted a depressing dark green color and the windows bare, without any curtains to cover them. The wooden furniture, hard and uncomfortable, needed various repairs. The kitchen supplies were rusted and the pipes corroded. Noises from the street were constantly assaulting them in the most annoying fashion. For the sensitive Sarah and her children, used to pleasant surroundings, it was a dramatic change. "How will we survive this?" she asked herself. She was lost in these reflections, when her sister's voice intruded on her musings.

"I know that the apartment is not in the best condition," Theresa commented in a voice full of regret, "but in this area it was the only place that could fit your budget. You know Joseph and I want to help you out. We are aware you are going through a hard time financially and we have the means to give you the help you need. We don't understand why Nathan refuses to accept our offer of financial assistance, which would make such a difference. Remember that everything in life is on loan, and at any moment we might be the ones who need your help. Please, accept our offer."

"Thank you, dear sister, it is very generous of you. We have already received so much help from Joseph, from you, and from the Kupperman family. What would have become of us without you!"

"We are family, it is only natural!"

"Mama, mama, we want to go back home. We don't like this place. It is dark and smells bad," Sarah's younger children chimed in.

"Don't worry, children, we will fix it up," she answered them sadly, knowing she couldn't turn back now. They would have to get used to their new life and she would have to do everything in her power to make it happen.

"God help me," she said aloud. Then, helped by her sister, she put herself to the task of cleaning everything from top to bottom, to turn it into a real home.

The children began to attend school. Sarah would walk with them early in the morning and after saying goodbye to them, quickly returned home to take care of the housework: cleaning, washing clothes, and cooking. Sylvia was not able to help much. Since Abraham's death, she had become withdrawn and did not share in family as she had before. Her children were worried about their mother, sensing her deep suffering. Her daily routine consisted in getting up early, saying her prayers and sitting for hours in front of the window of the room she shared with Max, her gaze lost in the distance. It seemed that nothing mattered to her anymore. The only person to interrupt her deep pensiveness was Sarah, when she appeared at the door with a tray of food.

"Mama, you must eat. You cannot go on like this. This melancholy will make you ill. Please! There is no longer anything that you or I can do for papa. He would not like to see you like this. Come, look at the delicious meal I have prepared for you."

Sylvia glanced over with a vague expression, smiled, and looked disinterestedly at the tray of food.

"Leave it there. I will eat later."

But she could see that her mother was getting thinner day by day. I must speak with Max and Theresa, she thought. Mama is going to get sick if she keeps up this way.

In the months that followed, Sarah managed to make her house into a cozy home. She painted the walls and furniture a pearly white color. She sewed some attractive curtains with scraps of fabric in various colors that she had obtained at a very reasonable price in a nearby shop. With the leftover fabric, she made cushions to cover the chairs so they would be more comfortable. She repaired the cabinets and, with Theresa's help, bought the pots and dishes she needed for her daily cooking. She placed some knick-knacks on the shelves to brighten up the place and make it more cheerful. The children's rooms were decorated with their favorite toys. Little by little, they began to feel more at home. Many times the children would leave sweet letters under the pillow, smiling impishly, just to see their parents smile when they found them. Nathan and Max were amazed by the changes Sarah brought about. It seemed like a different apartment. And if that was not enough, she managed to make the money stretch so that every Friday she would be able to prepare their favorite dishes, for the family to share as they met around the traditional Sabbath table.

Everyone tried his or her best to help Sylvia out of her depression. Their affection and efforts met with success and she began, bit by bit, to return to her family. At first, she didn't express her opinions. She would only listen. But slowly, she started to involved herself in the daily life of the household and there came a time when she was the same person she had always been. One day, as he gave Sarah a warm hug, Max said:

"My dear sister, we have done it. Mama is leaving behind her apathy."

"Yes, she answered. I hope that she won't fall back into that melancholy. She may not be able to recover a second time. One more tragedy in the family would kill her. I hope, from now on, that we will only be together for happy occasions."

"Amen!, added Max."

Chapter 7

Joseph and Theresa kissed the *mezuzah*[1] they had given a few months before to their relatives as a good luck amulet on their move to their new apartment, and excitedly rang the bell. They heard quick footsteps approach and the door opened.

"How happy we are to see you here!" exclaimed Sarah, giving them a kiss on each cheek. "Come in. We are sitting in the drawing room having tea with pierogis."

After exchanging hugs and words of welcome, Joseph began to speak of his summer vacation spent in Otwock.

"It is a charming location. We rented a cottage near the Swiderek River, and every day we would sunbathe and refresh ourselves in the waterfall. We rested a great deal. Well, I really needed the break after working so hard! And

---

[1] *Mezuzah.* (from Hebrew: doorpost) Rectangular parchment containing two passages from Deuteronomy, transcribed in accordance with the same rules governing the writing of copies of the Torah and phylacteries. It is part of the Shema, one of the most important prayers of the Jewish people. See I. Abrahams. (Author's note)

how are you doing?"

"We are still working hard at the factory, answered Max."

"Yes, added Sylvia, but we are healthy and we are all together. I really appreciate this now after the difficult time we spent apart, when you decided to come to Warsaw trying to better our situation."

"Nathan, you seem tense. Are you worried about something?" Asked Theresa.

"The news about the Jews in Germany is worrisome. As you probably know, the spread of the plague of anti-Semitism started with the economic crisis suffered around the world in 1929. A lower-ranking Austrian officer named Adolph Hitler, with the backing of the workers' National Socialist Party, has risen to be an absolute dictator in Germany and is an anti-Semitic fanatic.

There are violent outbreaks on a daily basis. No Jew can feel safe in that country. They are being attacked in any place, injured, and their wives and daughter raped. There is no respect for human life and even less for religion.

The boycott on Jewish businesses is absolute, with the tolerance or even open approval of the government. They are plundering shops, breaking windows, beating the shop owners and throwing the goods into the street, so that it has become acceptable to loot and destroy private property.

In small towns, they are boldly attacking farmers. And in open-air markets, they go straight to the Jewish stands, kick over the baskets and stop anyone of a different nationality or religion from buying the products.

The next phase of this persecution is forced segregation of the Jews, which in some cases is violent. They are being excluded from the courts, the medical profession, law, and even prevented from teaching. Now they are passing racial laws so that anyone who is a descendant of Jewish parents or grandparents is not allowed to hold public office. They are being expelled from schools, colleges and universities, and deprived of citizenship and nationality.

"Oh, my God, those poor people!" Sarah exclaimed, upset by the news. "How can they survive without work, and when they are unable to provide education for their children?"

"I suppose that most will want to emigrate," commented Max with visible unease.

"It is not as easy as you think," countered Joseph. "Especially for professionals like me, because most university diplomas are only valid in the country where they were granted and if the professional decides to emigrate he will face a series of very difficult obstacles. In any case, there is a limited immigration quota for each country."

"If Nazism overflows from Germany and spreads throughout Europe, it will poison the society in those countries...", mused Theresa.

"It could happen," replied Nathan pensively. "We should join together to defend human rights."

Suddenly, everyone stopped talking and they were enveloped in a ponderous silence that lasted for several minutes until the mood was broken by the sound of children's voices.

"Aunt Theresa, Uncle Joseph, finally you are back! We missed you so much."

"Thank you, Samuel, and we missed you, too," she answered, squeezing him in her arms.

"How was your trip?" Rachel asked curiously.

"Marvelous. We hope that next summer we can take you with us," said Joseph with a smile.

The children looked at each other, pleased with the offer, and nodded their heads.

"Uncle, we hadn't had a chance to thank you for the *mezuzah*," said Saul, coming closer. "Can you tell me more about its meaning?"

"It is an ancient tradition. It comes from the commandment to recognize the unity of God, to love God and to place these words on the doors and lintels of your homes.

The passage written inside the *mezuzah* includes the basic teaching of Judaism:

- monotheism, the basic duty - love, the main discipline - to study *Torah*, and the fundamental method of the Jewish religion, which is to join the written word with the spiritual."

"It is all so beautiful!" exclaimed Rachel.

"And now, my dear family, let us have dinner," Sylvia suggested happily, getting up from the sofa. "I have prepared for you a delicious borscht with meat and potatoes, and a Polish cucumber salad."

"But, grandma, what about dessert? Apple strudel?"

"Yes, Etty, and it is delicious."

The next day, the two sisters went shopping downtown, and after a good deal of window shopping, they decided to stop for a rest in a small and cozy cafeteria. They ordered tea and cakes and Theresa began to speak:

"Sarah, for some time now, I have been anxious about a personal problem, but I hadn't had enough courage to recognize it or talk to anyone about it until now. Today, I want to take this opportunity and discuss it with you, and since you are so close to me, I know you will be able to understand. When we first got married, we were very anxiously awaiting my first pregnancy. Month after month, we waited for our miracle, but it never happened. Finally, we decided to consult a doctor recommended by our neighbor, Mrs. Epelbaum, who had been treated for a problem like mine and is today the proud mother of two children.

For a long time, I was going to this doctor's office and had all sorts of tests. When he found nothing out of order, he decided to see if the problem had to do with Joseph. The exams startod all ovei agaih. When he got the final results, he called us in to his office and briefly explained that he had not found any apparent physical cause for our failure to conceive. It might be, in his words, a psychological problem.

This seemed impossible to us. Joseph and I are very happy and our marriage is stable. He has a good job and is satisfied with his work, and as for me, I have easily adapted to life in Warsaw. I am deeply in love with my husband, surrounded by loving people who look out for me, and my husband and I have an excellent economic situation."

"Could it not be, that anxiety over your strong desire to be a mother is the real cause of your inability to conceive a child?" asked Sarah, seeing the anguish reflected in her dear sister's face.

"It is possible. This wish has become an obsession, and I recognize that. I would give anything to have a baby."

"I really do understand what you are going through," added Sarah, feeling sorry for her. "Every since you were little, you have had a strong maternal instinct, and we saw it expressed toward us, your siblings. When mother was sick or had to leave the house for any reason, you would assume all her responsibilities and would take the best care of us."

"Then why is God punishing me and preventing me from knowing the joy of motherhood?"

"Stop torturing yourself, Theresa. It is still too early to think that your apparent inability to have a baby is definitive or irreparable. Try to relax and keep an open mind. This may help your deepest wish come true."

"All right, Sarah. I will do that. I hope that this will bring me the answer to all my prayers."

Chapter 8

In the two and a half years that had passed since Sarah and her family moved to Warsaw, they had made a great effort to adapt to city life but part of them still wished to return to their village. One day, Max came over to Sarah with a worried expression and said:

- I need to talk to you about something important.

- I am listening, she answered, taking off her white apron. I have already finished prepared tonight's dinner. As you know, since it is Friday, I always try to make something extra special.

- Come, let us go into the parlor and have a chat, he said, gesturing toward the room.

He followed her in thoughtful silence. His attitude was a little odd. He was usually affectionate and playful with her, but now he seemed terribly serious and nervous.

- Is there a problem at the factory? she asked.

- You are partially correct, but it is a complicated situation and any decision on it may affect our family's future. I would like you to keep an open mind and listen to my ideas.

- She studied him for a moment, then nodded her head in consent.

- For the past three and a half years, Nathan and I have worked tirelessly to turn the factory into a good business. Up to a certain point, our efforts have paid off with a degree of success. As you know, we have many buyers for our sweaters throughout the city and some even come from nearby towns.

At first we lost money, but that was to be expected from any business that is starting up. Afterward, more or less at the time papa died and you moved to Warsaw, it began to produce enough to pay for the materials needed to make the sweaters. We didn't have to keep investing capital to keep it going, which was a great help from the financial viewpoint, and allowed us to spend more money on our personal needs. Now, the factory is actually making a profit, although not as much as we had hoped.

Most Poles buy just what they need, not only because they want to save their money but also due to their miserable salaries, barely enough to cover their daily living expenses. The country's economy is quite depressed and is affecting all businesses, including our own.

Max was silent for several minutes, while his sister began to digest these ideas, and then continued:

- Sarah, as you have noticed, during our time in Warsaw, our problems have not gone away to any great extent. I would like my family to not have to suffer privations. I will make every effort to make that a reality, and Nathan fully backs me up on this.

Various people we know have talked to us about a stable and prosperous situation in other countries, and about the salaries and quality of life for workers, which are much better than in Poland. We have started to find out about the possibility of going to work in South America, and the prospectives look quite good.

- South America? she asked curiously.

- Yes, it seems far away, but several people we know have emigrated to a country called Colombia and some of them have already sent for their families here.

- But, Max, how could we work there? We only speak Polish and Yiddish and nobody know those languages in those countries. It will be difficult or almost impossible to communicate with the people there.

- I understand your concerns, but by living among those people, we will be able to learn their language in a short time. And as for work, we already have some friends there who are willing to help us.

- Oh, brother of mine! complained Sarah. The move to Warsaw was difficult for the children and it was a big change. Not only did they have to leave their home, but also their aunts and uncles, cousins, and friends. Thank God, we had help from Theresa, Joseph and his family when we arrived. And now, when they have finally managed to adapt to this place, don't you think they will be affected all over again?

- You don't understand, he answered. The idea is not to move the whole family to South America right away. Nathan and I would go first to get things organized, and as soon as we are set up, we will send for you.

- For heaven sakes, Max, she protested, have you already forgotten how much we suffered when we were separated, when you came to Warsaw and we stayed in the village?

- No, Sarah, no I haven't forgotten. I know well how hard it was. And if we go, it will be repeated all over again. But we must be strong and persevere in our efforts until we manage to find a better life, so we can at least provide for our basic needs. And maybe, he added in a playful tone, we might even become millionaires.

Hearing her brother jest, she answered with a smile:

- You will never change. Even at the most difficult times, you always find a way out. If there is no other way, you still go on. Being apart from you again will be extremely hard on us, and even more so given the enormous distance between the two countries, but if you are so convinced that we will soon be in a better financial situation, then all these sacrifices will be worth it.

Over the next few weeks, they made some important decisions. The first was to sell the factory. It was not too difficult to find a buyer. With that money, they bought their tickets for the trip to South America, keeping some for their arrival in the new country and giving the rest to Sarah, who would be returning to the village with her mother and the children to live in Sylvia's building again, which had meanwhile been vacated by the tenants and was ready for their return.

They had mixed feelings about the endeavor. On the one hand, they were happy to be returning to their true home, and on the other hand, sad about leaving their family in Warsaw and over the prospect of Max and Nathan's coming voyage.

Life is such a paradox, Sarah thought as she watched the children shouting happily over the idea of seeing the rest of the family again and all their friends.

- Mama, isn't it wonderful? Rachel asked her. I am so happy! I wish we were there already.

- Calm down, my darling daughter. When we are back at home, our stay in Warsaw will seem like it was only a dream...

Chapter 9

- Here they come, mama! Pearl yelled excitedly, as she watched the horse and carriage approaching to bring Sarah and her family back home.

Pearl, who had always been Rachel's favorite cousin, had grown up with her. They had shared sadness and joy, laughed and cried together and built a strong and lasting friendship that had grown even stronger over time.

- Yes, I can see them, too, agreed Bertha, Pearl's mother, stretching to peek through the window. At least I finished cleaning the house already, so Sylvia won't have to find out how the tenants left it when they moved out. It is unbelievable how some people can live in such filth...

She turned her head toward her daughter, and then realized she had gone out already to meet the new arrivals. It is amazing how excited we all are to see our family return, thought Bertha. I am so glad they decided to come back.

- Rachel, Rachel! Pearl yelled as she ran.

- Papa, please, stop the carriage, Rachel asked anxiously. Nathan, seeing his daughter's excitement, pulled up on the reins of the horse, and the obedient animal slowed his gait to a halt. Helped by Max, the girl jumped down and ran as fast as her legs could carry her toward her cousin.

- Here I am, she called happily. Almost immediately, Pearl threw herself at her cousin and they hugged each other in a deep and joyful embrace.

- How I have missed you! she cried, and continued to hold Rachel in her arms...

- And I missed you, too. It seems like ages since I last saw you. Each girl looked at the other, trying to detect any changes. But, besides the fact that they had grown a bit, they were the same as ever. They both broke into smiles, and holding hands, started toward the door of the house.

- Welcome home! exclaimed Bertha, coming toward the carriage where the other family members were disembarking. I am so thrilled to have you back here again.

- Thank you, answered Sylvia, reaching over to give her a hug. We are also very happy to see you again. We couldn't wait to get back. We missed all this. Sarah climbed down slowly from the carriage, taking in the view over the countryside, and for a moment, thought she was dreaming. Night after night in Warsaw she had imagined this moment. And now, standing before it, she couldn't believe her eyes.

- Mama, please, can I get out? Samuel asked her.

Shaking off her reverie, she moved out of the way and then, hugging him lovingly in her arms, she said:

- My darling, we are here. We are home!

- Yes, thank God! I liked the city, but I love our village. My real friends are here and it is sad living far away from our family. I missed you all so much!

Bertha, standing nearby, was surprised to hear Samuel express his feelings so strongly about their return....and I thought he was shy and withdrawn, she thought to herself.

Max heard Sylvia calling from inside the house. He hurried over, leaving the two suitcases he was carrying beside the staircase, and asked as he came up beside her:

- Are you all right, mama?

- Just fine, son. I am happy to be back in Jalowiec, but my happiness is dimmed by your father's absence. Without him, the place looks different.

- You are right, he agreed sadly. Some things in life are beyond our control. We have to accept them and leave them in God's hands.

- I would give anything in the world to have your father again by my side, said Sylvia in a plaintive voice.

- I know, mama.

- Come here, Max! Nathan called from outside.

- I'm coming, he answered. He kissed his mother's cheek and went out to help Nathan, who was trying to lift an enormous box.

- Please, give me a hand to carry this up. It weighs so much and I am already tired out.

- I will help you, papa! Samuel yelled out from the door. I am very strong, you'll see.

The two men looked at each other and with a smile, Nathan accepted his son's offer.

- Thank you for your help, he said, when they finally finished unloading the huge crate.

- You're welcome, papa, it is always a pleasure to help you out.

Looking into his son's eyes gratefully, he gave him a playful pat on the arm and went out of the room. He went downstairs and back to the carriage to continue unpacking the rest of the things. At six pm, once the task of unloading and putting away the baggage was finished, they all went to the kitchen to rest for a while and have some tea and butter cookies, baked by Theresa before leaving Warsaw.

- How I will miss my daughter and her husband, Sylvia thought with distress. That melancholy thought contrasted with the happy shouts she could hear in the distance of the children playing with their cousins.

- That was a hard job, exclaimed Sarah, sitting down at the table beside Nathan. Thank heavens we are almost done. Tomorrow I will start finding out about school for the children, so they don't miss too many classes.

- Don't worry about it now; sit and rest, Bertha coaxed her. If you want, I can go with you early in the morning to speak to the director of the school. I know her and she is very nice and helpful. I will help you with everything.

- Thank you, I would love that. Is seven-thirty in the morning a good time?

- Fine. I will be waiting for you.

The next morning, they went to school to register the children. The whole process went off without a hitch and they were soon on their way out of the school buildings.

- Bertha, would you like to come for breakfast at my house? It is still early and we could chat for a while.

- I'd love to. You can tell me about your experiences in Warsaw.

- Let's go then, answered Sarah. It is so wonderful to feel at home and have a good friend like you.

When they arrived, she started to prepare the tea. The children were still asleep since they didn't have to go to school. The whole house was quiet. Nathan and Max had gotten up early to do errands in preparation for their trip.

- Mama still isn't up yet; that is unusual for her. She must be very tired after the trip. Moving is very tiring for a woman her age. I noticed that she was awfully quiet. It is probably due to the trip the men are planning, she added with a note of sadness.

- What trip? Asked Bertha.

- Oh, you still don't know! she said, placing two cups of tea and a bread basket on the table. Wait a moment while I bring the butter and jam. I will tell you all about it.

Bertha watched her, perplexed, waiting for the explanation. Could they be leaving again? she thought. That can't be; they had just got there. They wouldn't be leaving again so soon after all that work. Besides, they seemed very happy to be back.

- Ready, said Sarah, putting the rest of the things on the table and sitting down in front of Bertha. Please, have some toast. Here is the jam. I still haven't thanked you for the exquisite meal you prepared when we arrived and for cleaning the house. It looks terrific and I can only imagine how dirty the tenants must have left it.

- Don't mention it. I did it with a lot of love.

- Max told me he wrote you about our date of arrival in a letter, but the rest was all your doing. I apologize for having caused you to go to so much trouble.

With a flip of her hands, Bertha indicated that it was of no importance, and said:

- Now, tell me about the trip.

- Sarah sighed, and with a mournful expression, began to recount to Bertha the family's plans for the near future.

- As you well know, the economic situation in Poland is extremely unstable and this is affecting everyone negatively. When Max and Nathan decided to open the factory in Warsaw, they had hoped to tackle our overwhelming financial problems and overcome the hardship we were enduring, since we couldn't even afford the basic necessities. When father died and we moved to the city, instead of conditions improving, the situation became worse. The cost of living was too high, and we didn't have income from the fruit and vegetable shop anymore, since we had sold it when we left to get the money for our move. But the business was not as successful as we had hoped. The meager earnings would have been enough for Max and mama alone, but not for all of us, being such a large family. We tried to convince them to stay and keep trying, saying that we could return to the village, but they refused to even hear us out. The idea of splitting us up again seemed unthinkable. One day Max came home to tell me that he and Nathan wanted to go to South America to try their luck. According to one of the workers at the factory who spoke to them, the economy there is booming and full of opportunities. Also, it seems some of the men who went to those countries a few years ago have already sent for their families and they are not coming back to Poland.

- But, Sarah, interrupted Bertha. Do you really know how these people are doing? You can't risk going so far away without knowing all the details.

- I agree with you. We don't know very much about South America, but the men's idea is that they will first go and find out about the conditions and possibilities there, and if it is as good as we have been told, they will send for us as quickly as possible.

- And meanwhile, how will you all survive?

- I don't really know, answered Sarah. According to Nathan, as soon as they arrive, they will look for work immediately and start to send us money every month. Also, maybe I can work for the owners of the fruit and vegetable shop that papa used to own. I have enough experience after having worked so many years at his side.

- Don't count on those people too much, commented Bertha, as she got up to take the plates to the wash basin.

- Why do you say that?

- You don't know them. There are strange people, different from us. I even think I have noticed that they have some animosity toward Jews. When we go into the store, they seem to be very cold toward us. Our presence seems to bother them. It was very different when Abraham was alive....it was a real pleasure to go shopping then. I would often go in to buy any old thing just to spend some time and have a conversation...

- Yes, it is true. I also miss those happy days working alongside my father. We worked long days, but we were happy in our work. We enjoyed it when our family and friends would come in. I still remember when would tell me to keep the tea kettle hot to be ready in case any of you appeared unexpectedly, to be able to offer you a cup of tea.

- He was an excellent man, agreed Bertha. It is tragic that he died so young.

- Good morning, Sylvia greeted them as she entered the kitchen.

- Good morning, mama, answered Sarah. Did you sleep well?

- Yes. I really needed that rest. I think that being home again helped me to sleep so well.

- I am glad that you are feeling better, Bertha said. Yesterday you seemed to be exhausted.

- Yes, I was, she agreed. The trip was very long and the move was hard. I am no spring chicken anymore and these situations affect me more now. But today, I feel good as new.

- Come, mama. Have a cup of tea while I heat up the bread.

- Thank you, my dear daughter.

Sylvia sat at the table and delicately poured herself a cup of tea, adding a spoon of honey and mixing it, then looked over at Bertha.

- You cannot imagine how happy I am to be among my people again. Warsaw is a lovely city, but it didn't make up for having to live so far away from my loved ones. I was born here, grew up here, and there is no one in this world that can uproot me again from this place.

- But, how can you say that? asked Sarah upon hearing her comments.

- Yes, Sarah, you heard me. I am not moving from this place again. This is my house and Jalowiec is my village, and when I die, I want to be buried next to Abraham.

- You know Max and Nathan's plans, exclaimed Sarah. They are going to send for us once they are set up in South America.

- Of course, you will go with the children. Those trips are not for me anymore. Besides, after our experience living in Warsaw, I want to spend my last years here in the village.

- Mama, I have no intention of leaving without you. It would mean years, maybe a lifetime, before I would be able to see you again.

- Don't think that way. Your duty, you must always remember, is to stay beside your husband. Wherever he goes, you must follow. So, when the time comes for you to be reunited, you mustn't give it a second thought.

- Please, think about it some more, insisted Sarah. I cannot believe that you would want to stay alone when it comes time for us to go.

- I will never be alone. I have many people around me who love me, Sylvia concluded with a note of finality.

- Have you told Max what you are thinking? Sarah asked with concern.

- No, my dear, but I will when the right time comes.

Chapter 10

As soon as they arrived in Jalowiec, the men put all their time and effort into the somewhat complicated task of organizing their coming trip. In preparation, they spoke with various women whose husbands had emigrated to South American countries, and consulted pamphlets and books brought from Warsaw, in order to gather as much information as possible about the unknown continent where they would soon be traveling. The night before the trip, Nathan was in his room resting as Sarah finished her housework, when a sudden cloud of doubt came over him. Dear God, help me! How can I know if we are doing the right thing by leaving here? I don't know how my poor wife will survive now, since even by working together, we have not been able to cover the expenses that keep piling up. He tossed and turned in the bed and kept analyzing the situation. Of course, we are doing this for the good of the family, but I can't help worrying about how they will all manage until Max and I can send enough money to support them.

- Is something wrong? Sarah asked, concerned. I came into the room a few minutes ago and have been watching you adrift in your thoughts. I didn't want to interrupt you, but suddenly your face twisted with an expression of pain and I got scared. What are you thinking about?

- My darling, it is so good to be near you! I want to tell you what I am thinking about our trip. Please come and lie down beside me. If it was up to me, I would never let this night end so I could stay beside you forever. I was busy with the arrangements for my trip all day long and didn't stop to think about actually leaving. Now, it is hitting me hard....after tomorrow, I won't be able to see you anymore and only God knows for how long....

She came over to the bed as her husband spoke. She looked at him with a pained expression on her face and caressing his cheek with the back of her hand, said:

- Don't fret, darling. I know how difficult this all is. I myself have been fighting against a cloud of doubt for the past few weeks, not knowing if we are doing the right thing in allowing our family to be separated once again by the currents of life. As for me, I almost feel as though I am disobeying the divine commandment to follow you wherever you go, in spite of myself. And when I think of our separation, despite of my grieving heart, as heavy as yours, I know we must take these steps because we can no longer go on living like this. Every day, our fight to survive is more difficult. We don't have the resources to face the present and we are afraid to look toward the future, as we don't know what new problems may await us. We have brought our children into the world, and obeyed the precept to be fruitful and multiply. Now, we must fight to give them a better future in a land where they can be free, where they won't be hated for their religion and where they can be educated and work without facing discrimination or barriers.

With a determined gesture, Nathan dried his tears and those of his beloved wife, took her in his arms and hugged her to his breast tightly, then said firmly:

- I promise you, my sweet, to work without rest day and night, if necessary, and to bring you to my side as quickly as possible. I will spare no effort or sacrifice to shorten the time that we will be apart.

- Yes, she answered, I know you will and we will soon be together again.

Nathan responded by holding her even closer. For her part, she loved his caresses and began to kiss him fervently, forgetting her inhibitions and giving in to unbridled passion. It was an unforgettable night, a combination of joy and sorrow. As dawn began to break on the new day, bringing Nathan's departure closer, they held each other even tighter, wondering when they would see each other again. Neither was able to sleep all night. They wanted to be together and share the few remaining hours until daybreak. Nathan did not wish to leave, nor did Sarah want him to go, but both knew it was necessary. There was no other way.

Chapter 11

Max awoke with a start, feeling nervous and fearing that he had overslept. He felt exhausted, in spite of the hours he had slept. It must be from the intense work over the past weeks, the tension from preparing the trip and his subconscious worry at leaving his mother and sister with the burden of so much responsibility. For months he had been turning over and over the same question in his mind: was the trip to South America only a kind of escape from the overwhelming daily problems that just kept increasing?

An objective analysis of the facts using cold logic brought him over and over again to the same conclusion and served to reaffirm the clear conviction that if they continued on the same difficult path, fighting against the current, they would only arrive at a state of extreme misery, with the additional burden of knowing that they had rejected their opportunity to change that pathway and seek a better future. The decision that had already been taken was thus, the most sensible and reasonable one. Pulling strength from his deepest reserves, with a quick, decisive movement he got up, went to the washroom, and after an invigorating cold shower, began to get dressed.

Contrary to his fear, it was still early. Rays of sunlight and the cock crowing had yet to announce the start of the new day. He carefully closed the suitcases and took them to the front door of the house. I will have a cup of tea, he thought, as he walked toward the kitchen. When he got there, he was surprised to find Sylvia sitting beside the window, her gaze staring out into space.

- But, mama, he exclaimed, chiding her gently, what are you doing here so early?

She roused from her meditation and looking at her son, answered affectionately.

- Good morning, Max. Come and sit beside me. I will make you some tea. I was feeling nervous and couldn't sleep well.

She carefully arranged her delicate, pale rose-colored housecoat, and began to speak.

- I was tired of dozing in bed, and a while ago I decided to get up and have something to drink. I am happy to be able to spend these moments with you.

- Thank you, mama. I am also happy to find you here. This gives us a chance to talk before I have to leave, as I was hoping to do.

- Let me put on the water to boil, Max, and I will sit with you and chat a bit.

Sylvia got up from the chair and patting his hand, went over to complete her task under her son's affectionate gaze.

- You are as beautiful as ever and look younger than your years. I pray God will keep you always healthy. I want to remember you as I see you right now, and when you join us I will be proud to introduce you as the most beautiful mother in the world.

- Thank you, my dear. I wish you all the best of everything, said Sylvia sitting down beside him again, but I am afraid that our meeting will not happen as soon as we would wish. Please don't be angry with me for not wanting to go to South America. I am already too old, and for me to leave my ancestral village where I grew up and have lived all my life, is more than I can bear.

- I have given up trying to convince you, he said in a serious voice, but I am sure of one thing. When Nathan and I are established there, God willing, and Sarah decides to go with the children to be with us, you will go with them despite your attachment to this place.

She looked him in the eyes sadly and did not answer. She did not wish to add more worries to her son's many burdens, but she would not go to South America. It was her final decision and nothing could change her mind. With Abraham buried here in the village, she would not leave.

- Good morning, Nathan greeted them as he entered the kitchen. You two are early birds. They aren't coming to fetch us just yet. Max, do you have everything ready for the trip?

- Yes, my luggage is at the front door of the house. I didn't want to make Abel wait. It was very kind of him to offer to take us to the train station.

- You are right. I'd better go back upstairs and bring my suitcases down right away.

- Where are you going? Sarah asked him as she passed him on her way into the kitchen.

- I'm coming right back, darling. I am going to bring my cases down.

- Good morning, all. Sarah said, giving Sylvia a kiss. How did you sleep?

- Not very well, her brother answered. Mama had a restless night. She told me she hardly slept at all. It must be because of our trip.

- Abel is already waiting for us, Nathan called from the front of the house.

- I'm coming; I won't be a minute, Max called back.

Sarah hurried out of the kitchen and her brother went over to his mother, hugged her tightly and said in a voice choked with emotion:

- Mama, it is time to say good-bye. Please try not to suffer, I beg you. We will all be together again soon, I am sure of it, and this will all seem like a dream. Take good care of yourself while I am gone. Eat well and send me news of anything you need so I can try to help. We will work hard and send you back money as soon as we can.

Sylvia squeezed him tightly to her heart, and with a great effort held back the tears that would give away her sadness, saying to him in a thick voice:

- May God bless you, my son, and be with you wherever you are, give you health and happiness and help you in all that you undertake.

- I hope it will be so, mama.

They continued their embrace for a long moment.

- Nathan, where are you? Sarah called out.

- Here, outside. I am putting the luggage into the carriage.

- Good morning, Abel, Sarah greeted him.

- It is good to see you, he answered.

- It was very kind of you to offer to take them to the train station.

- That is what friends are for. Where is Max?

- He is still talking to mama in the kitchen, but he knows you are here.

Here they come! he exclaimed as he saw them approaching.

After exchanging greetings, they continued to finish loading the luggage. When it was all ready, Nathan went to his wife and taking her in a deep, emotional embrace, he whispered in her ear:

- Please, my love, take good care of yourself and the children. I will come and get you soon. I promise.

- I know you will, my beloved. I will be counting every minute until you return.

- Come, Sarah, Max called. I want to say good-bye to you, dear sister. The two hugged each other with profound affection.

Tears of sorrow rolled down Sylvia's cheeks, as she wondered whether she would ever see her children together again.

- Mother, don't cry, Nathan implored. Our departure should not be a cause of suffering. We are doing it all for the good of the family.

- Yes, son, don't worry. We will be fine, Sylvia assured him, as she dried her tears and tried to hold back more.

Nathan hugged her and started to get into the carriage, where Max was already waiting for him.

Sarah stood beside her mother and put her arm around her shoulders in a protective gesture, and with the other hand began to wave good-bye, exclaiming:

- We will see you again soon! May God protect you.

Chapter 12

Mr. Flint chatted amicably as he drove the carriage to the train station at an easy pace. He was a good-hearted and sincere fellow, and because of these fine qualities, he was well-known and respected in the village. His wife, who was somewhat sickly and fragile, wasn't able to bear children and even though the couple had given up the idea of having their own children, they could not help wishing for the joy of parenthood. This unfulfilled desire had left a small mark of frustration on Abel Flint's life. An affectionate soul, he had managed to fill this void by turning his paternal affection toward Nathan's children, and treated them as if they were his own.

- Don't worry about your family, he said to them sincerely. You know how much I care about your children. I will be looking out for them and I will do my best to fill your shoes while you are gone.

- Thank you, Nathan answered him, giving him a affectionate pat on the back. We have always appreciated your friendship and we are truly fortunate to have someone like you to turn to in our times of need.

Abel interrupted the conversation and pulled up on the reins of the horse to let a herd of cattle cross the road. Nathan, meanwhile, started to drift off as he recalled the events of the previous day...

- Sarah, please, he remembered asking her, tell the children to come here. I want to speak to them. Tomorrow we leave at dawn and I won't have a chance to explain to them the reason for our trip to South America.

- Yes, I will call them right now, she answered as she walked over to the staircase.

She hurried down to the front door and opened it, then stopped a moment to catch her breath.

- Children, come here, she called out as loudly as she could.

- Coming, mama. What is it? asked Rachel, who was playing with a rag doll near the house.

- Your father wants to speak with all of you. Please, go find your brothers and sisters and when they are all together, come up to our room.

- Yes mama.

She obediently left her rag doll in a box that served as a cradle, and ran off.

- Samuel, Saul, Etty, Hannah, Mendel, where are you? she called out in her high-pitched child's voice. Please, answer me.

She waited a few moments and since nobody answered her call, she continued to run ahead. After a bit, she stopped on hearing some voices from the other side of the fence along the road. She came closer to see who was moving around and found the children playing hide-and-seek.

- I have been calling you for quite some time, she said angrily. Haven't you heard me?

- What is the problem? Samuel asked her curiously.

- Papa wants us to come in so he can talk to all of us.

Please, help me to find everyone.

- All right, let's go, he answered.

Between the two of them, they found their other brothers and sisters and went up to her parents' room. Standing in front of the door, Rachel knocked lightly and on hearing her father say, "Come in!", she turned the doorknob. They all went in together and approached their parents. Sarah looked intently at the tableau formed by her children and could not help thinking: How beautiful they are! What happiness they bring to us in the midst of our problems. I wonder how the departure of their father and uncle will affect them. I hope I can make up for their absence.

- My children, Nathan began, getting their attention. Thank you for coming so quickly. Please, sit down beside me; I want to speak with you.

Samuel and Rachel sat down on the two armchairs near their father and the rest went to sit on the bed, where Sarah was leaning against the headboard.

- As you know, he continued, your uncle Max and I are leaving tomorrow for South America, and before I leave I wanted to tell you all that I love you all very much. You are my reason for living. I would never have thought of going on such a long trip if it were not for the need to earn more and improve our family's situation. Your mother and I want only the best for you and that is why we have decided to make this sacrifice and be apart for some time, so that your uncle and I can find good jobs in South America and earn better money. He paused, looking over at where Sarah was sitting, and saw a silent tear roll down his wife's cheek, which she brushed away quickly. He turned his attention again to his speech and watching his children's faces, innocently upturned toward him, he continued:

- I would like to give you a lovely house, because that is what you deserve, with many rooms and surrounded by a beautiful garden full of flowers. I would also like to send you to better schools and be able to satisfy mama's every wish, because there is no better wife and mother in the whole world than your mother. Please, while I am gone, take care of her for me and for you.

- Yes, papa, they all answered in chorus.

On hearing their answer, Nathan opened his arms to his children, who ran excitedly toward him to give him kisses and hugs as soon as he finished speaking.

- Papa, asked Samuel curiously, after some time, when will we see each other again?

- I think I haven't explained things fully, he answered immediately. Our idea is to work hard until we have earned enough money to send for you.

- I don't understand, said Rachel. Can you explain the part about sending for us?

- It is very simple, he answered patiently. I am saying that as soon as I have the money, I will send you tickets so you can come to join us in South America.

- And who will stay with grandmother if we all leave here? Saul asked with a worried frown.

- Don't worry about her, Sarah said, smiling. When we go, she will go with us. Of course we won't leave her behind.

- What about our house and our friends? asked Etty as he looked at his father doubtfully.

- Don't worry about a thing. You will have a house to live in and new friends to play with, Nathan answered as he glanced at Sarah, while silently wishing fervently that he would be able to make these promises come true.

- You are very quiet, Nathan, Max commented, rousing him from his thoughts. Any new worries, other than all those we already have? he added in a jesting manner, showing off his famous sense of humor.

- I was thinking about Sarah and the children, he answered as a twinge of regret passed across his face. It was very sad to have to say good-bye yesterday. I tried to explain to them the reason for our trip, but I wonder if they are not too small to understand our family's problems. I still have many doubts about whether we are making the right choice and I tremble at the thought that we might regret all this in the future.

- Here we are at the station! exclaimed Abel, stopping the carriage in front of the building.

- Do you need some help with the luggage? a polite young fellow asked as he came up to them.

- No thank you, answered Max. We can unload it ourselves.

The fellow moved on with a disappointed look, while they began to place the baggage on the sidewalk.

- Max, do you know where they sell the train tickets? Nathan asked him after a moment, picking up his two suitcases.

- No, we had better wait for Abel and go together to find out.

- Agreed.

As soon as their helpful driver and guide came back, they went into the building. They bought their tickets and after a short while, heard the boarding call over the loudspeaker. They said good-bye to Abel with many hugs and reminders to take care, then began to board the train. Max went ahead through the narrow aisles, looking for their seat numbers. Nathan followed with his head down, brooding and plagued by doubt about their decision to undertake the risky trip.

- Nathan, called Max. Here I am. Come and sit down. The train is about to leave.

Chapter 13

One day, Sarah was resting on the chair in the sitting room that had been Abraham's favorite when he was alive. The curtains were closed and absolute silence governed the dimly lit space. Somber thoughts filled the anguished woman's mind. My God, could something terrible have happened to them? They have been gone for two months already and we still have had no news. I remember as if it were yesterday when Nathan asked me not to worry, and that he would contact us as soon as he arrived at his destination and tell us how they were getting along. And now, nothing! I have had no news from them and no one to ask. Abel tells me not to worry. He thinks that they are fine, but just have not been able to get in touch with us. I can only hope that this is the only reason we have not heard from them.

Sarah got up listlessly. Fatigue and tedium overwhelmed her. The hard work and strain of the past months were beginning to show. Since the men left, she had been accepting any type of work, no matter how humble or demanding. And then, last week, she visited the doctor without telling Sylvia so as not to worry her, and her suspicions were confirmed. She was pregnant! On hearing the news, she felt immense joy, but as the surprise faded and she began to reflect on her family's precarious situation, she was terrified. Bringing a new child into the world would mean new problems for everyone. I have to tell my mother, she thought and started toward her room decisively. She called at the door several times before finally hearing Sylvia's voice inviting her to come in.

- Sorry, mama, I didn't want to disturb you. If you are sleeping, I can come back later.

- No child, don't worry. I was just napping for a moment. You know....at my age, I have to rest more often. But come in and take a seat. I am happy to have some time with you. You have been so busy working lately. Thank God, the children seem to have noticed your efforts to take care of the house and are behaving like angels. Sarah was quiet for a few moments, then in a pitiful voice blurted out to Sylvia:

- I am pregnant!

- What did you say?

- Yes, mama, you heard me correctly. I am expecting a baby. The doctor confirmed it a couple of days ago and I am so upset, she said, breaking into an emotional sob.

- My dear daughter, you couldn't give me better news! Why are you crying? I don't understand.

- But, don't you see? she asked, wiping away the copious tears. As the pregnancy goes on, I will just get weaker and you know how much we need the earnings from my odd jobs. If I can't keep up the pace I have now, the money coming in will diminish or disappear altogether. Plus, having a baby is very expensive. Where will I get the money we need to take care of a baby, if we can barely make ends meet with the expenses we have now?

- Sarah, please, don't fret. These past few months have been very difficult for all of us, especially since we have had no news from the men. But I am sure this situation won't last forever. Max and Nathan's silence is probably due to a delay in the mail delivery. There is a vast distance between Europe and South America and this country is also very large, we must be optimistic. God willing, we will soon receive not only good news from them, but also the financial help they promised us.

Chapter 14

Sarah finished reading Nathan's letter with a sigh, and looking over at Rachel, who was sitting nearby, sensed her daughter's barely contained anxiety to hear how her beloved family was faring.

- Thank God, your father and uncle Max are fine. They had a hard trip over in the ship, but they have already made their way to Bogotá, the capital city in a country called Colombia, in the northern part of South America. They rented a small room in a boarding house for the two of them. They don't say too much about the city in the letter, but I am relieved to hear what they say about their efforts to find work. They have met several people who they knew from Poland, and who are trying to help them. As we thought, they are having some problems with the new language. When people there come over to speak with them, they don't understand and even though they are polite and respectful, they try to stay away because they can't communicate with them. It is a truly difficult situation! Rachel giggled happily on hearing her mother's words.

- Mama, may I go and tell my brothers and sisters about papa's letter? she asked excitedly.

- Of course, child, run along and tell them the news.

As Rachel skipped out, Sarah looked over at Sylvia, who was absorbed reading Max's letter. She waited a moment, understanding her mother's deep feelings on receiving the anxiously awaited letter from her distant son, and watched as her eyes filled with tears, undoubtedly due to the relief felt after her months of worry and fears.

- Didn't I tell you? her mother said, overjoyed. They are well. I felt it in my bones.

- Yes, you were right, Sarah answered, hugging her. How happy I am to see these letters! Nathan told me about the city and the people there. They are different from us, but he is happy and seems to be doing quite well.

- Max is also optimistic about the efforts they have both made to find work, added Sylvia. Some of their friends have given them samples of cloth to sell from door to door, in the neighborhoods around the city. He also mentioned the problems they are having with the language and because they don't know their way around the city. They often get lost as they try to find their way, but are very grateful for the help they are getting from our friends. They have already started to make a little money.

- About the money, mama, Nathan says he is sorry they cannot send us anything right now. It seems they haven't earned very much and they need a little money to get along themselves. However, he told me not to worry. He thinks he will be able to earn more soon to help us.

- You see, daughter? Things are not so bad, and as the old saying goes, "A child is born bearing his own fortune". The news of your pregnancy comes together with the happiness of receiving good news from our loved ones. And as soon as they hear of the new baby, be assured that they will spare no effort to give that little child a better life.

- Thank you, mama, for your understanding and help. I feel much better already, and am rejoicing inside to imagine a new son in my arms.

- And what if it is a girl? asked Sylvia, with a mischievous smile.

- I will be just as delighted, Sarah answered happily.

Chapter 15

Time passed with an inexorably slow pace. It had been four years since Sarah had seen Nathan and she missed him terribly. Sometimes, in the middle of the night, she imagined him close and wondered sadly when she would have the joy of seeing him again.

Many things had happened in the past few years, some of them wonderful, like the birth of a beautiful baby girl who she named Miriam, and who had brought much happiness to them all despite her birth into such inauspicious circumstances. Sarah vividly remembered the birth, when she had desperately missed not having her husband by her side, as it had been during the birth of the other children. During her labor, she didn't know if the pain of the contractions was worse, or the pain of Nathan's absence.

After she recovered from the delivery, she managed to get work in the store that her parents had once owned. The previous owners had left town and the new owners knew of Sarah's experience there and decided to offer her work. She delightedly accepted the job and felt a huge relief that she was able to stop taking in clothes for washing and doing other tiresome odd jobs that she had to accept for lack of other opportunities. Nathan sent her a little money every month from South America. This sum, together with her own earnings, allowed them to live a little better and provided a small amount of ease in their otherwise meager existence. By being careful with her money, she had managed to save a few zlotys. Sarah used these savings to spruce up the house.

She painted the house a pale color, which made it seem larger and covered the chairs in a deep blue floral pattern. If Nathan and Max could only see these changes! she thought sometimes, with a mixture of hope and chagrin. She left only one chair as it had always been: her father's old chair. She couldn't bring herself to touch it, with all the memories it still contained for her. The curtains had come down from the rods and she had spent one whole afternoon washing and starching them until they looked new again. Their beige color set off the cream tone of the walls and the whole place looked bright and cozy. The children were thrilled to see all the positive changes in their home.

One day, Sylvia came over to her daughter and said:

- My dear, you are working too hard. All day you toil in the shop and when you come home, take care of the house and the children, and on top of this keep working to fix everything without any rest. You cannot go on like this; you will make yourself ill and all your efforts will be wasted.

- Mama, answered Sarah, This is the way I can numb my worries and stop thinking so much. It has already been four long years since our loved ones traveled so far away. If I had know how long this separation would last, I would never have agreed to it, or at least, I would never have let Nathan go. Miriam is already three years old and her own father has never met her. My children are growing up without a father to help them and I am here without a flesh and blood husband by my side.

- Sarah, Sylvia said, stroking her hair, when you see your husband again and have a better life, you will know that he made the right decision. All your suffering will have been worthwhile.

After a few days, Sarah received another letter from Nathan. In it, he asked her to send his son, Samuel, as soon as possible. Money to purchase the train tickets and ship's passage was included in the letter. He felt he needed the boy's help to be able to earn the money needed to bring them more quickly.

Samuel was ready in a matter of days. Sarah and Sylvia, with Abel's help, took him to the train station, where he set off on his voyage alone, with all his father's instructions for the trip. Finally everything was ready and he boarded the train, his mother's embraces almost crushing him, as she said to him:

- My dear son, please take care of yourself and be very careful. With the help of God, you will be well. We will be praying for you until you reach your father's side.

- Good-bye, mama. Don't worry about me. It will all be fine.

But as soon as he was inside the train car, he began to weep as he looked out at his mother and grandmother waving their tearful farewell.

It was a long trip. He had to travel by rail from Warsaw to Germany, then to Holland, where he took a ship to the Colombian coast, (Puerto Colombia). He did not want to admit it, but he was truly afraid.

Chapter 16

The ship had been docked at Puerto Colombia for a few hours already. Nathan wiped the sweat from his brow over and over again. The heat was stifling and the mosquitoes wouldn't stop biting him for an instant. Nevertheless, he stayed there motionless, staring at the gangplank where the third class passengers had started to descend moments before.

For a split-second he thought he recognized Samuel among the passengers. He spotted a young man who appeared to be exhausted after a long and hard trip, moving down the gangplank with a slow, hesitating gait. But his hopes were dashed as he watched the young fellow's parents grasp his arm to prevent him from falling down.

Nathan was consumed with anxiety. While Samuel had been traveling across the ocean over the past few weeks, Nathan had been imagining any number of tragic accidents that could have happened to his son: from death by drowning to not being able to find him at the pier when the ship finally docked. He felt guilty over having sent for the boy, who was still so young. But he absolutely needed some help to be able to keep up the struggle for his family.

Things had not been as easy as Max, the eternal optimist, had imagined. The fact that they spoke no Spanish was the biggest hurdle they had to overcome, in addition to the fact that they knew nothing about the people and customs of the country. They also knew little about selling fabric, but thanks to their audacity and determination to make a go of it, they managed to earn the respect and trust of those they went to visit. When their potential customers saw the immigrants' efforts to make themselves understood, they took pity on them and even corrected their mistakes, trying to help the salesmen. Given this friendly reception, the men found the confidence to go back and continue to offer their merchandise.

One of Max and Nathan's greatest sales successes was setting up a system of deferred payments or layaway, which was a good incentive for the immigrant buyers since they could purchase without having to pay the full amount, and just put down weekly payments according to their ability to pay. Sometimes, because they didn't know their way around the city, Max and Nathan would be unable to find their way back to the client where they had sold the merchandise and would have to give it up as a loss.

Little by little, they were able to overcome these obstacles and began to feel more comfortable with the work. Yet, at night they would return exhausted from walking through all the neighborhoods of the city and often would even forget to stop at a market to buy some food so as not to faint from hunger. But they had to go on. There was no turning back if they were to bring their family here. Nothing else was important.

Nathan squinted, peering into the distance. For a moment he looked away from the gangplank but he would not allow himself to take his eyes off the scene for fear of missing the boy when he finally came off the ship. The pier was crowded with people and it would be very difficult to find him later.

The passengers continued to pour off the ship. Fatigue and the intense heat made disembarkation a trying experience.

A space opened up among the people in front of him craning their necks to look for their various family members, and he tried to reach the first row to be able to see better and look closely at every single person arriving at the pier.

Suddenly, on the upper part of the gangplank, a handsome young boy appeared carrying an enormous packsack with all his possessions.

- It's my son! Here I am, Samuel! Here I am!! he called out in a booming voice, while waving his hand as energetically as the small space allowed. Samuel, Samuel! he kept calling out in Polish, trying to draw the boy's attention to him.

People turned around to look at him, surprised by the strange language, and he, excited as he was by the joyous arrival of his son, hardly noticed the inquisitive glances. Samuel continued slowly down the passageway. His heart beat quicker than usual. During the whole trip, he wondered what he would do if he wasn't able to find his father once he arrived. The instructions he had been given took him up to the moment he got off the ship. From there on, everything depended on finding his father. He looked around carefully, studying the people grouped at the end of the gangplank.

All of a sudden, he noticed a man pushing his way through the people in the first row. Samuel, Samuel! he heard the voice calling out in his native Polish.

- Papa, here I am!, he answered and began to push and elbow his way through the passengers around him in an attempt to hurry down. After such a long separation, father and son reunited in a silent embrace, broken only by the occasional sigh of happiness breaking through.

Nathan held his son for a time in his arms. His joy at seeing his eldest son, after four years, filled him with deep emotion. Thank God, you have arrived here safe and sound. I am so happy! he said, holding the boy at arm's length and taking in every detail. How you have grown over the past few years! I can hardly recognize you. When I left Poland you were but a child and now you can come to me a man!

- Time passes, papa, and we all grow up. I am fifteen now and you are right, I am not a child anymore. – Of course, Samuel, you have already had your Bar Mitzvah[1]. In our religion, every boy who has reached thirteen years old is considered an adult, but I am still amazed to see how big and strong you are. May God grant you a long life.

- Thank you, papa.

- Now, come my son, let us not linger here anymore. There are too many people and it is far too hot. Tell me, do you have any more luggage besides this packsack, which I must say is quite enormous all by itself? Nathan asked with a smile.

- No, papa, I have everything in here. Mama thought it would be best to pack like this, so I could take care of everything more easily. Nathan, on hearing his wife mentioned, hung on Samuel's every word, wishing to question him fur-

---

[1] *Bar mitzvah.* The name means son of the commandment or age of majority (bound to fulfill religious duties). It is the initiation of the young Jewish man into the religious community at the age of thirteen. This ritual constitutes one of the most important and fundamental of the Jewish rites. (Author's note.)

ther, but noticing the boy's forehead bathed in sweat, he decided to wait for a better time to find out every detail of his family's life and experiences. He suggested they leave.

- Where are we going? Samuel asked curiously, walking along beside his father.

- We still have quite a way to go before we arrive at our destination. We have to take a train to Ambalema; from there we will go by car to the city of Ibagué, which is the capital of Tolima, and then on from there by train to Bogota. Your uncle Max is anxious to see you. So, let's not waste any time getting on our way.

After several exhausting days of travel, they arrived at their destination....the guesthouse where Max and Nathan were staying. They bounded up the stairs, oblivious to the weight of the large packsack. Nathan put the key in the lock and opened the door.

- Uncle Max, where are you? We are here, yelled Samuel from a corner of the room as he set down his luggage.

- Where is my favorite nephew? answered Max excitedly, opening his arms.

Samuel ran to him, answering with a strong, manly embrace.

- Why who are you? exclaimed Max incredulous, holding him away to get a better look. It can't be; you have turned into a grown man.

- It is me alright, uncle. Time marches on and you know it has been quite a long time since you have seen me. I have been anxiously waiting to be reunited with papa and with you. I have missed you both so much. If mama could only see us together now! She wishes every day for our family to be together again and prays to God to keep you healthy and that you may save enough money to send for them soon.

- Samuel, Nathan stammered out apprehensively, tell us more about them. You know that Max and I have been sending some money every month. Is it enough to cover the basic expenses?

- To tell you the truth, papa, the first months were very hard on mama. She was so worried because she had no news of you and it was a constant strain on her. She was working day and night, without resting, in any job she could find. Then she found out about her pregnancy and slowed down a little, and began to work a bit less both in the house and outside the house.

- My poor Sarah, exclaimed Nathan remorsefully. I have made you suffer so much!

- Then, Samuel continued his report, with the money you sent things began to improve and mama was able to take it a bit easier; up to then, she had been quite worried that she wouldn't be able to keep up with the heavy work because of her advanced condition. She was doing odd jobs for different people to make ends meet at home. Then, as you know from our letters, once my sister, Miriam, was born, mama got work at the shop that used to belong to our grandparents and this was a great relief for her.

- And how is your grandmother? asked Max with a trembling voice.

- She is fine now, uncle Max. Right after you left, she was very sad and depressed. She didn't want to eat or speak to anyone, and even we couldn't seem to cheer her up. We were very worried, especially when she used to sit in front of the window in your room, uncle Max, and spend hours sitting there motionless staring vacantly out the window. He dropped his head in grief as he listened to Samuel's story, but the boy continued. Little by little, and with a lot of patience, she began to come around and today she is the same grandma as before. She takes care of us, helps us when we are having problems, and helps to cheer up mama and keep her going.

- And physically, how is she doing? asked Nathan with interest.

- Generally, she is in good health, but it seems to me she has aged a lot in the past few years.

- What I wouldn't give to be with them! Max said pensively, especially with my mother. I am afraid that something will happen to her before I have the chance to see her again.

- Please, don't say that, Nathan pleaded. When you speak like that, I start to doubt all over again the wisdom of our coming to South America to try and improve our family's lot in life. Where is your optimism? Are you going to weaken now, when we are half-way there? Let's be positive, and with God's help, we will soon have enough money to bring Sylvia and Sarah and everyone else.

Chapter 17

Two years had passed, although it seemed more like two hundred years to Sarah, since Samuel had left Jalowiec to go and meet his father in Bogota, the capital of Colombia, in South America. Despite this, she carried in her heart the image of her boy, already becoming a man with the beginnings of a muscled chest, carrying a huge packsack on his shoulder, boarding the train...

Over the past twenty-four months, with the dual absence of her husband and her eldest son, she felt even more abandoned. Each day, each hour, each minute, she wished fervently to be with them, but her long-cherished illusion that this would happen in the near future, began to fade and die. When Nathan left, she had thought it would only be a few months before she would see him again, but the months had turned into one year and the year had turned into five more, and meanwhile Sarah suffered the anguish of seeing her family separated.

The arrival of letters helped her to bear the burden, but she couldn't help worrying about the risks faced by her husband and son....and her brother, Max, so far away in that strange country with such different people.

Sylvia had aged greatly. Her face revealed the passage of time and the pain she had to bear. In contrast, Sarah's children were growing strong and healthy, and had become accustomed to the idea of an absent father, and their eventual reunion with him and Samuel. One day, they received a letter announcing the arrival of Max. From that moment, they rejoiced in the happy news.

Preparations for his arrival started weeks in advance. The house had to be spotless and shining. Sarah prepared her brother's favorite dishes and watched happily as her mother began to undergo a transformation as a result of the marvelous news of her son's arrival.

The long-awaited day arrived and Sylvia sat nervously in the kitchen, her eyes fixed on the wall clock. She didn't know the exact time of his arrival, but she could not control the pounding of her heart. How much longer? she thought. After so many years, and now with only a short time left to have my son in my arms again, I feel like a schoolgirl on her first day of class or a teenager on the first date. Sometimes, we humans are so complicated; I don't know why I suddenly have no patience. I should simply be happy and grateful for his return home, but I feel so nervous and anxious. It has been a difficult test over these years and now that we are so close to the end, I somehow can't believe that Max will soon be here.

- Mama, come here, Sarah called to her from the living room. I want to show you something.

Sylvia's heart started pounding even more on hearing this. For a moment she thought her moment of happiness had come. She slowly got up from the chair and went into the living room with a racing heart.

- Doesn't our house look lovely? When Max comes in and sees all the changes, he will think he has come to the wrong address. I am so excited about his arrival. I wish that Nathan and Samuel could have come with him, she added in a sad voice.

- Yes, my dear, I would also like to see our whole family together again.

- When Max arrives, he will tell us about his plans and will explain why they couldn't come with him on this trip. I can't help worrying about them, and whether they are keeping well.

- Don't worry, dear. Don't torment yourself. You will soon know everything about their lives in South America.

A few more hours passed and at nightfall, Rachel heard a knocking at the front door. She opened the door and on seeing her uncle Max, ran to hug him without saying a word. It had been so long since she had seen him! But it really was him, here at the house.

- Oh, my girl, how you have grown! he exclaimed, taking a long look at Rachel, after lifting her away from the embrace. It seems like yesterday that we left on this trip and you were just a little thing, but you have turned into a woman...and a very beautiful one, at that.

- Thank you, uncle. Please come in, don't stay in the doorway. Everyone is anxious to see you.

Max brought in his luggage and leaving it in the entranceway, started toward his mother's room and knocked twice on the door. Sylvia opened the door and her incredulous eyes filled with tears of joy.

- My son, finally you are here!

Max hugged her affectionately and tears sprang to his eyes.

- Mama, how I longed to see you! You cannot imagine how I have missed you. Sylvia answered by squeezing him hard with her old, but still vigorous arms. At last she had her beloved son back. After a short while, Sarah came in, followed by Rachel.

- Welcome home, Max! she exclaimed, moving in between Sylvia to give him a hug and a fraternal kiss on the cheek.

- Thank you, Sarah. I am very happy to be back. I missed all this.

The rest of the children came in then to welcome Max. Their joy was palpable and their faces reflected the enormous affection they held for their fun-loving uncle. He had been a very important paternal figure in their lives and his return home after such a long absence was a cause for celebration.

Max told them many stories and details about the country where he was living with Nathan and Samuel. He spoke for hours about their good and bad experiences and told them how much their father and brother were missing them.

Sarah and Sylvia watched him entranced. They never tired of hearing him speaking to the children, but they also wanted to be alone with him to bombard him with their own questions.

-Now children, said Sylvia after a time, Uncle Max has just arrived and he must be very tired from his trip. Leave him alone now and tomorrow, when he is rested, he can keep telling you more stories.

- Yes, that's right, agreed Sarah. Tomorrow is a school day and it is getting late. Say goodnight and go to bed.

- Yes, mama, they all replied in unison, with a look that belied their true feelings. One by one they came over to him, and hugged him lovingly before leaving the room.

- I must congratulate you, Sarah. They are wonderful children. You have brought them up very well. I said the same to Nathan, when Samuel came to stay with us. And you, mama, must have certainly had a hand in that area. You are close to your grandchildren and I know how much you love them.

Sylvia nodded her head in agreement, and then silently listened to her son continue.

- Sarah, Max went on, first of all, I want you to know that Nathan and Samuel are doing very well. They are working terribly hard and don't let up for a second in their determination to bring you over as quickly as possible, but in every part of the world it is hard to make a living. Also, part of their earnings must, of course, pay for their own expenses and the rest they send here every month to help out the family, so their savings to buy the tickets for your trip are not as much as they would have liked. But, don't despair. They work very hard day after day, and I am sure that they will soon manage to achieve this goal.

Max paused, and watching the concerned faces of the two women, continued talking. As you know from our letters, as soon as Samuel arrived in Bogota, we decided to buy two knitting machines. With these machines, Nathan and Samuel began to knit sweaters and I would take them to the marketplace and sell them there, but after a time, I was offered a better paying job in a stocking factory. So I decided to try my fortune and leave Nathan to try and earn more for himself by leaving him the machines. I am a bachelor and besides earning the money to pay for mama's trip to South America, my expenses are not much compared to Nathan and the rest of you.

- And they know how to work these machines? asked Sylvia curiously.

- Of course, mama. At first it was difficult, because of some small but very important details. We didn't know how to place the yarn in the machine, or the proper tension or how to do different stitches. But we learned all these aspects and now, Nathan and Samuel have become very good at it.

Naturally, he had brought along some sweaters as gifts, and they could see the results of the process he had just finished describing. In addition, Nathan was working two days a week as a volunteer, slaughtering animals using the kosher[1] butchering technique. It had to be done very precisely and only a person with Nathan's religious training could carry out this type of work.

- But, do they pay him for this work? asked Sarah.

- No, sister, as I explained, it is volunteer work, so Nathan doesn't receive any pay, although he gets a lot of satisfaction from the work. In the Jewish community in Bogota, everyone knows him and likes him. He is making a very good name for himself due to this noble activity.

- Tell me about Samuel, interrupted Sarah anxiously. How is he doing? What jobs is he doing?

- He is a great boy, Sarah. As soon as he arrived, he started working hard to help his father get together enough money to send for the family. At the beginning, he just did basic tasks, like threading wool, separating colors, putting samples in order, and other odd jobs that didn't require too much expertise. But Samuel is a clever boy and before we knew it, he not only learned how to communicate with people in Spanish, but also to experiment with the machines and he has been able to create modern sweaters that some clients like very much.

- God bless him! exclaimed Sylvia with emotion. I am glad to know of his contribution during these times that are

---

[1] *Kosher.* (Hebrew: proper, acceptable), a term that in Rabbinical literature is used to designate that which is permitted and legitimate in accordance with the rituals of the Jewish religion. Even where permitted foods are concerned, a series of conditions must be met before these are considered kosher. Due to the knowledge required for ritual slaughter, this is left to professional butchers (shohet) who are authorized by a Rabbinical College, which has issued them a special certificate.

so difficult for the family. Besides, this will help him to become a responsible and serious young man, and form him for the rest of his life. Good habits acquired in childhood and adolescence stay with a person his whole life.

- That is true, mama. You are so right, Max added, looking at Sarah, who didn't miss a word of Max and Sylvia's conversation.

- And how is Nathan? Sarah asked, impatient for more news.

- If you mean his health, thank God he is very well. In terms of his mood, he varies. Some days he is very optimistic, thinking of being reunited with you soon, and other times he gets depressed when he starts doubting as to whether leaving here was the right thing to do. For some time, there have been rumors about a possible war in Europe and this has caused him an unbelievable amount of worry. His concern over this doesn't let him rest. Day after day he imagines that something may happen to you and he suffers because he is not here to protect and help you.

A few days ago, we went to the El Cometa cafeteria, owned by a Mr. Max Szapiro. As Nathan has told you in his letters, almost all the immigrants from Poland and the other European countries meet there. After dinner, most sit and play cards and share their thoughts, but that night, no one could concentrate on the game. The news about a possible war had us all scared to death.

Since about five years ago, the Hitlerian threat began to be felt, but no one paid it the proper attention at that time. Max paused briefly and then continued, an expression of unease on his face. The Germans have made public their plan to conquer the world at any price. They consider themselves to be a superior race and are ready to prove it. It is feared that their first objectives for planned attacks will be the countries that are strategically important to achieve these ends, and Poland, since it is in the center of Europe, is one such country.

- What would be the consequences of all this? asked Sarah with consternation.

- I cannot answer that question exactly, but it would seem that there could be great damage to us. The so-called Nazis don't like Jews, or should I say, they hate us, and they may decide to wreak vengeance on us simply because we practice the Jewish religion.

- But, why is there such hate? Sylvia asked, unable to contain herself.

- I do not know, mama. No one understands it. It seems that Hitler suffers from an inferiority complex and wants to cover it up by seeking power. They also say that he had a difficult experience while an adolescent, when he found his mother in the arms of a Jewish lover, and supposedly from this incident he has developed a hatred of everything related to Judaism.

In nineteen twenty-three, Hitler was the head of the National Socialist Workers' Party and hoped to defeat the government in Berlin, loyal to the principles of the constitution of Weimar. After inciting riots and failing, he was put in prison and in his jail cell wrote a book titled, "Mein Kampf", which is a doctrine preaching hatred of Jews and humanity. In this book, he classifies nations according to race and purity of their blood, instead of according to their spiritual and cultural development.

In any case, the news are not good. We have heard of isolated attacks on people in Warsaw just because of the simple fact of belonging to our religion, and this is very alarming. The stories we have heard are horrible. Among them, we have heard of girls in the community being raped, attacks on private Jewish establishments, and even burning down synagogues while people are there praying.

- Oh no! exclaimed Sylvia, it cannot be.

- Mama, don't worry, said Sarah, coming over to her in a protective gesture. It cannot be as bad as they have heard in South America. You know how things are exaggerated when they go from one person to another.

- You are right, my dear. I had better settle down and get some rest. I am quite tired now.

- Go ahead, mama. In a minute I will come in and see you, said Max, giving her a hug.

- All right, my dear son, I will wait for you, answered Sylvia, going out of the room.

As soon as she had left, Sarah closed the door and spoke in a low voice to Max.

- Mama got very nervous just then and I understand her. She thinks her family is in danger. But, be honest with me, Max, is the situation really that dangerous or do you think it is only a lot of rumors?

- Yes, Sarah, I believe that it is real and it is worrisome. Nathan and I have spoke on a number of occasions and we have come to a conclusion. We have to get you out of the country as soon as possible. The only problem is the economic issue. We still don't have enough money for tickets for the whole family.

Nathan's suggestion is to make the move in two steps. Mama, you and the four smallest children will go first and you will leave Rachel, Saul and Etty with Abel and his wife, and as soon as the rest of the money is together, we will send for them.

- No, absolutely not! Leave my three children here? Absolutely impossible. Either we all go or we all stay and face whatever happens here, but I will not be separated from my children.

- But, Sarah!

- I will not accept any discussion, Max. It is clear for

me. Either all or none.

He lowered his head, defeated. When he had spoken with Nathan the last time before leaving for Poland, he had promised to convince Sarah to travel with Sylvia and the four children. But he had failed in this task. He knew her too well, and realized just how impossible it would be to change her decision.

Chapter 18

Nathan stretched his arms in an attempt to relax his tired muscles after a long day at work, and, yawning, looked over at the clock on the wall. It was six o'clock in the afternoon. Four hours ago, Samuel had left to take some sweaters to some clients and he had continued working. At various points during the afternoon he had thought of taking a break, but, without quite understanding why, had felt anxious and preferred to keep busy. He stayed in his chair at work for a few more minutes, then looked around at the modest room around him.

It was a small room, used by both him and Samuel for their living space and to work. On one side of the room they had placed two cots against the wall and had improvised a couple of night tables using wooden boards held up by bricks.

Leaning against the second wall was an old chest of drawers in dark wood that Max had picked up second-hand to store his belongings. Parallel to this wall they had placed two knitting machines, where each one sat most of the day, and a storage bin to hold wool, thread, needles, samples, booklets and any other necessary materials or work tools.

Light filtered in through long windows set into the upper part of the wall, which, because of their height, made it practically impossible to see the view outside the building. At first, Max and Nathan didn't like this arrangement, but over time they stopped noticing it and grew used to their surroundings, which were otherwise sufficient for their modest needs. And to make up a little for the lack of garden greenery, they bought a picture of a lovely tropical paradise and hung it on the wall above the cots.

A wall clock hanging over the knitting machines reminded them every day when to start and finish their work day. They had access to a common bathroom at the end of a long hallway lined with other rented rooms, but the inconvenience was balanced out by the modest rent they had to pay. This allowed them to save more money to reach their goal.

When they had just arrived in Bogota, they rented these quarters, but as soon as Samuel came from Poland, Max decided to give up his place and move to another small room in the same part of the building, two doors down.

Nathan stood up languidly from the chair and walked over to the chest of drawers. He took out a thick gray overcoat and placed it on his shoulders. He wanted to take a short walk, to see if any mail had come in from Poland.

The sun had already fallen low in the sky and it was starting to get dark in the city streets. Nathan inhaled the fresh air deeply, enjoying the freedom from being shut in all day. After asking the owner of the building if there were any letters for him, and receiving a polite shake of the head, he decided to take a stroll to settle his thoughts.

In the front of his mind was Max's absence, since he

had left two months ago. The trip had been more than justified and they had already had news from him, but still they missed him. Samuel, of course, partially filled the void, but Max was a very special person. Naturally generous, he sincerely cared for his brother-in-law and showed a great willingness to help him at all times, and because of this, Nathan grew to love him more each day.

Since Max had left to work in the stocking factory, there had been a certain distance between the two brothers-in-law, but they had agreed to meet every afternoon after work to take a walk and talk about what had happened during the day and find a solution for any problem that came up. Nathan missed these lively exchanges of opinions, concerns, and often, memories of the family and their native land, and waited anxiously to be able to take them up again.

He continued pensively on his way, and suddenly, came upon a rubber ball that had been thrown in his direction. He kept it in his hand and watched a group of children coming over to look for their ball. One of them caught it as Nathan tossed it back, stammered a timid thank you and smiled broadly, then ran to join the others.

Oh God, he thought, if only these were my children! If I could only see them like these ones, so healthy and happy, running after a ball, but they are so far away. It has been years since I've seen them and I cannot share their games with them. Maybe they don't even remember their father anymore....he held his face in his hands and remained still for several moments.

- No, no, I cannot let myself drown in despair, he said, shaking himself. I will soon bring them here and I need to have courage more than ever at this time. This is what Max would say if he were with me now.

With this resolution of spirit, he hurried back to the

building, where his son would most certainly already be back.

The next day, as they were getting dressed to begin the day's activities, they heard knocks on the door of their room. Nathan hurriedly finished dressing and as soon as he opened the door, saw the owner of the building with an envelope in his hand.

- Mr. Ratovich, a telegram just arrived for you. Since it says "urgent", I decided to bring it up immediately.

- Thank you for your consideration, he answered nervously.

- I hope it isn't bad news, she added, before moving to go back down the staircase.

Nathan closed the door, feeling a heavy pressure in his chest.

- Who was it papa? Asked Samuel curiously.

- Mrs. Gonzalez, he answered, tearing open the envelope with trembling fingers and beginning to read:

Mr. Nathan Ratovich.
Carrera 13 # 24 - 25
Bogotá - Colombia.
Sorry to inform. accident at school. Mendel dead. burial today.
Max

- Nooo!... he yelled horrified, falling on his knees to the floor.

- Papa, for God's sake, what is the matter? asked Samuel, running over beside him.

- Nathan began to sob with hoarse moans emanating from the deepest recesses of his being.

- Speak to me, please, his anguished son begged him.

He kept crying without answering and began to pray:

Baruch dayan haemet[1], when Samuel found the paper by his father's side. He picked up the telegram and as he read its contents, started to cry with his father.

Mendel, my dear brother, he thought, I will never see you again. We will never again run together through the fields, we won't grow up together side by side as we had hoped. Today they will bury you and I won't be able to see you ever again. Why, God? Why is there so much injustice?

Samuel wrapped his arms around his father, hugging him, not letting him go for an instant. They stayed like this for some time and at length, Nathan spoke to him hoarsely.

- Come, my son. Finish dressing. Let us go to the synagogue and pray for your brother for God to help him wherever he is and to help us find a way to bear this terrible pain.

As he spoke, he began to tear his clothing[2].

For seven consecutive days they didn't work and sat on low chairs[3], sharing their enormous loss. They didn't shave[4] and they kept the flame of a candle lit in Mendel's memory[5]. Nathan asked Samuel again and again to tell him stories about the family during his years away.

---

[1] The Baruch dayan haemet blessing (Hebrew: Blessed be the true judge) is pronounced upon receiving the news of a death or seeing a death. (Author's note.)

[2] Tear his clothing (Hebrew: Keria) ceremony to express resignation and mourning (Author's note.)

[3] Sitting on low chairs symbolizes for the person in mourning his recognition that life is no longer the same and his wish to be closer to the earth where the loved one has been placed (Author's note.)

[4] Not shaving is an expression of withdrawing from society (Author's note.)

[5] In the Jewish tradition, a candle is the symbol of the body and soul. The flame is the soul and there is a belief that we should keep it lit during the intensive mourning period (Hebrew: Shiva) to help the soul during its journey (Author's note)

- But I've told you so many times.

- Yes, son, I know. But I feel closer to them when I hear you share your memories. Please don't get annoyed, because it helps me when you remember all of them.

- It is all right then, papa, if I can help relieve some of your suffering by this.

The following days were for Nathan the most melancholy and painful that he could remember in his whole life. If only he could be beside his beloved Sarah, then together perhaps they would be able to bear the suffering, but alone and far from his country and loved ones, this pain marked his daily existence. Sometimes, depression and anguish would come upon him with particular force. He imagined his wife crushed by her suffering and unable to face life after her son's death.

The intensive mourning period came to an end and they began to work again.

Samuel was worried about his father. Mendel's death had affected him greatly, and he would eat very little, sitting up all night praying until the early morning hours.

- You will make yourself ill if you continue like this, he said to him one day.

- Don't worry. I will be all right. I need to work harder to bring them here sooner. I don't want to get any more bad news.

- Yes, papa. We will continue as we have until now with our struggle and soon we will bring them.

- May God make this true, my son.

One afternoon, two months after Mendel's death, Nathan was in the butcher shop working as shohet[1], when

---

[1] Shohet. (Hebrew: slaughterman) a person in the Jewish community who is given the task of slaughtering animals in accordance with ritual laws. Special studies are undertaken to receive the authorization (kabalah) that permits him to exercise this profession. The person must be an observant Jew (Author's note.)

Mrs. Rabinovich came in to ask for some chickens for her Friday night meal.

- Good afternoon, she greeted him warmly.

Nathan interrupted his work and wiping his hands on the white apron he wore over his clothing, he came over to her and answered her greeting:

- Shalom alehem[1].

- You are still sad and I don't blame you, she said. One never gets over the death of a child. But besides your sadness, I see that you are very worried. Is there something else that is disturbing you?

- Oh, Mrs. Rabinovich, I don't want to burden you with my problems, but I am so worried about my family! Working here, I hear many things from different people, and over the past few days everyone is talking about a war that is imminent in Europe. I can't stop thinking of how I can get the rest of the money I need to pay for the trip to bring my two oldest children here. I tried to convince Sarah, through my brother-in-law, to come with the four smaller ones, but she wouldn't even consider it.

- Of course, she exclaimed. I would not leave a child and go to another country, either. My worry as a mother would not let me live one moment in peace. Her reaction is completely natural and logical. But I have an idea. Let me speak to my children about your situation, and perhaps we can find a solution.

- God bless you, he answered with feeling. Thank you so much for you kindness.

That night, Mrs. Rabinovich explained the desperate situation of Nathan and his family to her own family.

- Mother, answered Nahum, her eldest son, we cannot take care of the whole world. And besides, ship passage

---

[1] Shalom alehem. May peace be unto you (Author's note.)

from Europe is very expensive.

- I know, but you are forgetting something important, even fundamental, in my view. God has been very good to us and we have managed to gather some wealth in this country that has been so welcoming to our family. How can we ignore the pleas of man that has been such a gentleman and so helpful to us and other members of the Jewish community? Also, when he was our guest at the Friday night meal, he spoke so much of his family that I feel like I know them already and I would feel guilty if anything bad were to happen to them.

- What is your idea to help them, then?

- I will make up the money to bring them here, with a personal loan.

- But, mama!

- No buts. It is already decided.

- As you wish, answered Nahum, with a voice of resignation.

The next day, after his work at the butcher shop was finished, Nathan came running home to the building where he lived. In his excitement to get home faster, he almost tripped over the stairs and fell down, but recovering his balance, continued forward until arriving at his own room.

- What is the hurry, papa? You have been running, I can see.

- My dear son, we have done it! At last we have enough money to bring your mother and all your brothers. I hurried home to tell you, because I couldn't wait one more minute to share this happiness with you. Can you believe it? We will soon have them here with us. You don't know how I have dreamed of this day.

- But, how did you do it?

- Samuel, it is a long story, but the fact is that we have a loan of the money we need to pay for the last two tickets.

- A loan? I don't understand.

- Remember Mrs. Rabinovich, that sweet lady who invited us a few months ago to share the Friday night meal with her family and who we told about how we came to Bogota?

- Yes, papa.

Well, she has lent me the money. And thanks to her generosity we will be able to all be together again.

- Halleluiah! exclaimed Samuel with a voice full of feeling.

- Now, come, son. Sit beside me and we will start planning for their arrival and where we will move. We can't stay living here. We will have to find a larger place where there is room for us all.

- Do you have any place in mind, papa?

- No, Samuel, but as of tomorrow, we shall start to look and we shall surely find it.

Chapter 19

Once Sarah received the letter containing the passages to Colombia, she felt as if she were swimming in a sea of doubt. So many years waiting and now, with the tickets in hand, she began to feel a profusion of conflicting emotions.

On the one hand, her heart thrilled at the thought of soon seeing her dear husband and beloved eldest son once again. But, she would have to leave her country, so much a part of her heart and soul, despite all the difficulties she had suffered here. She had been born and raised here, surrounded by the love of family and friends, and most of these people would stay behind in Poland. How she would miss them all! She was also fearful of the unknown, in spite of the news she had received in the letters from Colombia describing life there. She felt afraid that she might not be able to adapt to a world so different from what she knew and overwhelmed at the thought of not being able to learn to speak Spanish. How would she manage to communicate with the people there?

Then, reconsidering, she realized how important it was to put aside her concerns. The idea was to be reunited with her loved ones wherever they were. They were making an enormous effort to seek a better economic and social situation for all of them and she would not be the one to take away that possibility.

Finally, she was fully convinced that the move to Colombia was the right course for her and family and she proceeded to tell Sylvia of her decision.

She was worried she would find her mother staunchly opposed to the idea of leaving Poland. Sylvia had clearly expressed her agreement with the idea of Max, Sarah, and the children traveling, but did not include herself in the plans. She argued that she wanted to remain near the gravesite of her departed husband, Abraham, and would not accept the idea of leaving her country and her group of friends and family.

- Sarah, you must understand, she would say to her daughter. This is my life and I have already made my decision about this. I will live the rest of my days as I see fit. I do not want to leave this place where I have everything that matters most to me. I am already old and cannot deal with such a total change in my life. I wish with all my heart that I could keep living with you, Nathan, and your children. I have been happy beside you, but the most important thing for me now is to stay here in my country, with my people and close by your dear departed father's resting place.

- But, mama, do you realize that years may pass before we can see each other again?

- Yes, but even so, I have decided to stay. You must soon leave to be with your husband, and this is your place. Too much time has passed since Nathan left for Bogota, and this lengthy separation is not good for your marriage. You must always protect your own family, above all.

Sarah decided to speak with Max as a last recourse to see if he could convince their mother to go with them, but it was all in vain. Sylvia obstinately refused to listen to her children's arguments. Preparations for the trip had the whole family busy and in a constant state of uproar. Sylvia's family grew closer to her than ever, given their imminent departure and the expectation of her absence in the family.

One night, Bertha arrived at Sarah's home, and after warm embraces of welcome, came into the kitchen. Over steaming cups of tea and conversation, she began to raise a delicate matter.

- I am loathe to raise this ...she began, stammering. I only dare to talk to you about this matter because we are family and because of our great friendship since we were young.

- Tell me, her cousin said, encouragingly.

- Both Moses and myself have been worried about Pearl. From everything we have heard, the future of the Jews in Europe looks very uncertain. You and your family have a chance to emigrate to another country, at a time when the war is literally knocking on our doors and I am very happy for you. Unfortunately, our current economic situation does not allow us to follow you on your trip to Colombia, but I need to ask of you an enormous favor before you leave.

Sarah watched her curiously, nodded automatically, and waited for her next words.

- Our daughter is the most precious thing in our lives and we are willing to make any sacrifice, no matter how great, to give her the chance to grow up without fear, and to become a young woman who can one day marry an honorable and loving husband. We are terrified for her safety in case a war breaks out. So, we have decided to ask you, thinking of all these dangers and problems that even the most optimistic of our friends are predicting, in the event our fear does become a reality, if you will take her to live with you. We have been saving money to have it ready for an emergency, but you are the only ones who can help us with these plans.

- Of course, Sarah answered, with an embrace, noticing her cousin's efforts to hold back her tears. Unable to restrain herself any longer, her tears began to flow freely, thus relieving the pain that she had been holding in for so long as she faced the mounting torrent of terrible events for her family and country.

- As soon as I arrive at our destination, I promise you, I will make the necessary arrangements to send for her. She will grow up beside my children and as long as I live, your daughter will never lack anything, she reassured her cousin with feeling. Then she added, "I hope that soon you and Moses will be able to come and join us".

- Thank you, I hope that one day I can repay all your kindness to me.

- Don't worry about a thing. Pearl is my niece and besides, you know I have always loved her like a daughter.

As soon as Bertha had left for home, Sarah went to her mother's room and told her about the conversation.

Sylvia was very happy that Sarah had agreed to take Pearl in, in case of danger.

- And you, mama, asked Sarah once again, will you finally decide to come with us?

- No my daughter, do not insist any more. I will not leave this place. I cannot physically withstand that trip, but you have my blessing. God willing, you will all be happy and make your most precious dreams come true in that far-off land.

Chapter 20

Sarah and her children were about to begin their exodus to South America. The waiting luggage had been lined up in the front hall of the house. On the upper floor, the children's excited voices could be heard, busily checking the rooms over and over again, and Sarah was assuring herself that the various rooms in which they had lived until that day were absolutely spotless.

Sylvia left her room, planning to help her daughter with the last-minute tasks and to enjoy the last few moments in the precious company of her loved ones, when she began to feel a strong pain in her chest as she went up the stairs. The pain grew stronger, making her almost double over with the intensity.

She started to tremble, bathed in a cold sweat, and had to stop and hold onto the handrail to try and recover from the sharp, intermittent stabs of pain. Am I dying? Was I ill and didn't realize it? No! This must just be the stress and anxiety over my children's and grandchildren's trip to South America.

The pain continued, but began to decrease in intensity.

She tried to stand upright, but once again a sharp stabbing pain doubled her over. My God, she pleaded, do not let me die just as they are about to travel. Sarah must be reunited with her husband. Help me to recover quickly.

Sylvia clearly heard her son calling and still feeling weak, she made a great effort to go back down the few stairs she had climbed then, leaning heavily on the rail, turned to go into the kitchen.

She sat in a chair and rested her head on the table. After a few minutes, the pain began to subside and she started to feel somewhat stronger. She waited a while more, and when she could straighten up, looked outside and gazed at the familiar old tree with her rheumy eyes. Its beautiful trunk had thickened over the years and it was crowned by a myriad of leaves that fluttered in the wind, and a bird's nest that could just be glimpsed high up in the branches. Smiling, she remembered when she and Abraham had decided to plant it so many years ago.

Oh, dear God, this is my home and always will be! My children are leaving but that is the nature of life. They grow up and they leave. I must stay, because only here will I be happy. I have my memories and perhaps soon, I will join my husband in the life beyond this one.

- I was looking for you, mama, said Max, coming toward her. We must leave and we wanted to say goodbye to you. The children are waiting in the front hall with Abel and Sarah will be down any minute. But, you look so pale. Are you not feeling well?

- No son, don't worry, answered Sylvia, getting up from the chair and coming over to give her son a hug. If you notice anything, it is just that I feel sad thinking that this moment is finally upon us, and now the time has come for you to really go.

- Are you really sure you won't come with us? There is

still time for you to change your mind. We can wait a while more for you to pack your things.

- No my dear, I don't want to go. But I will be counting the days until you return. I hope to see you again soon. Sarah will not be able to come and visit me, of course, because she will have much to do with her family, not to mention the cost, but you will come. I won't lose hope of that day coming.

- I promise. As soon as I am able, I will come and spend a few months with you.

- Thank you. That is what I wanted to hear.

Sylvia embraced him with great emotion, and after a short time, he took her by the arm and they went together to see the rest of the family.

- Grandma! exclaimed Rachel, as she caught sight of her grandmother arrive with her uncle. You don't know how I will miss you! Rachel came close and affectionately took her hand. Every day I will think of you and your good advice.

- That is what I like to hear, sweetie. Try to keep being a good and obedient girl, help your mother with her chores and always remember me.

Rachel hugged Sylvia firmly and after caressing her grandmother's tired, lined cheeks, she let her brothers and sisters come up to each say their farewells.

Sarah came running down the stairs. She had taken longer than she thought, but was satisfied with her last tidy-up of the upstairs apartment, which had been her home for so many years. Everything was spotless, gleaming, just as she liked it. From the entrance, she watched the luggage being loaded onto the carriage. She came silently up to Sylvia and, with a sob escaping her throat, embraced her mother lovingly.

- Mama, she said, recovering slightly, the time has

come for us to leave and I almost cannot believe it. It hurts me so much to have to leave you here alone. If it were up to me, you would be coming with us. Please, write to me often and as soon as Max comes back and you sell the house, go with him to South America. We will be there waiting for you with open arms.

- Yes, I will write to you in detail about everything that is happening and about the rest of the family, so don't worry. You know, I will be surrounded with people who care about me. They will be watching out for me.

- I know, but I can't stop thinking about how great a distance there will be between you and us.

Sylvia embraced her tenderly and then, moving away, let her brother come close for one last farewell.

- Goodbye, mama.

- Goodbye, my dear children. May God go with you.

Max lovingly kissed his mother's hand and, with his arm around Sarah, led her to board Abel's carriage, where the children were already waiting, fidgety with anticipation. Already tearful, she turned to look upon her mother one more time, and asked God to give her the chance to see her mother again.

Sylvia waved goodbye. She felt a knot in her throat and an enormous weight upon her heart. She would never see them again, she thought. This is the final farewell. As she waved, she felt a profound ache, not in her chest but in the depths of her soul. As if in a dream, she watched Abel pull up on the reins of the horse, saw her grandchildren squabble over who would get the best spot to see their grandmother off and observed them waving animatedly, while Sarah broke down into tears and Max gazed back with a mournful expression as they pulled away.

The carriage left and Sylvia stayed pensively for a long while watching the road where her children had just driven

away. Suddenly, the tears began to stream down her cheeks and she exclaimed aloud:
    - Dear God, how alone I am now!

Chapter 21

As Abel drove the carriage, they began to travel farther away from the town, rocking along the unpaved road. The two-story house and thick tree planted by Abraham and Sylvia began to shrink in the distance before Sarah's gaze as she turned for the last time to see her old home, becoming tiny dots and finally, disappeared forever into the horizon.

No one said a word. There seemed to be an unspoken agreement to not break the silence. Sarah repressed a sob from time to time and surreptitiously dried her tears.

After some time, when they had covered a good distance, she leaned her head on her brother's shoulder, and watching the view over the road, tried to shake from her mind the vivid sight of her mother standing in front of the house, with her deep, blue eyes and her gray hair impeccably combed, her broad forehead, soft, pale cheeks, and her whole face lit up by the sun, waving goodbye to them. She remembered how, the night before their departure, she sat down with all the family.

During the gathering, Bertha and Pearl seemed to be

trying to draw out their last moments together, repeatedly hugging all the family members about to leave on their trip. The next day they would be gone, who knows for how long…

Moses gave them various pieces of advice, including how to stay away from the sections of the train where there might be groups of Nazis, who had lately taken to carrying out subversive activities such as creating problems among the travelers and, then taking advantage of the ensuing confusion to cause various type of damage. Esther watched the children sorrowfully, as they had until then filled the great void due to her barrenness, and wondered how her life would be now without the innocent happiness that Sarah's children brought to her household.

On many different occasions, her husband had mentioned this to her. Thanks to these young ones, their frustrated desire for parenthood had been alleviated to some degree. But now, who would replace them?

Abel listened with interest to the children's comments on the preparations and expectations for the trip, and smiled at every ingenuous outburst and childish description. Pearl, with her lively personality, was strangely silent during most of the evening. She barely said a word to her good friend, Rachel. She seemed to understand the significance of this departure and deep inside, she believed they would be saying goodbye forever.

Sylvia, watching her closely, came up to her.

- I notice you are not feeling sociable tonight, she said in a mildly chiding tone. Even Rachel has not managed to cheer you up. Come over with the group of young people, instead of sitting all alone in the corner.

- Yes, aunty, you are right. I have been staying outside the group, but it is because I feel very sad that after tomorrow I won't be able to share my life with my cousins anymore and I love them all so much. Without them, I will feel so lonely.

Sylvia hesitated for an instant, then smiling down at Pearl's angelic face, asked her:

- Wouldn't you like to visit them?

- Of course, she answered feelingly. But the trip is very expensive and my parents probably cannot afford the expense.

- Don't lose hope. You never know what is around the corner and when you least expect it, you might find yourself in South America, answered Sylvia with a grin, and added:

- Come on, now, let's turn that frown into a smile and join the others. If not, they will be unhappy for your sake on this special occasion.

Hearing these wise and kind words, Pearl's face lit up and she quickly went over to rejoin her cousins. Moments later, she was happily conversing with them.

Oh, what an unforgettable night of embraces and farewells! thought Sarah. As long as I live, I will never erase that evening from my memory. So many beloved friends and family together, all giving their best wishes for our success and happiness. All of my dear uncles, aunts, cousins and friends from a whole lifetime. I will cherish this forever!

- Sarah, said Max beside her ear, making her return to reality. A penny for your thoughts?

- She, amused by him as always, answered with a smile:

- Nothing, nothing important. I was just remembering our family gathering last night at home.

- How I will miss Pearl! sighed Rachel with a sad expression.

- I understand your feelings completely, my dear, Sarah said taking Rachel's hand in hers, but remember your grandmother's words. Maybe one day, and maybe even quite soon, she will be able to come and visit us.

- Do you really thing so, mama? she asked with a look of radiant expectation.

- Nothing is impossible, and especially not when it is a wish from your heart.

- And will grandmother also come with her? asked Saul with concern.

- Naturally, Max answered immediately. In three months, with God's help, I am planning on returning to bring her back with me.

- Hurrah! shouted the children excitedly. We want grandma to come!

Hearing Max's words, Sarah questioned him.

- But you don't really think she will be happy living alone knowing we are thousands of kilometers away!

- Thank you, Max, said Sarah, hugging him. You have made me very happy.

From there on in, the mood in the carriage was joyful and newly enthusiastic for the voyage they were about to undertake. They chatted and sang for a long time, and took short naps to shorten the considerable distance between Jalowiec and Warsaw.

Chapter 22

Children, wake up! We are in Warsaw, exclaimed Abel.

- Remember when we lived here a few years ago? Sarah asked them as they stretched and yawned.

- Yes, mama, answered Rachel, looking curiously about the streets as the carriage moved forward.

- I really don't remember, said Hannah, confused.

- Well, that is entirely possible my dear, her mother answered tenderly, for you were very small and did not know where we were.

- I don't remember either, Miriam lisped.

-You weren't even born yet, Rachel answered her with a giggle. How would you remember?

- I remember where our house was, said Saul. I didn't like that apartment. I much prefer grandmother's house, where we were so happy. The Warsaw streets are dangerous and I couldn't run there for fear of being hit by a carriage. The school was different. My teacher wasn't nice and there were too many children in the classroom. I dreamt every day of going back to the town, where I could be free. I would love to keep living there forever. By the way, uncle

Max, what is it like in South America? Is it like Jalowiec or like Warsaw?

Max looked at him, perplexed. He wasn't expecting that question. He should start by explaining to the boy the difference between the small town of Jalowiec, the city of Warsaw, and South America, an enormous continent, then go on to explain about Bogota, where they were going, which was a city comparable to any European capital.

On the other hand, how could he make the child's mind understand the reason why he and Nathan had to emigrate to another country, when they, just like Saul, had been so happy in Jalowiec close to their family and friends?

- You will see, Saul, Max began to answer slowly.

Here is the train station! Rachel shouted with excitement.

Max breathed a sigh of relief that he had not been forced to completely answer his nephew's question, and turning to face forward again, saw that they had indeed reached the end of the first leg of their journey. Abel pulled up on the reins, and the horse came to a abrupt stop. Max climbed down from the carriage and started looking for a porter to help them carry their luggage to the train. Meanwhile, Sarah made sure all the children stayed together.

- Stay with me, children, she coaxed them nervously. There are many people here and you don't want to get lost.

But the children, ignoring their mother's please, ran out to meet their uncle and aunt.

- Theresa, Joseph! How happy I am to see you. Thank you for coming to see us off! exclaimed Max, accompanied by the baggage porter, as he spied them hugging their nieces and nephews.

Sarah, hurrying alongside her children, gave a shout of joy as she met up with her sister. When they saw each other, each one rushed to welcome the other in an affectionate and prolonged embrace.

Joseph was watching them protectively when he heard his brother-in-law call out, asking him to come while he purchased the train tickets.

The boys dashed to and from around the women, who were deep in conversation, trying to catch up on the events that had taken place in their families in the long year since they had seen each other.

- My goodness, how I will miss you! said Sarah. I wish you could travel with us.

- We would love nothing better, but it is impossible. Joseph's profession means we have to stay close to Warsaw. He is in charge of various construction projects and without him, the work will not progress efficiently. But, I have some wonderful news.

- What is it? Sarah asked curiously.

- I am pregnant. Finally we are expecting a baby, after so many years of frustration.

- Mazal tov, my dear sister. This is truly a marvelous surprise, exclaimed Sarah with tears of joy in her eyes. We must hurry and tell everyone. This good news cannot be kept a secret.

Theresa and Joseph received with jubilation the congratulations from their family, with their best wishes for the baby and for the parents' long life.

- Where is Abel? asked Max.

- Here I am. I am so happy for them, that now they will have the child they dreamed of for so long.

- We are all thrilled about this good news. I can't tell you how grateful we are that you have helped us by bringing us here to Warsaw.

Do you remember when you brought me and Nathan six years ago? It seems like only yesterday, doesn't it?

- Yes it does. You don't know how much we will miss

you. Now that you are all leaving, there will be such an emptiness.

- Passengers for Gdynia, please board the train, they heard over the loudspeakers.

- They are calling us, exclaimed Max.

- It is our train, said Sarah, and began to move her children toward the boarding platform.

- Until we meet again, Abel, my good friend. Keep well, and say goodbye to Esther for me. Please keep an eye on my mother, added Max.

- I will take good care of her, of that you can be sure.

-Goodbye, Theresa, and write to me about your pregnancy, said Sarah, holding onto her sister in a strong embrace. Thank you for coming to the station. Visit mama as often as you can. She will be very lonely.

- We will, don't worry.

- Farewell, uncle Joseph, I will miss you very much, said Rachel as she came close to him. He lifted her up to take a good look at her and for the first time, smiled between his tears, saying:

- Take care of yourself, my sweet one, and take good care of your brothers and sisters. Don't forget to write.

- Yes, uncle, we will write.

After saying their goodbyes, they rushed on so they wouldn't miss the train. Sarah ran behind them, counting and recounting heads.

Max gave over the tickets and went to sit beside his sister. As soon as the engine started to leave the station, he leaned in close to her and whispered in her ear.

- Now we are really on our way. Soon you will see Nathan and Samuel again.

- Thank God, I can hardly believe it!

As the hours passed, the children kept their good humor for quite some time. Even the strident sound made by the metal wheels of the train against the rails seemed exciting to them. When the chimney spewed smoke from the carbon igniting, this made them think of witches and frightening stories. The winding climb of the train made them shout with joy.

Max and Sarah watched them tenderly and exchanged knowing glances. How they were enjoying their first trip in a train! The happiness was clearly etched on their innocent faces.

The rhythmic sound of the metal monster wending its way inexorably along the railway ties gradually began to sink them all into a pleasant stupor. Finally, fatigue won out and they all fell asleep.

They continued in peaceful slumber until arriving at the port to leave for South America.

Chapter 23

- Uncle Max, look at the ship, Saul called excitedly. I have never seen one before, and this one is enormous!

He bent down to his nephew's height and with a smile said to him:

- It seems large because you haven't seen other ships. You will soon change your mind, he added, standing up and tousling the boy's hair.

They had arrived in the port of Gdynia and were impatiently waiting their turn to board the ship that would travel to the port of Bologna, in France. The long line was advancing very slowly and the wait seemed eternal.

- Mama, how much longer will we be here? I am tired, Etty complained with a pout.

- I don't know. I hope not much longer. Don't lose patience; they will soon let us on.

But Sarah had been very optimistic in her prediction. The boys began to complain they were hungry, thirsty and tired. Two long hours later, they were finally called by the official in charge.

- Your papers? the official asked them.

- Here they are, answered Max quickly.

- Are you traveling with someone else?

- Yes, sir, with my sister and her six children. Here are their documents.

They were checked over carefully and the official seemed satisfied. All was in order. Next, he motioned for Max to go to a room nearby, where they should continue to wait.

- More waiting? Sarah asked Max, irritated. I thought we were ready to get on board.

-Relax, this is all routine. You will see that soon we will be sailing.

Anxious from all the waiting, they sat down in their seats.

- Who is Mrs. Ratovich? asked a women coming into the room where they sat waiting.

She was an older woman with a hard expression and dark hair that poked out from under her nurse's cap in a grotesque fashion.

- That is me, answered Sarah, getting up.

- Follow me, the woman ordered and turning on her heel, left the room.

- Max, please take care of the children, Sarah said as she hurried to keep up.

- Don't worry, I'll take good care of them.

Sarah left right behind the nurse and they went past various doors until reaching the last one, where they entered and she was asked to remove her clothing. She didn't have a chance to ask the reason for the examination due to the woman leaving the room hurriedly, with a fairly unfriendly attitude. She was mystified, but began to undress.

Almost immediately, the door opened and a doctor entered.

- Good day. Please lie down here. I am going to examine you.

- Sarah followed his instructions and while the examination took place, observed him in detail: an older man, almost in his seventies, his hair ash-gray with abundant flecks of silver, pale skin, round glasses perched on the bridge of his nose, rather short and with an enormous belly, all giving him the appearance of a jolly fellow.

- I have finished the examination, he said after a short while. You are in good health. You may get dressed and wait for the nurse.

- Sarah quickly got ready and as soon as she saw the nurse approach, began to leave.

- Not so fast! she yelled at her. Sit here.

Without a word, she obeyed and the woman rather brusquely began to check her hair, causing her to cry out with pain.

When this was done, Sarah stood up and ran back to where Max and the children were waiting. But, to her surprise, she found the room empty.

- Where have they taken them? she wondered anxiously. She thought of going back to the doctor's examination room, but when she tried the door handle, she found it locked. She resigned herself to wait and sat down, trying to suppress her worry. Fifteen minutes passed and finally, Miriam appeared.

- Mama! she cried, throwing herself into Sarah's arms.

- Why are you crying, my dear? Sarah asked her with concern.

- A horrible woman grabbed my head and pulled my hair many times until I started crying and then said: "No sick person or anyone with lice may get on board the ship".

She kept crying as her mother soothed her and tried to calm her down, by saying to her sweetly:

- Don't worry, my dear. They did the same to me. This examination is not very nice but it is necessary.

Necessary, but humiliating! thought Sarah to herself. No one has ever treated us this way before. Just then, she heard childish voices coming closer and Max came in with his nephews, who looked at her pitifully.

- Let's go! he said, and looking straight at his sister, he explained: The results of the examinations were satisfactory. We should be happy, since otherwise they would not have allowed us to continue the trip.

They quickly picked up their belongings and left the room, trying to forget the unpleasantness they had just undergone there. When they arrived at the ship, they gave in their tickets, got on board and following instructions from a sailor, found the bunks that were assigned to them in third class.

- Sarah, her brother said to her, as he looked at her tenderly, I think I can guess your thoughts. This place may not be very comfortable nor clean, but at least we will only be here for three days; afterward we can rest for two days in Bologna before taking the next ship.

- It is fine. We will get along. Anyway, the children seem happy. Since it is their first time on a ship, it is all a big adventure for them.

- Come, Sarah. Leave all the baggage where it is. Let's go to the deck to watch the ship leave port. We have to say goodbye to Poland. From now on, we will be far away from our country, just some more immigrants in a new land.

The ship began to pull away slowly from Gdynia harbor, leaving in its wake a large white flume on the silent sea. Max and Sarah looked back one last time at the place where they were born, their beloved homeland. The children shouted with joy. Some passengers began to wave their handkerchiefs in the air to bid farewell to those on shore. Some of those on shore, looking sad, waited at the port until the last bit of the ship disappeared over the horizon.

The first day of the trip was peaceful. The sky was transparent over the crystalline teal water. The air was light and comfortable. Most of the adults tried to accommodate their belongings as best they could in the cramped space, while the youngsters began to strike up friendships with the other passengers as they roamed around the quarters. By sunset, they were all exhausted and fell into a deep and restful sleep.

At dawn the next day, they saw that dawn had given way to the gray vault of heaven, which was showing signs of a coming storm. With incredible speed, giant thunderhead clouds began to erase the last traces of the brilliant dawn from the sky. A strong wind began to blow and the previously tranquil sea transformed into a tumultuous tide with ominous choppiness, followed by huge whitecaps stirred up by furious rising gales.

The ship, at the mercy of these elements, was dragged over the crests of the frightening hills of water only to be dropped precipitously. The worried captain changed direction to face the wind, but the current began to break against the bow.

Blinding streaks of lightening cut across the near blackness of the sky, accompanied by dreadful thunderclaps. The electric storm that had been unleashed was the most frightening thing that Max, Sarah and the children had ever seen, and the smaller children, terrified, ran to take refuge in their mother's skirts.

- I am so afraid, mama, exclaimed Etty, crying and trembling pitifully.

- Me, too, Miriam cried out with terror, as the swaying of the ship made her fall to the ground with a thud. Sarah squeezed them both in her arms, trying to give them courage that she herself did not have at that terrible time.

- Rachel is running around like a crazy person and Hannah is hiding under the bunk and won't stop screaming, Saul reported with distress.

- Oh dear God, prayed Sarah. Please help us! Protect us from all danger. Allow us to arrive safe and sound to our loved ones.

Meanwhile, Max, who was up on deck, was helping the sailors and several passengers soaked by the torrential rainfall, to secure the objects that were being thrown about by the rolling waves. Suddenly, they heard a deafening noise and a crewman yelled out:

The lifeboat is untied!! I need help! Hurry, the ship's railing is breaking apart and the lifeboat will fall into the water!

Several of the men, hearing his call and grabbing onto whatever they could reach so as not to fall, began to arrive at the site of the emergency and with great difficulty began to tie up the ropes of the small boat, to prevent it from continuing to bang about and cause more damage.

When Max finally went below deck, drops of sweat mixed with rain covered his forehead. He made his way through the narrow passageways and observed the frightened passengers trying to stay together out of the storm, but the powerful swells continued to break against the ship's hull with the strength of a monstrous sledgehammer, and each breaking wave made the terrified travelers stagger under its force.

- Max, you look worn out, Sarah exclaimed as she saw him arrive.

- I am exhausted. I only came for a moment to see how you all are doing. I have to keep helping out because the situation is quite dangerous. As soon as the bad weather calms down a bit, I will come and rest a while.

The storm lasted a day and a half more. Little by little, it began to die down until the sea was totally calm once again.

- Thank you, God, for hearing my prayers, Sarah exclaimed aloud.

- Is everything all right now, mama? Rachel asked anxiously.

- Yes, my dear daughter, have faith and the sun will soon shine again.

Later, the captain called the crew to a meeting on the bridge, where he informed them that due to the storm and the course they had taken to outrun it, the ship had shifted from the original course and therefore, the trip would last three to five days longer than scheduled.

Chapter 24

The terrifying storm had been a traumatic experience for the passengers. Sarah's children were quite upset and for nights after would be awoken by nightmares in the middle of the night. Perhaps they were reliving in their dreams the horrifying crash of the waves breaking against the ship's hull, the bone-chilling howling of the wind and the resounding cracks of the blinding rays of lightning. After all this, poor Sarah, despite having lived through many hardships over the past years, felt a deep relief when one day, the distant horizon showed signs of a shoreline.

When Max, who was always checking on their progress and had made friends with some of the crewmen, gave her the important news, she thought: God has accompanied us and has allowed us to arrive at the end of this stage of our journey.

She felt even happier at the thought of having two days of rest in a hotel before having to embark again on the majestic Atlantic Ocean to reach Barranquilla, Colombia.

- We should start packing our things immediately, Max told her. We are nearly arriving at port and we should try to be the first passengers off the ship. I feel as if we have been at sea for months instead of five days. I have had enough of the sea for now. While you pack, I will get the children ready.

- I wlll be there right away, she answered, moving quickly about the quarters.

A few moments later, she heard Rachel coming into the bunk area.

- Mama, do you need some help? I promised grandmother to help you all the time, remember?

- Of course, she answered with a smile. If you like, you can get your brothers' suitcases ready. They will come and get them when the ship has docked.

She started to pick things up where her mother had shown her, gathering up the various articles of clothing strewn about the bunk and exclaimed:

- I have never felt happier! We are already in France and each day brings us closer to papa and Samuel. I wonder if we will again be the united family we once were.

- Do you remember those times, Rachel? Sarah broke in. So many years have gone by!

- Well, I don't recollect as well as I would like. But, I do remember my father so gentle and caring, always studying except when he would take time for us and to teach us religion.

- Yes, that was his way. He was always watching out for you. I can only imagine how much he has suffered from being so far away from you all for six years. This painful and long separation will surely have left its mark on him.

- Will he be the same papa that we remember so dearly? I wish for, and yet, fear the day we will meet again.

- I understand your worry, but you must put your fears to one side. He will surely be anxious to have us all by his side again.

- Yes, mama, she answered, continuing with her work.

Nonetheless, her daughter's words had sown seeds of doubt in Sarah's heart. Had Nathan changed very much during their long years apart? Was she going to meet a stranger? She felt such anguish that it seemed to reach the depths of her very soul.

- Dear God, please let it not be so! I hope I will find the same man who I married.

- Come, we are here, called Max, almost yelling from the door of the quarters as he tried to organize the family and get them ready to disembark.

Thank you, God, for bringing us here safe and sound after this difficult trip, Sarah prayed fervently. And then she hurried to catch up with Rachel, who was running after Max and the children, as they watched the captain maneuver the ship into the pier.

The passengers began their descent from the ship, passing through passport control, picking up their baggage and finally, they found themselves in a velo-taxi[1] on their way to the hotel.

- Oh, mama! Finally we can rest in a real bed on solid ground, Saul said with a sigh of relief.

- I'm with you, agreed Etty. I am exhausted.

- Yes, we all feel the same, Rachel added. I hope that tonight we can take a nice, hot bath and sleep until we are completely rested.

But as soon as they arrived at the hotel, they received news that was as unexpected as it was unpleasant and discouraging. Their next ship would be leaving in the morning. Due to the weather, they had been at sea for two extra days crossing to the port of Bologna and in fact, they were lucky not to have missed the ship traveling to Barranquilla.

---

[1] *Velo-taxi.* A carriage pulled by a bicycle.

They would not have as much time as they had hoped for their well-deserved rest. The first light of dawn found them already embarking on a ship sailing under the Dutch flag.

- This ship is a real beauty, Uncle Max, said Saul with delight. Now I understand why you said there were ships bigger than the one that brought us from Poland. This one is truly incredible.

- You are right, my boy. Thanks to the generosity of Mrs. Rabinovich, who insisted that we travel in style, we are able to enjoy this wonderful ship. But come now, let us go see the quarters, as your mother must already be waiting for us.

- Uncle Max, said Rachel excitedly as they came into the room. This is real luxury! There are even goose down comforters and pillows. It will marvelous to sail surrounded by such comfort.

- Yes, Sarah agreed with a smile of amusement. There is a huge difference between this ship and the other one.

- We had better hurry, Saul added seriously. I don't want to miss a single minute of this trip. It is going to be very interesting.

- And comfortable, Etty said happily.

That night they put on their finest frocks and went to the dining room all abuzz. They had never seen such elegance. As soon as they arrived, an attentive waiter approached and graciously pulled out the chairs at the table for Sarah and Rachel to sit down, and politely helped them to settle in.

Etty watched them a bit jealously, thinking it would be great to have someone help her sit down so elegantly. It was a shame to be so young, she thought to herself.

The menu was brought to them and they read it with amazement, to see such a selection of food available.

Then, admiring the silver serving platters and Rosenthal china, they watched as each course was served to them.

- Mama, this all seems like a fairy tale, exclaimed Miriam innocently.

They all laughed at her observation and the night passed happily.

Another happy event occurred that night. Max and Sarah met up with several other passengers traveling from Poland, like them, in search of better economic horizons.

The following morning, wishing to get to know their fellow shipmates a bit better, they met on the deck and engaged in pleasant conversation for several hours, exchanging ideas and enjoying the pleasure of traveling under such excellent conditions.

The children also struck up friendships with the children from these families who were the same ages, allowing the adults to enjoy some private time.

The days passed quietly. The trip, in some ways, seemed more like a pleasure cruise for those wealthy enough to pursue such luxuries.

One morning, the collective tranquility enjoyed by the immigrants was abruptly shattered. Cries and shouts were heard by the group where Sarah was animatedly conversing with her newfound friends, and they began to ask with concern:

- What has happened? Has someone fallen overboard?

Soon they found out the bad news. A crew member came briskly over to the group and told them in a voice choked with concern:

- It is war! War has broken out!

- What are you talking about? Max asked, still not understanding.

- War has begun in Poland. The captain has just received the news over the radio. The Germans are invading the country.

- Oh, no! he exclaimed and blanched at the thought.

- Mama, mama! Sarah began to cry inconsolably.

Max, recovering his senses somewhat, came over to Sarah and put his arms around her shoulder, then said to her quietly:

- Calm down. If we panic, then the other passengers may also start to panic. You know, many of them are also Polish.

- You are right, Sarah said, drying her tears. But, what will become of mama? And what of Abel, Esther, Bertha, Moses, and all of our family and friends? Oh, dear God, our beloved Pearl! she added, starting to sob once again.

- Please, you must try and control yourself. Don't cry any more and just let me try and find out the true situation.

Sarah nodded as she bit back her tears, and looked around at the others, who were as anguished and concerned as she was, and in her mind the words resonated over and over: War! War!

September first, nineteen hundred and thirty-nine would be forever marked in their lives. The horror and killing that began on that date would go beyond anything that was humanly possible to imagine, but by a twist of fate, they had set sail a few days earlier without even knowing the importance that this act would have for them: to save their lives.

Chapter 25

Hitler and Stalin's pact in August of nineteen thirty-nine meant that both countries went on to conquer and divide up Poland. Germany occupied the western region and Russia took over the eastern provinces. Given the simultaneous occupation, the fighting was over quickly, despite constant efforts by the Poles and the Jews[1] to try to maintain the country's independence.

Air bombardments and military assaults left thousands dead and prisoners of war.

Adolph Hitler's dearest dream was about to become a reality: the Slavs, considered to be an inferior race, would be dominated throughout Europe by the pure-blooded and superior Germans. To this end, he carried out a series of murders and expulsions of the Poles, taking away their property, dividing families and moving some groups to other regions to work as slave labor for Germany.

---

[1] There had never been real solidarity between Poles and Jews due to the anti-Semitism that existed before the invasion, which cast a heavy pall that was impossible to overcome. (Author's note.)

But the nightmare was especially horrible for European Jewry, for whom total extermination was planned.

As the Germans entered Poland, thousands of Jews, hearing about what was happening to the Jewish population in Germany, decided to flee to the eastern provinces occupied by Russia, believing that they would thus save themselves. However, upon arriving there they faced an equally cruel fate. They were sent to inhuman work camps where most of them perished.

The Nazi invaders divided western Poland into two parts: the territory taken over by the Reich[1] that was to be immediately settled by the Germans, and the General Government[2], where the Poles and Jews were deported to create a reserve work force to serve Germany's needs. Certain neighborhoods in Warsaw, Lublin, Krakow, and other cities with Jewish populations, were turned into ghettos[3] where the Jewish population was corralled in overcrowded conditions.

Anita Kupperman hurriedly came into her husband's jewelry shop and glanced around, then found her husband in conversation with a customer.

I have to interrupt him; this can't wait, she thought with anguish and nearly bolted toward him in her haste.

- Marcos, I need to speak with you. It is urgent.

- Wait for me in the office. I will be right there.

---

[1] The territory taken over by the Reich included the provinces of Pomerania, Danzig, Upper Silesia, and the region of Lodz and Poznania. (Author's note.)

[2] The General Government had jurisdiction over the regions of Warsaw, Krakow, Lublin, and the rest of central Poland. (Author's note.)

[3] Ghetto, Jewish. During the Nazi occupation this term referred to prisons surrounded by a wall and barbed wire placed strategically on all entry and exit points to prevent leaving or contact with the outside world. (Author's note.)

A few minutes passed, which seemed like hours to Anita and when Marcos finally opened the door, he found a nervous wreck waiting for him.

- Is something wrong, my dear? I have never seen you like this.

- Have you not yet heard about the decree issued by the Germans?

Intrigued, he raised one eyebrow wordlessly and allowed his wife to go on.

- They want to take away our possessions and confine us to a sector of the city that is cut off by a wall that is three meters high and nearly seventeen kilometers long.

- How do you know so much about this wall?

- Because our neighbor, Mr. Chaim Kohn, was one of the people in charge of building it.

- But,… he said protesting, I and many other wealthy Jews in Warsaw have already paid large amounts of money to prevent these places from being set up and the Germans promised us that they would not take any such measures.

- By paying that money, I am afraid that you only managed to postpone the plan that was already in place, she continued anxiously. The governor of Warsaw, Fischer, and his delegate, Leist, have issued a series of orders including the ghetto borders, movement of the Jewish population in the city to these areas and the expulsion of all Aryan residents from the same area.

- As if it were not enough to have already suffered the humiliations they have inflicted upon the Jewish community! he exclaimed angrily. They make us use special markings, like the yellow Star of David on our clothing and on our businesses. There are restrictions on our use of trains, streetcars and other means of transportation, and we are forced to ride on the back of trucks. We are not allowed to go to parks, beaches or public places upon pain of imprisonment for any violation. How far do these damn Germans think they can go?

- The most painful of all for us and all Jews, Anita added, is not being able to send our children and grandchildren to school or universities. How can they prohibit the education of young people, when our whole future depends on this knowledge? They don't care at all what happens to our people and they show this by trying to take away every right that exists under divine and universal law.

Marcos, let's close the jewelry shop and go find out what the true situation is. I have a very bad feeling about this. I sense that terrible things are about to happen, and we had better not be unprepared.

Giving in to his wife's premonitions, Marcos decided to take with him his most valuable gemstones and keep them safe at home, in order to be prepared for anything that might happen.

The Germans had set a two-week period for relocation to the ghettos, where the situation of overcrowding and tumult began to take on a nightmarish quality.

Handcarts and wheelbarrows were the only means available for the transportation of household goods and personal effects.

The buildings inside the designated limits were overpopulated, and the majority of inhabitants were Jewish mixed with a minority of Catholic and Protestant residents.

Joseph, with Teresa's agreement, invited his parents to share their apartment on Franciszkanska Street, which by chance happened to be located inside the ghetto limits. Rivka, Shoshana and Golda, along with their families, found lodging in a nearby building that had been vacated by a poor Aryan family.

After a short time getting used to these new circumstances, Mr. Kupperman decided to reopen the jewelry shop. Along with his son, he would go out for a walk on the street every day and they would hear about the latest news in Warsaw.

One day, when they arrived at the entrance to the ghetto, some SS[1] officers and Jewish policemen prevented them from leaving.

- This is an outrage, exclaimed Joseph with irritation.

A policeman came over and in a mocking tone, asked to see his judenrat[2] pass.

- We don't have such a pass, but we must go to work. We haven't been out for two weeks now.

Several uniformed German officers, standing nearby, heard Joseph's comment and began to laugh loudly and derisively.

- I do not understand why you are reacting like this, Mark commented with a serious expression.

- You don't have to worry about the business. It is no longer yours, answered a German wearing a gray shirt with a swastika on an armband and tall, polished black leather boots.

- What are you saying? Joseph asked, incredulous.

- You heard me. By special decree issued by the Führer, all property, business establishments, furniture, and bank accounts owned by Jews and Poles living in the terri-

---

[1] SS (German: Schutzstaffel or independent guard) The initials of the repressive Nazi troops whose members were indoctrinated in the Nazi credo and eventually gained control of the entire Nazi structure through the Gestapo (German: Geheime Staatspolizei or secret state police) and the SD (German: Sichesheits Dienst. Or security services)

[2] *Judenrat* (Jewish councils). The basic function of the judenrat was to ensure the compliance with the authorities' Anti-Jewish policy to terminate the Jewish population. A board of directors, who controlled all aspects of community life, headed the council. (Author's note)

tory of the Reich and Poland has been confiscated.

- Oh, no! exclaimed Mark in disbelief, and turned on his heel to look away from the soldiers so as not to give them the pleasure of seeing the tears of sadness and anger that were welling up in his eyes.

- Come, papa. Let us go back home.

- Fifty-one years ago, Marcos said to his son, your grandfather, Neftali, founded that jewelry shop by the sweat of his brow. I have proudly kept the business going all this time and now a maniac who calls himself the Führer, has snatched it from me as easily as taking candy from a baby.

A sense of martyrdom and despair began to penetrate the ghetto inhabitants, fed by the torture, rape, and murders perpetrated by the German army soldiers.

Food became scarce and epidemics, mostly contagious typhus and eruptive viruses, began to break out and decimate the population. Many traded their belongings for food. Objects began to lose their true value. Hunger and thirst became severe problems. The Nazis would cut off the water supply for a week or two weeks at a time, in the hope that nature would take care of the task of annihilation and extermination that was being planned by their evil minds.

Deportation happened daily and thousands of persons died from overcrowding and starvation.

Every morning those who died were taken out and left piled up, nude, in front of the buildings. Every article of clothing was priceless to the survivors. The Germans charged exorbitant amounts for a burial and so the Jewish police would pick up the cadavers in large carts pulled by skeletal horses and take them to mass graves at the cemetery where they would be thrown one on top of the other, without a shred of respect or a religious ceremony.

The odor in the streets was suffocating and unbearable. There were not many people in the streets during the day, and at night they would meet in a maze of trenches and bridges that they secretly built between the buildings. It was forbidden by the SS to go out between nine PM and five AM without written permission. Violators were killed under cover of darkness.

The implementation of forced labor by Poles and Jews older than 12, depleted their strength and accelerated the process of annihilation.

- I am very hungry, mama, said Abby, Golda's youngest son, rubbing his stomach in an attempt to relieve the constant spasms of pain from lack of food.

- I am sorry, son, there is nothing to eat in the house. Yesterday we finished the last crumbs remaining from the food that your grandfather obtained when he traded a handful of gemstones.

- How can we get more food? The child asked sadly.

- I don't know, she answered, weeping.

My family will not die from hunger, decided Abby determinedly. I will find some food no matter what.

After a short while, he slipped out of the apartment and moved stealthily toward the wall that surrounded the ghetto. After carefully studying it, he picked up a small board and began to dig, lifting his head from time to time to look around in case he was being watched. It took a little over two hours to dig a hole the right size. Then he covered his board with a little earth to hide it and slid into the tunnel noiselessly.

- Where is Abby, aunt Golda? asked David, Rivka's son. I have been looking for him for a while.

- He must be over at Joseph's house. He is such an active boy.

- I will go over there and look for him.

But, after looking all around, he couldn't find Abby. The minutes turned into hours and the family grew concerned.

At nightfall, when they were already beside themselves with worry, they heard knocking and opening the door, found their neighbor carrying in her arms a child who was sleeping deeply, hugging in his arms a paper bag.

- I found him lying in the street, she explained.

- Abby, where did you go and where did you get that bag? Golda asked with concern.

The child continued sleeping. He seemed to be in fine physical shape but his clothing was very dirty. As she could not wake up, Golda called her husband, Elias, and they carried him to the room. They placed him gently on the bed and let him continue in his peaceful slumber.

The bag in Abby arms fell to the floor and her mother picked it up. She was bowled over with surprise to find some food inside.

- Where could he have got it? she asked, looking at her husband.

- I haven't got the slightest idea

The next day, Abby told them about his odyssey to the world outside the ghetto.

- When I climbed out of the tunnel, I ran toward some nearby bushes. From there, taking shortcuts, I got to a huge house and rang the bell. I was trembling with fear. I didn't know who lived in that huge mansion.

An older lady, who was rather large and seemed kind, wearing a very clean uniform, opened the door.

"What do you want, boy?"

"I am starving. I haven't eaten for many days and I cannot stand it anymore."

"Poor child. How old are you?

"I am nine years old."

Right away, she let me in to the house and showed me into the kitchen. When we got there, she put an enormous slice of bread and a good piece of cheese on a plate.

"Am I dreaming?" I wondered, but I couldn't resist the temptation any longer and began to devour the food.

"Not so fast, young man", the nice lady said to me. "You will make yourself ill".

When I finished, I thanked her and turned to leave the house.

"Drink this glass of water", she told me kindly, while I prepare a package of food for you to take with you."

I thought I hadn't heard her properly, but then I saw her looking for something in the pantry.

"How did you manage to get out of the ghetto?" she asked me in a hoarse voice.

"I dug a small tunnel between the two sides of the wall".

"The bag shouldn't be too big so that you can carry it. Otherwise, you won't be able to get through the opening again."

Her helpfulness and words overwhelmed me. I could not control myself and began to cry and hug her. I thanked her for giving me some food to take back to my family and then hurried back. Night had fallen and despite the darkness, I was afraid I would be found and asked God to protect me. I ran through the deserted streets and as I reached the building, I must have fallen asleep from sheer exhaustion.

- Oh, my darling grandson! exclaimed Anita. You should not have taken such chances. The Nazis are heartless and might have done terrible things to you.

But Abby, ignoring his family's warnings, went back again and again. One day, carrying food as usual, he tried to pass through the opening but the bag hidden next to his body got stuck and he began to cry out with fright.

A girl from inside the ghetto tried to pull him out, and unfortunately, was spotted by a German soldier. That devil in a human body killed the young boy with a single shot and began to strike the girl repeatedly with his rifle butt, killing her as well. He then called out to his companions to boast of his exploits.

David, who often would follow behind his cousin, saw what happened and ran to tell his parents. Elias came immediately and managed to pull his son out from where he was wedged in.

On arriving home, Ariel examined the boy and found he had multiple fractures. He died without making another sound, his life snuffed out like a small bird killed by a stone from a heartless bandit.

Nazi power was an instrument in the hands of a bloody maniac to round up and attack the Jews relentlessly, but the intelligence, conviction and life force of the long-suffering victims were unshakeable.

The Jews, locked up in the ghetto, made tremendous efforts to defend themselves, organizing mutual aid societies, medical assistance and searches for contraband food. They created a network of schools, workshops, and clandestine businesses.

On Walowa Street, near Franciszkanska where the Kupperman family lived, a theater company flourished under the capable direction of Bluma Furswerk. Janusz Korczac's famous orphanage was used as a base to print and publish various newspapers edited both in Hebrew and Polish. A small symphony orchestra was formed, headed by Simon Pullman, the famous musician, and this group performed a great variety of concertos.

Despite the walls, barbed wire and daily deportations and humiliations of all kinds, the Germans could not destroy the cultural life of a people who had always been known for their erudition.

But the horror did not end there and in nineteen forty two, human slaughterhouses were built to speed up the European and Jewish extermination, and death camps in Treblinka, Maidenek, Auschwitz and several other camps were supplied with lethal gas chambers and crematoriums.

- Quickly, hurry and hide! The Gestapo is inspecting the building, Rivka cried out hysterically one early morning. They want to deport us to the work camps.

Upon hearing her voice, they all began to run in terror to find a safe place to hide. But, this time, although they didn't realize it, the Germans had come with the intention of checking each and every hiding space with a fine-toothed comb, since they had been given specific orders to evacuate the whole area. One by one, they were found where they had tried to take refuge. "*Alle juden raus. Raus, raus! Hinunter! Alle juden hinunter!*" All Jews out. Get out, get out! Come downstairs! All Jews downstairs now!

Shoshana, desperate with fear, managed to hide in a tight corner of the pantry, making it almost impossible to find her. The carpenter who had made the pantry had made an error calculating the dimensions and had been left with a small empty corner, and he had covered it with a plank of wood to hide this fact.

From that corner she could hear the screams and cries of her family, fearing the worst as they were pushed and shoved by the Nazis out of their own hiding places. She was sorely tempted to run and help them but convinced of her impotence to do so. She could do nothing. If they found her, she too would be lost.

After some time had passed, there was total silence in the building and Shoshana, thinking she was alone, crept out of her hiding place. How shocked she was to find herself face to face with a Gestapo officer. The beast watched her with eyes filled with brute strength and lust.

- Dear God, save me! she exclaimed fearfully.

The German came closer and grabbing her by both

arms, he bent her backward until she was forced to the ground. He roughly ripped off her clothing until she was naked and pulling down his pants to the knees he thrust himself upon her, ignoring her cries of anguish and despair.

Once he had satisfied his morbid and sadistic desires, he murdered her coldly with a bullet to the head.

The evacuation continued. A ghetto police squad, made up of about two dozen men, blocked the entrances and exits of every building in the area, until all the residents came out to the street, at which point the Jewish police[1] checked their documents and searched them. From there, they were taken to the boarding platforms at the station.

Shots rang out constantly, quelling any thought of rebellion by the prisoners. Anita hung on to her husband with all her strength and copious tears flowed from her eyes.

- I haven't seen Joseph, Theresa, or Shoshana, Marcos commented with concern.

- They were not arrested with us, Ariel answered quickly.

- Where can they be? May God help them! exclaimed Golda in distress.

Form a line!! yelled the Lithuanian and Ukrainian cadets, as they tried to force an enormous sea of people gathered in the station into a line.

The selection process began. An officer dressed in a SS uniform, seated at a desk, decided the fate of each person based on his personal appearance, work papers…or his own discretion.

Right…left…left…left…life…death…death….death.

What will become of us? Marcos wondered distraught.

---

[1] It is regrettable that the Jewish police in many cases supported the Gestapo operations, mistreating and in many cases, acting in the most cruel fashion against their own people.

Will I ever see my family together again, or is this the end?

- Your papers! the officer barked at him officiously.

Without saying a word, he gave them over.

After a few moments, the Nazi gave his final decision: left.

He stayed there wavering for an instant, then after moving forward a short distance, he stopped to listen to the verdict that fate would deal out to his beloved wife.

Upon hearing "left!" he stretched out his arm and weaving his fingers into those of his companion of so many years, they boarded the train with heavy hearts.

Elias looked at the cattle cars in which they would be transported to the concentration camps. Most of them were made of steel with wooden walls, from German, Czech and French factories, worn from use.

The line advanced slowly, punctuated by sighs, screams and shots. Any act of rebellion against the SS by the prisoners was punishable by death.

Many people straggled behind, weighed down by the load they carried on their backs, straining in a weak effort to save their last few belongings. The Germans pushed them along in an attempt to speed up the process. *"Schnell! Schnell!"* Quickly, quickly! They shouted.

Once aboard the train, the prisoners were moved toward the back of the convoy where, to their dismay, the air was dark, heavy and malodorous. The ventilation shafts were closed and the only fresh air came in through a small window covered by barbed wire.

When the train was fully loaded to capacity, the officials closed the doors from the outside.

A terrible panic erupted inside the car and most of the people began to scream in desperation. Ignoring their clamors for help, the heavy engine belched smoke as its metal wheels screeched on the tracks to being the journey.

Anita held tightly to her husband, while he, weaving in between the persons squeezed in about him, moved forward to try and find a place near the ventilation shaft where they could rest. With great difficulty they managed to sit down on the floor of the cattle car.

Absolute silence now reigned. Resignation was carved into their faces, along with deep sadness and worry over the unknown future.

Visions of the past began to pass through Marcos' memory. His childhood, youth…so happy and full of life. The peace and tranquility of his home…raised with so much love. His wife and four daughters…always trying to do better, the jewelry shop…where he had worked so hard.

The wrenching cry of a hungry child brought him back to reality. He closely observed the miserable people squeezed in around him and his heart twisted with despair.

How can the Germans be the masters over our destiny and over all Europe? Why is the rest of the world ignoring our cries? Where is divine justice?

Suddenly, he found it hard to breathe. An oppressive knot had formed in his throat. He tried to get up, and he barely made it to the window, where he began to take deep breaths and try to relax. Looking outside at the light of a beautiful autumn morning, he could see lush green fields stretching out far into the horizon. The sight of a passing brook with its riverbed full of sparkling stones reflecting the morning rays of sun and a flock of birds going by made him think of freedom.

- Nooooo!! I must be dreaming. This is only a nightmare, he exclaimed aloud.

At that moment, the train shook sideways as it passed from one track to the other. It slowed down slightly and rolled through the Siedlce station, where a group of teenagers running along beside it drew their fingers along their

necks to mime death, as they taunted the unfortunate passengers by predicting their final destination.

From there the convoy advanced slowly onto another
track where there were various train cars, SS soldiers, and
an ominous sign: Treblinka. The train stopped for a short
time and then began to move in the opposite direction toward a side track. It made its way through a dense forest
with enormous trees and after a time, a huge area surrounded by a barbed wire fencing on wooden posts appeared.

The train stopped. The door opened with a great crash
and they began to hear booming voices bark the order for
them to get out...*Schnell, Schnell!!* Quickly, quickly!

The platform filled up quickly with disoriented people
looking for their family members and friends, carrying their
belongings on their backs and holding their children as
close as possible, for fear of losing them in the midst of the
tumult.

Cries, sobs and despair filled the air, intensified even
more by the cracks of the whips lashed pitilessly by the SS
officers, and by the fear of the Ukrainian soldiers in their
black uniforms, arms at the ready to shoot.

Anita climbed down from the train, accompanied by her
daughters, sons-in-law and grandchildren, but she could not
find her husband and she searched for him desperately.

- Where could he be? she asked the others, distraught.

- We will go and look for him, offered Ariel, taking Elias,
his brother-in-law, by the hand and setting out into the
crowd.

- Dear God! exclaimed Golda, seeing an armed Ukrainian guard moving in their direction.

- Schnell, schnell!! he yelled angrily, striking out with
his rifle butt and pushing the women toward an opening in
the middle of the fence.

- We have to move mama, her worried daughters said, perceiving the hate reflected in the deep black eyes of the guard.

They anxiously made their way through the doorway and found themselves in a yard surrounded by a hedge of dried-out bushes, and along the sides were long wooden barracks.

"Women to the left, men to the right!" The orders came from a fellow with Jewish features wearing a red band on his arm, who was trying to organize the tumultuous wave of people flowing in, helped by other guards identified by similar distinctive markings. Halinka and David, Rivka's children, held tightly to their mother, fearful from the violence they had experienced.

- You, young man, go over with the men on the right, one of the officials said to him.

- David looked at his mother in supplication as tears of frustration and distress began to roll down his thin face.

- Find your father, Anita managed to say to him.

Rivka looked on paralyzed as the soldiers beat her son while they took him away.

- *Alles herunternehmen!!*[1] yelled out an SS soldier, ordering the men to completely undress.

- Quickly, quickly!! the Ukrainians kept yelling.

Following the Germans' orders, the women, terrified and holding their small children tightly, went toward a cold, dark barracks building. They took off their clothing, leaving it scattered on the ground, and then were forced to sit on benches in front of other prisoners who had the task of cutting their hair.

Panic, pain and sadness were the overwhelming emotions on the faces of these unfortunate women, thrown by

---

[1] *Alles herunternehmen.* German: take everything off.

an adverse destiny into this horrendous place and submitted to the most inhumane and degrading treatment imaginable. Yet, there was still a faint light of hope shining in the depths of their eyes as they felt the rough hands run over their heads, and they consoled themselves with the thought that the haircut would be followed by a disinfection process and after that they would be left alone.

Once their hair had been shaved off, they were ordered to walk along a narrow corridor some two hundred meters long, which was lined on both sides by green barbed-wire fences leading to a strange-looking building.

A brick building…unfinished walls, no windows….three rooms….a narrow corridor…floors covered in terracotta tiles….doors with hermetic seals…valves.

It was particularly surprising to see the ironic classified ads that had been posted in the first fenced areas: carpenters, road construction workers, masons, tailors, cooks. It seemed to be a cruel way of planting the false idea in their minds that their future depended on this classification, and that they would be chosen to perform one of these tasks.

An SS officer explained to them in a calm tone:

- After the bath and disinfection, your property will be returned to you.

The women walked along the corridor completely nude, each one holding a small bar of soap in their hand as they went through the door toward the supposed showers.

Once inside the enormous room, Anita noticed through her tears her daughters' and granddaughter's extraordinary and striking youthful beauty, which had not been affected by the abusive shaving of their lovely long hair, nor affected in any visible way by the torments they had suffered at the hands of the Germans in the Warsaw ghetto.

A sudden premonition made her shudder and embracing each them strongly, they leaned one upon the other and dissolved into heart-wrenching sobs, like an island of pain and suffering in a sea of unfortunate humanity that was made up of some four hundred women and children crying with terror in that cramped room.

For about fifteen minutes the room filled with gas, flooding the air with its lethal vapors, until all the bodies lay still and lifeless.

After forty minutes, various Jews led by capos[1], identified with a distinctive yellow symbol on their knees, picked up the bodies to be transported to the common graves. The burial was carried out by several tractors and the hum of their diesel motors was a constant sound in the background at the Treblinka death camps.

A large group of young people, among them Elias and Ariel, were led to a barracks building after having been separated from the larger group of naked men who, having been beaten into submission, were led through a fenced-in corridor to the gas chambers.

What will happen to us and our families? Ariel asked worriedly.

One of the prisoners who had already been at the camp for several weeks heard his question and came up to him sadly:

- Your family is already dead and as for you, what awaits you is a hard life of heavy labor, misery, hunger and torments, just like me. The time will come when the Germans will kill us, or we will kill ourselves or try to run away without any hope of making it, he said to them quietly in a voice filled with emotion.

When the prisoner had finished, Elias exclaimed:

- My God, it cannot be true!

- Please, believe me. Why would I lie to you?

---

[1] *Capo.* German: the person in charge of the prisoners (Author's note)

Ariel looked into his eyes and seeing sincerity and truth in them, began to cry inconsolably, and started to pray:

- Itgadal veitkadash shemeh raba bealma di vra hiruteh.[1]

Immediately, all the men present joined into the prayer in a sorrowful clamor.

David, searching for his father, had managed to move away from the group of persons being held in the yard and had hidden in the latrines. He stayed there for about an hour in a state of anguished indecision. Finally the fetid odor hanging over the place was more than he could stand and trying to feel brave, he decided to step out and continue looking.

Suddenly, a soldier dressed in an SS uniform appeared wearing high, polished boots and a soft cap decorated with a shining skull on a black background. Upon seeing David, the dark face of the executioner lit up with a smile of cold satisfaction.

The boy began to back away, trying to escape from this man with the twisted expression on his face. But the soldier came at him with long strides, moving the boy back into a corner until he had forced him into the infirmary[2] where a flag with a red cross on it was displayed. He ordered the child to undress and guided him onto a plank that had been placed over an enormous common grave, full of cadavers

---

[1] "Glorified and Sanctified be God's Great Name": The first words of the Kadish – mourning prayer. This is an ancient Aramaic poem which is an expression of faith by the bereaved, who despite his sadness, continues to affirm his faith in God and in the value of life. It expresses the submission of man to the will of God. It is recited during prayer services at the synagogue. (Author's note)

[2] Infirmary: in the concentration camps, the sick, the elderly and children were killed here to make them believe there were entering a military hospital. (Author's note)

that were burning in an unholy bonfire.

David stood there, shivering from the cold, when a Ukrainian soldier spotted him, aimed his rifle and shot. His wounded body rolled into the pit as he fell from the plank and was received by the giant dancing flames, which, swallowed him with a horrible squeal. Seconds later, the body of that poor soul whose only crime in life was to be born Jewish, disappeared in the blackness of an immense column of smoke.

In nineteen hundred and forty three there were only forty thousand survivors left of the four hundred thousand inhabitants who had been locked into the Warsaw ghetto by the Nazi army, and well aware of the sad fate that had been decided for them by the most eminent Aryans, decided they would not go quietly.

They organized brave and resourceful guerrilla groups with members such as Mordechai Anilevich, Joseph Kupperman, Michael Klepfisch, Tschemerinski and many others, who were ready to keep watch day and night over the ghetto streets and to defend the inhabitants with their lives.

On April eighteenth of the same year, Theresa arose early one morning to clean and tidy the apartment on Franciskanska Street in preparation for the first day of Pesach[1], celebrated according to the religious calendar on the following day, while her small son, Jonathan, played with some kitchen utensils and pots on the floor nearby.

- Honey, where are you? Joseph asked her as he came out of the bedroom.

- Here I am, in the kitchen, she called out.

---

[1] *Pesach*. (In Hebrew: to pass over) This is the Hebrew name for Passover, the religious holiday celebrated in remembrance of the Jewish people's time in Egypt, when God passed over their homes and kept them safe. (Author's note)

- You look beautiful today, he said gazing at her with adoration and taking her into his arms.

- You are just a flirt, that's what you are, she answered him with a smile of contentment and returned his embrace with a surge of tenderness.

The war and its atrocities had awoken in them a very special sensitivity born of the awareness of how important each and every minute of life was and how fortunate they were to have managed to survive until that moment.

- I must be going. In a few minutes my guard shift starts on Mila Street.

- Please, be careful, she begged him with concern. Do not take such great risks with your life. You may do it to save the people here in the ghetto, but remember that we need you, too.

- How could I forget? he answered with a smile, taking from his pocket a precious photograph of the whole family.

They kissed passionately and minutes later he closed the door, leaving his wife behind with a sinking feeling in her heart.

Dear God, she prayed silently, protect him and bring him back to us safe and sound.

As night fell, she observed the results of her efforts with satisfaction. Despite the general scarcity of food in the ghetto and the special requirements for Passover, she had managed to obtain in tiny quantities, the foodstuffs she needed to comply with the basic precepts of the Seder celebratory meal[1].

The table looked festive set with an embroidered white tablecloth, which had been a wedding gift, and the ritual

---

[1] *Seder.* (Meaning: order). It applies to the order in which a ritual banquet must be carried out on the first two nights of Passover. During this dinner, the story is told of the suffering of the Jews in Egypt and their liberation from slavery. (Author's note)

silver candelabra, with its four branches each holding a pure white candlestick.

The Seder platter (ke'arah) miraculously displayed the required items: a leafy vegetable, celery (karpas) and to the left of the celery a glass of salty water; behind this a piece of horseradish for the bitter herbs (maror)[1]; on the other side a paste made from grated apples, nuts, almonds, cinnamon and ginger (charoset)[2], which had been generously donated by a kind neighbor; a shank bone with some meat on the bone (zeroa)[3]; a boiled egg, three matzo[4] crackers, each covered with a cloth; and enough wine so that each person could drink the traditional four cups of wine (arba kosot)[5] plus one more for the symbolic arrival of the Elijah, the prophet.

Theresa hugged Jonathan with deep emotion. At last, she had finished the day's tasks and could fully enjoy her child, the light of her life. From the bottom of her heart she thanked God for having allowed her to experience the joys of motherhood, and blessed the moment she found out she was expecting a child. But, in one of life's great ironies, she had not been able to share the delight of her son with her nearest and dearest.

---

[1] *Maror.* A bitter herb is used as a reminder of the years of suffering and bitterness the Jews endured as slaves before their exodus from Egypt. (Author's note)

[2] *Charoset.* This symbolizes the work of the Hebrew slaves when they made clay bricks. (Author's note)

[3] *Meat and egg.* These symbolize the Passover sacrifices and the flight from Egypt. (Author's note)

[4] *Matzo.* This refers to the unleavened crackers or bread that the Jewish people eat on Passover in memory of the exodus from Egypt. (Author's note)

[5] *Arba Kosot.* This symbolizes the four aspects of God's promise: "I will bring you out from Egypt...I will free you...I will redeem you...and you will be my people" (Author's note)

An involuntary tear slipped down her cheek as she remembered the dreadful day that she and her husband, coming back from a judenrat meeting, found out about the deportation of their families and neighbors to the concentration camps. Then she shuddered thinking of how terribly far away she was from her sister Sarah from Nathan and her nieces and nephews.

- If only I could see them again! she sighed aloud, and with the child in her arms she went into the bedroom.

The night seemed peaceful. Joseph lit a cigarette and blew exaggerated smoke rings as he watched his mate on guard duty, Mordechai, who was sleeping deeply and snoring from time to time. He smiled as he remembered his beloved wife and darling son, who he would soon see again, and felt so lucky to be able to share his life with two such special people. He took his photo of them out of his pocket and a smile of happiness lit up his face.

At dawn, the Nazi death squads, with their black uniforms and heavy weapons, came in along Zamenhof road with tanks, vehicles armed with machine guns, and armored trucks and continued along Kupetska, Mila, Muranovska and Franciskanska streets.

Joseph heard from afar the sound of the war machinery entering the ghetto and woke his companion. They both ran to warn the other sentinels who were placed around the building.

- The troops are approaching! they yelled agitatedly. Prepare to attack!

When the Germans arrived at Mila Street on the corner of Zamenhof, they met up with a band of resistance fighters who began to throw homemade bombs, molotov cocktails and grenades. With the few weapons they had managed to build secretly, they fought desperately, killing various Germans and setting afire two armored tanks.

- We've done it, Mordechai yelled excitedly, as he saw the Germans retreat.

- We must double the guard, said Michael Klepfisch. They will most certainly attack again.

The next day, the Nazis came back fully armed and well-equipped, after first having cut off the supply of water and electricity to the ghetto. But, as they advanced, to their surprise mines that had been strategically placed by the guerrillas began to explode in their midst.

Given the strong resistance by the Jews against the army, the Germans decided to demolish the ghetto using fire and cannon shot.

- Dear God, cried Theresa blanching. The city is burning. There is fire everywhere. How will we ever get out of the building?

She lifted Jonathan from his bed and wrapped in a warm blanket, then began to hurry down the stairs, only to meet with a cruel fate. As they arrived on the lower level, a column that had been weakened by the fire fell on top of them and killed them instantly.

The Nazi attack continued with a rain of artillery, fire bombs and poison gases, converting the ghetto into a true scene from hell, with burned bodies and the screams of the wounded and mutilated everywhere. The resistance continued heroically, trying to defend their families, but the battle was terribly lop-sided and the chance of mounting a real defense became ever more distant.

The battle for the Warsaw ghetto lasted for forty days and at the end of this time, a large area of the city was left in ruins. Very few survived the Nazi's ruthless hunt. And even fewer, among them Joseph Kupperman, managed to escape.

Chapter 26

Colombia, September 1939

Leaning on the deck railing, Sarah strained her eyes to make out the Colombian coastline. Given the history of her people and the centuries of persecution that had gone before her, she couldn't help feeling a kinship with her ancestors and their search for the promised land as the answer to all their problems.

Once she and her family set foot in that unknown land, a new chapter would begin in their lives. The certain knowledge that she had left behind her life in Poland once and for all made her dwell with nostalgia and regret on all the things that were lost to her forever. Mendel, her beloved son, his life cut shortly in an untimely fashion, would be forever buried on Polish soil; her mother who would one day likely lie beside her grandson and dear departed husband in the same graveyard; the ancestral house, the shop that had been their business and center of their lives, the flowering fields, glorious dawns and delightful sunsets, happy moments with the family, all the hardships they had overcome...and the apocalyptic horseman of war galloping on his blood-red steed across her homeland.

When, in the middle of the ocean, Sarah had heard of the war breaking out and the Germans entering Poland, she had been unable to sleep at night and could only rest during short naps. She would close her eyes and imagine her mother and the rest of her family at the hands of those barbarians and her heart would break at the thought.

- Look mama, we are almost there, Etty cried out excitedly.

- Yes, darling, she answered rather unenthusiastically, still distracted by her gloomy thoughts.

- Do you see that ship, with a huge waterwheel on the back, on the stern? Saul asked her, pointing at the horizon. Uncle Max explained to me that it is a steamship. When the captain is approaching the coast he has to be very careful, because otherwise he can run aground on the sandbanks at the bottom on the sea. When that happens, he has to call for the "rowers", who go in their canoes to bring a strong chain from the shore that they attach to a large tree. Then the captain orders "Full steam ahead!" and the ship moves with the help of the chain. They do it over again every time the ship gets stuck. Isn't that interesting?

She nodded in agreement and answered him with a measure of pride,

- I am happy to see that you are learning a lot on this trip.

- Me, too, interrupted Miriam with a spark of jealousy.

- Of course, sweetie.

- Come over here, you all. Rachel called them from the other end of the hall. Leave mama in peace.

- Coming...

Sarah smiled at her eldest daughter's attempts to protect her from being disturbed. She gazed out again at the immensity of the ocean and fell back into her reverie. She had been constantly submerged in her thoughts from the moment she had heard the captain tell them the news of war, been silent and distant from her children. All her initial excitement and happiness had vanished. Again and again she asked herself why her mother had so insisted on staying in Poland.

- Dear God! she sighed, what will be her fate?

Max, who was standing near his sister, heard these words murmured aloud and scolded her.

- You should not let yourself get swept away by worry. We still don't know anything definite about the Germans and their location. They may still be far away from the town and our family there.

She looked directly at him, her brow wrinkled in doubt.

- Do you really think so?

- Please, have faith.

- I shall try, she answered, somewhat unconvincingly.

Slowly the ship approached the Colombian coast. They could hear the captain's voice shouting orders to the crew. As soon as the ship docked in the port, the passengers began picking up their baggage and the debarkation process began.

Max hoped to see Nathan on the pier, but his efforts to find him were fruitless. After half an hour of constant and agitated searching he came back to his family. They were about to hire a car to take them, when a young man came up.

- Excuse me, sir, the fellow asked them respectfully, are you with the Ratovich family?

- Yes, I am, he answered cautiously. I am Sarah Ratovich's brother.

- Very pleased to meet you, sir, the young man said to him, holding out his hand. My name is Jacob Lempert. Two days ago I received a phone call from Mrs. Rabinovich, who was a very good friend of my mother, and she asked me to come and meet you at the pier when the ship from France arrived. So, here you have me at your disposition to help you with anything you may need.

- Why, thank you, Max answered him and shook his hand. You are too kind. Please let me introduce you to the rest of the family. Sarah, come over here.

She came over nervously, seeing him with a stranger.

- This young man has kindly offered to show us around and help us, he said to her in Polish. His name is Jacob Lempert. Let me introduce you.

- Please to meet you.

- The pleasure is mine, Mrs. Ratovich.

- And these are all my nieces and nephews, Max continued, pointing out each one: Rachel, Saul, Etty, Hannah and Miriam.

- Nice to meet you all, he answered, looking at Rachel a bit longer than necessary. Feeling his gaze upon her, Rachel suddenly blushed.

Jacob immediately turned to Max and Sarah.

- I will bring my automobile over so we can load the luggage.

- Good idea. We will wait for you here.

- That young man seems very respectful and pleasant, Sarah said to her brother.

- Yes, I like him, too.

Rachel, hearing her uncle's words, began to blush again.

- Here he comes, Saul yelled out. We can finally get going.

They placed the luggage in the automobile's spacious trunk and as soon as they were all settled, Jacob started the motor and they began to move.

At first no one spoke. They were all gazing curiously at their new surroundings.

What a difference between this city and Warsaw, they thought, observing the narrow streets, houses built closely together, intense humidity and suffocating heat alleviated only by the occasional sea breeze. The pedestrians walked unconcernedly along the pavement, the women attired in bright-colored, lightweight dresses. Most of the people were wearing sandals.

- Mrs. Ratovich, Jacob addressed her. Would you like to come to my house? I would like you to meet my father. It is still early and you have several hours before the next boat leaves for the Magdalena River.

- Of course we would love to meet him and thank him personally for sending you to meet us.

- It is a pleasure to be able to help you. As he said these words, he turned to look at Rachel, who immediately looked down at her shoes shyly.

- The pleasure is ours, Max answered, patting the young man on the back. Sometime in the future, we hope to repay your kindness.

- You can come and visit us, Etty said quickly.

Rachel glanced over at her sharply, but Jacob smiled and answered the child:

- Why, thank you, young miss. I will keep your invitation in mind.

Jacob began to honk the horn to give notice of his arrival and turning into the semicircular driveway in front of his house, stopped the car.

- We are here. I would like you all to meet my father.

They got out of the car one by one and as they approached the front door of the house, were impressed by the majesty of the place.

It was a beautiful hacienda house, with a thick, healthy

lawn that formed a green carpet on all sides. The house was built from dark wood and flanked by huge climbing vines blooming with enchanting shades of pink and violet, providing a lovely, welcoming view for all visitors. As they went into the parlor, they saw various objets d'art that had come from places all over the world.

- Ah, you have already discovered my treasures, exclaimed a voice belonging to Jacob's father, as he entered the room. These are my most valuable possessions, because every one has a happy memory attached to it.

- I am pleased to meet you, sir, Max said as he came over to introduce himself.

- My name is Billy Lempert; very pleased to meet you. Any friend of Mrs. Rabinovich is a friend of ours. But, please, don't just stand there. Come in and sit down. Make yourselves at home.

They all made themselves comfortable, feeling the warm welcome offered to them by both father and son. Mr. Lempert, a considerate host, brought out drinks of all kinds, from vodka to the local liquor, aguardiente, and soft drinks for the children. A short while later, Jacob appeared with a variety of delectable homemade pastries, which were devoured happily by the adults and children.

Max and Billy discovered they had much in common as they conversed, and as both were Polish, they naturally began to chat about the recent events in Poland.

- I think our countrymen will fight back against those Germans and soon we will be getting good news from our homeland, their host said.

- I am not so sure about that.

- But, Max, you know how we Poles are. We will defend our homeland with all our might.

- Yes, I do agree with you there, but the way I see it, the country is at a dead end. For centuries, since 1240 when the Tartars attacked, we have bravely tried to fight for our land. In the fourteenth century, under the government of Ladislav I, the country enjoyed a golden age and became wealthy and powerful, after defeating its old enemy, the Teutonic Order. His son, Casimir, added other territories. Casimir's granddaughter married the grand duke of Lithuania and both countries formed an alliance. At that time, Poland attained its highest level of prosperity. But, Billy, you know as well as I do that our country has a strategic position in Europe and we have been invaded by border countries many times in their desire to divide up our land and increase their holdings. Between seventeen hundred seventy-two and seventeen hundred ninety-five, Russia, Austria and Prussia invaded repeatedly and conquered our land until they had basically erased our country from the map. It didn't reappear until twenty-three hears later, thanks to the struggle by our brave soldiers.

The situation now is a different, and worrisome one. For five years we have been watching the Hitlerian plague and have not taken it seriously enough. I am very worried. I have heard horrifying stories about that dictator, Adolph Hitler, and his ideas, and especially about his intense hatred for our people

Billy had begun to these comments, when Max came over and whispered quietly to him.

- Sarah is coming. I would prefer not to keep talking about the war in front of her. She has been very affected by the news and I am afraid it will just upset her further.

Billy nodded his head in agreement.

- Come, Sarah, and sit down beside me. We were just talking about Billy's fascinating travels. Would you like to hear about them?

- Of course, I would love to.

Meanwhile, Jacob had taken Rachel over to a corner of

the parlor and they were chatting animatedly. She was captivated by the young man's charming manner, and from time to time, a happy sigh escaped her lips.

For the first time in her life, she felt like a grown woman talking to someone of the opposite sex. During her school years, she had had a few girlish crushes, but these paled in comparison with shining illusion before her.

- You are so lovely! he said to her again and again.

- Thank you, she responded, her cheeks reddening.

- You have the most seductive eyes I have ever seen, he told her, gazing at her intensely.

- If you say so, it must be true, she answered with a contented sigh.

Several hours passed thus, and during this time, Mr. Lempert recounted his life story for his guests.

Nine years before, he had decided to emigrate to Colombia with his wife and son, with the idea of seeking a better economic situation. From the beginning, fortune had smiled upon them. They were able to save enough money to buy the house and their business of buying and selling fabric grew over the years until they had created a healthy company. But his dear wife, Anna, began to fall ill and despite the doctor's desperate efforts, she never managed to recover. As each day passed, she continued to fail, like a flickering candle, until she could finally resist no longer and passed away leaving them disconsolate and alone.

Ever since then, Billy had been unable to fill the void left by his dear wife's absence.

- Oh, Billy, I am so sorry, Sarah offered her consolation as she watched his face darken with suffering over his recollections.

- Please, excuse me, he begged, as he struggled to regain his composure. I am not being a good host, carrying on about my tragedies. Why don't you tell me about yourselves? Your escape from Poland is a true miracle, coming at this time.

- You are right, she answered him. But we were unable to convince my mother and my husband's parents to come with us. We are so worried about them and the rest of our family.

- I also have family living there. Perhaps we are being excessive in our concern. I am sure everything will turn out well.

- The idea of the war terrifies me, exclaimed Sarah.

- Naturally, we are all frightened when we hear that word. But you will see, in a few months time, it will all be over and we will be able to see our families again.

- I truly hope it is as you say. I cannot help thinking that something terrible will happen to them.

- Don't torture yourself. In order to get to the town, the Germans will have to go through Warsaw and they will encounter a great deal of resistance by the Polish army there.

- Thank you for your kind words. They are very encouraging.

- You are just nervous, Max said to her. It will pass when you see your husband again in Bogotá. Oh no! he exclaimed as he glanced at his watch. It is getting late. We had better be leaving to go to the river dock.

- Billy, thank you so much for your gracious hospitality, Sarah said as she shook his hand. We would love to see you in Bogotá. We would like to repay all of your help to us.

- We hope you will make it soon, Max added with a smile.

The children began running up and one by one, they bid farewell to Mr. Lempert.

Finally, it was Rachel's turn.

- Thank you very much for letting us spend such an enjoyable time in your home.

- It was nothing. We hope you all come back soon.
- I also hope so, she dared to answer.

They left the house and went to Jacob's automobile, where they had left the luggage, and quickly got inside.

With a rumble of the motor, the vehicle drove off to take them to the jetty.

Chapter 27

The boat trip along the Caribbean coast to the Magdalena River was an extremely difficult but interesting journey, and finally they arrived in Honda where they could board a train to Santafé de Bogotá.

The train ride was long and monotonous, with the constant hammering of the engine a constant accompaniment. To relieve her boredom, Sarah stared out the window, admiring the impressive mountain plains as they approached. They were majestic with their emerald green grass extending into the distance, grazing land for the large herds of cattle. Along both sides of the railway track she could see robust, leafy trees scattered here and there, with their low branches fanned by the wind, as the long, noisy metal machine snaked its way to the southwest. In the distance there were narrow, winding roads visible, some following the pathway of rivers and brooks.

Outwardly she displayed a calmness that she did not feel. Her heart was heavy with a multitude of confused emotions. On one hand, she was terribly worried about the threat of war and its effect on her family and friends, and on the other, she felt nervous about the meeting that was soon to take place with Nathan.

Will he have changed much? she thought to herself. Six years of separation with only the meager contact of a few letters, which had come frequently at the beginning, but became less and less regular as time went on...

How is he going to feel when he sees me? Will he be happy that I have come or will he feel that it is the end of his freedom? Perhaps he will have got used to living alone with Samuel so that having a wife and his many children with him again may seem to be bothersome. Will I have made this trip only to find myself with a stranger? What will it be like when we meet again? What will he think when he sees how I have changed over the past few years?

Endless doubts shook her confidence and tortured her spirit.

- Sarah, we are nearly there, Max said to her happily. Let us get all our belongings ready and put on our jackets. Bogotá is at an altitude of two thousand six hundred meters and it will be quite cold outside.

She nodded her head and began to follow her brother's instructions. Suddenly she felt overcome with emotion. Soon she would see Nathan and with the approach of that moment, a new wave of fears and doubts flooded in.

The strident whistle of the train interrupted her thoughts as the conductor braked and the train began to slow its pace. Sarah focused again on the present as she observed the commotion created by her children in their anxiousness to get off the train, after such a long and tiring journey.

- This way, Max pointed her to the door, and stepped aside to leave a space for her to pass.

She moved slowly, carrying her travel bag and as soon as she peeked her head around the opening of the door of the train, she saw Samuel standing on the platform.

- Mama, mama, over here, he yelled excitedly.

- My son, my dear, dear son, Sarah burst out, and began to hurry her steps to reach him. Oh, my darling boy, she exclaimed, squeezing him with all her strength amidst sobs of joy.

- It has been so long, mama!

- Sarah, my sweet Sarah, at last you are here.

She let go of Samuel, and turned to find herself face to face with her husband, who took her in his arms and brought her in close to his chest. She hesitated for a split second after the long years of distance, but immediately recovered and began to embrace him with affection, exclaiming:

- Oh, my dear Nathan. It has been such a long time, such a terribly long, hard time.

For several minutes, they were both overcome with tears of emotion. Despite the time that had passed, their love for each other was still unscathed. With her husband now before her, Sarah's doubts melted like ice under a warm sun. He was still the Nathan she remembered. Centuries could pass and their marriage bond and love would still remain rock solid.

- Mama, you aren't sharing papa with us, Saul said, slightly miffed. We want to see him too.

- Be patient, Rachel scolded him. Our parents have not seen each other for many years.

- And neither have we seen him for all those years, retorted the boy immediately.

- You are right, Sarah agreed, releasing her husband from her embrace and turning to look at their children.

- How you have all grown! marveled Nathan, as he moved closer to hug them all effusively.

- Hello, Nathan, Max said, greeting him.

- Thank you, thank you so much for bringing my family to me. You have been a true guardian angel.

Just then, he noticed a small arm hugging Max's leg.

- Who is this adorable child? he asked in wonder.

- It is your daughter, Miriam, Sarah answered proudly.

- Miriam? he repeated, his voice choked with emotion, looking at her through a veil of spontaneous tears. He squeezed her to his chest in an embrace so tight the poor child began to shy away in fear.

- My darling, I am your papa., he said to calm her. You don't know me yet but we are going to be great friends.

- Yes, sir, she answered seriously.

- Yes, papa, you should say, Etty added, correcting her.

- Uncle Max! Samuel called out as he spotted him.

- My nephew! Max answered, opening his arms wide as the young man came running toward him.

- Uncle, I have missed you!

- Me, too.

- Let's leave, Saul sulked. There are too many people here and I don't like it.

The picked up their luggage and began walking to the exit to look for a taxi.

- Will we all fit in one automobile? asked Rachel, surprised.

- No, of course not, Max answered her. I will take a separate car and some of you will come with me.

- I will go with you, Samuel offered. We rented a house and you don't know the way yet.

Max raised one eyebrow inquisitively and Nathan, noticing his gesture, said:

- Well, we couldn't fit the whole family in two rooms...

- But, what about me? asked Max, a little confused.

You are coming with us. We already moved out of the two rooms and moved your things as well.

- Then, let's be on our way.

As soon as they arrived, they unloaded the luggage and Nathan, with his arm around his wife's waist, took her on a tour of the house.

- Sarah, I hope you can forgive the size of the house. I wasn't able to rent anything larger because I don't have much money with the debt I owe to Mrs. Rabinovich. I am working very hard to pay her back as soon as possible.

- It is wonderful! she assured him happily. It isn't very spacious but it is pretty and it will do just fine. The really important thing is that we are all together again.

- That's my girl! he exclaimed, embracing her tenderly.

After a moment, he looked directly into her eyes and saw her love and compassion reflected there.

- I love you, Nathan, she said with deep emotion. I have always loved you.

- I know, my love, he answered and bent in close to kiss her on the lips.

- Eh–hem, coughed Max as he approached. Sorry to interrupt.

- Don't be. I was just showing the house to my darling wife, Nathan answered.

She blushed at her brother's unexpected intrusion. She was acting like a teenager. After all, it was her own husband kissing her.

- Come on, Max, I'll show you my latest acquisition.

As soon as they had left, Sarah took the opportunity to look over her new home in detail and vowed to make it cozy and homey.

- Nathan, how can I stay with you if you only have three bedrooms?

- I've got it all planned out. In this room, he said, pointing to the largest bedroom, the girls will sleep, and in this one, you and the boys, and in the other one, Sarah and I will sleep.

I understand that for you it will be a bit of a sacrifice to stay with my two boys, but we will save on the rent that we were paying for your room and we must make the best of things.

- But...

- No buts, my dear brother-in-law, you are staying with us and that is all there is to it. End of story.

- Max laughed at Nathan's use of the idiomatic expression and giving him a slap on the back, gave his agreement to the arrangement. He would live with them. Better times would come and then they would be able to rent a house with more bedrooms.

The boys ran around unchecked looking into every corner of the house, asking Samuel where each one was going to sleep and engaging in general horseplay with him, trying to make up for lost time.

Nathan, whose expression it seemed to Sarah, had been transforming noticeably from one of happiness upon their arrival to one of wistful sadness after they had arrived at the house, asked Max and Sarah with a bleak look to meet him in the kitchen. She felt anxious as she watched an ever-greater gloom take over her husband's face. Once they were all seated, he began to speak to them in a serious voice:

- I am very sorry to have to give you bad news so soon after your arrival when we should all be enjoying the day, but life is ironic and sometimes when we are at our happiest, the most tragic events occur to try our strength.

- Please, Nathan, we are on pins and needles, said Sarah, with a sudden sinking feeling.

- Sylvia has passed away.

- What are you saying! cried Max, visibly shaken on hearing Nathan's words.

- She died five days after you left...

Sarah looked at him aghast, speechless with shock.

- But, why did we not find out? Max asked, incredulous

- Bertha sent a telegram telling me what happened. She had a heart attack one night in her sleep. I tried to get news to you on the ship, but I could not reach you, and so Samuel and I decided to go ahead with the ritual mourning prayers.

- Mama! Suddenly a heart-wrenching scream of pain surged unbidden from the grief-stricken Sarah. Mama, mama! she cried inconsolably.

- Please, don't ... Nathan begged her anxiously. There is nothing more we could have done for her. We must thank God that he has given her a death without suffering.

- Oh mama! How could I have left you there? Sarah sobbed with deep regret. Why couldn't I convince you to come with us? She cannot be dead, it can't be, she repeated over and over again.

A tear trickled down her brother's handsome face as, his heart heavy, he started reciting the prayer for the dead, Itgadal veitkadash...

Dear God, Nathan prayed silently, help them with their pain. It is so hard to lose a mother and even harder when it is like this. Help them find the strength they need to face this terrible loss.

- I want to go to synagogue, Max said suddenly. Please, Nathan, come with me.

- Yes, right away. Come, Sarah, let us all go and pray together for Sylvia. May God grant her soul eternal peace!

Chapter 28

Sarah settled herself in the bed as best she could, trying not to wake up Nathan, who was deeply asleep after a hard day of work.

She watched him with loving concentration as her eyes adjusted to the semidarkness in the room, and suppressing a smile, she thought what a good-looking fellow her husband still was even after all the time that had passed since their first meeting back in far-off Poland. With him back by her side, the tribulations of their separation and the difficult years apart seemed no longer important. Their lives had settled into a pleasant and for her, satisfying routine.

She closed her eyes for a moment and happy memories floated through her consciousness. Her parents' house, standing so tall and proud against the horizon as they departed for Warsaw. Now, she wondered if it was even still standing.

Suddenly, reality came flooding back in an abrupt and painful wave as she recalled the rumors she had been hearing in recent days from some of her countrymen living in Bogotá. They had been talking about the war in Poland

and the atrocities being committed by the Germans. They were recounting how their families and friends had had their homes, businesses, and bank accounts taken away and they had been forced to build a restricted area in Warsaw surrounded by a high brick wall with barbed wire to hold all those whom the Germans considered to be undesirables. They were prevented from leaving the ghetto on pain of death.

They had been allowed to bring a few of their most precious belongings with them, but with the ever-increasing famine they had been obliged to trade even these few material possessions for food.

Sickness had laid waste to their numbers and under these adverse conditions, which were intentionally made worse every day by the invaders, survival began to seem impossible.

It is incredible, sighed Sarah, to see the world's passive indifference to Poland's tragedy. After all, are they not human beings who are being robbed of their right to life and their dignity day after day? I wonder how Abel, Esther, Moises, Bertha, Pearl are all doing…. Are they starving, too or is anyone taking pity on them?

She could still remember the day she promised Bertha to bring her daughter with them in case war broke out. Only God knew how much they had tried but the consulate had refused to listen their arguments and in any case, they didn't have the money they needed for the trip. I will never forgive myself for not having brought her with us when there was still a chance. But, how could anyone have predicted the future? How could they have even imagined the possibility of the subjugation of our people by the Nazi monsters, and that they would treat the Poles worse than animals?

Dear God, please let this nightmare end and give us

back our country's dignity. Don't allow hope to be destroyed and the children to suffer permanent damage, since they will carry in their hearts the pain of these days. The future of the world is in their hands. Please, God almighty, let this be a short war. She sighed in torment and after a while, began to sob when she could not contain her despair any longer.

- Sarah, Sarah! Nathan cried out, waking up with a start.

He turned on the light and asking her what was the matter, tried to console her by holding her in his arms.

- Nathan, she answered between sobs, you have heard the news of war. How can I go on with my life as usual when I think of the horrendous outrages that the Germans are inflicting on our people?

He bent his head in consternation. He wanted to give her some consolation for her pain, but she was right. They could not live peacefully knowing of the tragedies in Poland. He had been trying to insulate himself from his pain day by day, trying to forget what was happening. But tortured thoughts would cross his mind and he often found himself silently crying, suddenly aware of the tears flowing down his cheeks.

- I am sorry, Sarah said to him, drying her tears with a handkerchief. I should not have woken you and shouldn't be burdening you with my fears, but I am so sad and feel so terribly impotent.

- I know how you feel. If I could have done something for all those people who have been victims of the Nazis, I would have gone to fight with all my strength, but it would do no good. The Germans have decided to take over Poland and all of Europe. The war has become a good business for them, especially their treatment of the Jews, since Germany is getting rich from all the goods and property they have illegally seized from our people. They will trample any country and any person who tries to interfere with their plans.

She nodded silently. It was sad, but he was right. A handful of people could not fight as powerful an enemy as the Nazi forces. It would have to be the whole world, but the world had turned a blind eye while innocent citizens were being annihilated.

- You know, Nathan, mama was lucky to have died in her sleep. Can you imagine the terrible suffering she would have had to face if she had been alive now?

- You are right, he answered pensively, focusing his mind to see his parents' faces and praying for divine protection for them. Let us go back to sleep. It is getting late.

- I am sorry to have bothered you. You work so hard all day and need your rest.

- Good night, he said, drawing close to her and planting a loving kiss on her cheek. Don't worry so much. Powerful countries will soon react, putting an end to the Nazi outrages and crushing their plans for domination.

As the months went by, Nathan felt his faith in humankind's intrinsic goodness begin to slip away. The Germans had tricked thousands of people to supposed work camps where they were told they would be given food and lodging, but once they arrived, were led to fake showers and murdered with poison gas.

- Have you heard the news? he asked Sarah in horror. They are killing everyone, children, young people, old people. They are destroying our families, friends, and whoever doesn't die right away has to suffer so much he only wishes for death to free him.

- Oh, Nathan, tell me: Can we do anything?

- I wish I knew the answer to that question! he answered sadly. At times like this, the only power to help these poor unfortunate souls lies with God. Let us devote our prayers to them and ask for pity on them. Maybe we will receive an answer through prayer because mankind has failed us.

Chapter 29

Nathan tried to find consolation in justice as he railed against the world's indifference to the outrages suffered by the Poles at the hands of the Nazis, and in particular by the Jews, who were the main victims of the unbridled racist vendetta, a retaliation for supposed historic crimes against Germany, led by the maniacal Adolph Hitler and his sadistic lackeys.

However, even though he was not fully aware of it due to his limited language abilities and limited social interaction as an immigrant, Colombia, the country where he had sought refuge, was a true land of opportunity for individual freedoms and rejected any type of discrimination based on religious or ethnic origins. Its citizens generally shared Nathan and his family's horror at the crimes and injustices committed by Hitler's henchmen, despite the fact that there was relatively little in the way of real news about the events occurring reported by reliable sources abroad.

The upper levels of Colombia's government expressed similar feelings. When Sarah and the rest of her family moved to Bogotá, President Eduardo Santos had been in the seat of power for a year. Eduardo Santos, a journalist, was a member of the Liberal party and his family owned Bogotá's daily newspaper, "El Tiempo", one of the best dailies in the southern hemisphere. Mr. Santos, in an interview granted to a visiting North American reporter, commented on the German dictator with aspirations to take over the world, the so-called "Fuehrer", and according to that reporter, gestured to indicate the impressive view of the Andean mountains that could be seen through the picture windows of the presidential palace, saying:

"Hitler sees from his offices a landscape similar to this one. This is the only thing we have in common".

A daily routine settled over the Ratovich's home. The adults went about their tasks and work and kept up with the news from Europe. Much of this news was communicated to them by the large chalkboards on the sidewalks in front of the El Tiempo newspaper offices, where employees from the newspaper would use chalk to write the front-page headlines for the next edition, together with a brief summary of the most important national and international news stories.

There was always a generous fellow countryman who had learned enough Spanish to explain to Nathan or Max the information appearing there about the developments in the war in Poland and the Nazi plans for conquest.

The children began to get used to the house, the new language and their friends. Their previous life began to take on the sense of a fuzzy chapter in their childish memories. Of course, they remembered their grandmother with affection, but the pain of her loss began to blur and for the youngest, the memory became every more vague. Nonetheless, Samuel and Rachel remembered her vividly. With her tenderness and goodness and wise advice, she had left a permanent imprint on Rachel's life and Rachel constantly tried to live up to this model.

- Tell me, mama, she would ask curiously. What would grandma have thought about this fashion? Would she have liked to see me dressed like this, with my blue woolen skirt and this gray plaid sweater?

Sarah smiled at her eldest daughter's questions. What a vain child! But, it wasn't for nothing and with each passing day she became more lovely. Her attractive figure turned the heads of young men, and as she walked down the street, she would receive more than one compliment, which only served to swell her head even more. Her eyes were deep, wide and dark and she had a curious and bold expression, while her ivory complexion was the envy of all her friends.

- Mama, wouldn't I look prettier if I was only a little taller?

- What a thing to say, child! Each person is how she is. Maybe being shorter has some advantages. The important thing is to be yourself and to be positive.

- But you are tall and slim. Why can't I be just like you?

- Looking like one or another person in the family is a question of luck, and determined by what you inherit, but just look in the mirror and tell me what you think.

At her mother's insistence, Rachel looked at herself long and hard and liked what she saw there.

- You are right. I am not ugly, but do you think I can attract a handsome young man?

- Of course, no doubt about it. Besides being beautiful, you are hard-working. Your father is very proud of you. He says it would be hard to find another person as able as you are to help him in the sweater factory. Your contribution has been invaluable to increase production, and this has allowed us to achieve some economic stability. We have already managed to pay off our debt to Mrs. Rabinovich and this has been thanks to you and your brother helping us. From now on, with God's help, we will have a better life.

- Especially with papa's new business partner, Morris

Liberman. He is a good businessman and will surely help us to make a lot of money.

- I truly hope so, my dear. We could certainly use it.

- And Uncle Max? It has been days since we have seen him.

- Ever since he bought the stocking factory, he has been very busy working to make improvements. Besides, every spare minute he spends with Ruth. If you ask me, there will be a wedding soon, she added happily.

- I would love that, Rachel answered her enthusiastically. I really like her. Even Saul's bad temper disappears when she comes over, not to mention the others! They don't miss a moment of her company. No wonder Uncle Max doesn't bring her here more often. The children don't leave them alone for a minute.

- I didn't realize you were so observant.

- Well, I am. I am growing up, you know. I am becoming a woman.

Sarah startled to hear these words. Rachel certainly was not a little girl anymore. She was already nineteen years old. Heavens! she thought suddenly. Rachel was old enough to be married. Time has flown by and I didn't notice. All those looks by the boys seemed to me to be only a game. I had better speak with Nathan and tell him my thoughts. It is time to do something about this, especially being so far from our homeland, where it will be difficult to find her a groom in accordance with our traditions.

- Mama, mama, where are you? asked Hannah anxiously from the doorway of the house.

- Here in Rachel's room

She hurried over to find her mother.

Sarah looked aghast at her daughter.

- What happened to you, my darling? You are completely filthy.

- Oh, mama, when we went to play in the fields we got all dirty and on top of it, I had a fight with Miriam and she started crying.

- Oh no, not again, her mother answered crossly.

- Where is she? Rachel asked exasperated.

- Outside, sitting on the stairs at the front door. But it is her fault, she started it.

- I am going to check on her, Sarah answered, worried. Meanwhile, you go and take a bath and stay in your room.

Miriam was even dirtier than her sister. When Sarah asked her gently about what had happened, she answered hotly:

- Hannah pushed me. She always is pushing me because she says she is bigger than me. Why couldn't I have been born first?

- That was decided by God, Sarah answered, half of her feeling cross and half laughing. Come on, my dear, let us get you cleaned up and then we will talk.

Sarah came back to Rachel's room, still looking a little perturbed. Trying to console her, Rachel said:

- Don't look so worried. All sisters fight. We are not the only ones.

- That is true, my dear. Between us, it is not so much these little children's squabbles that upset me so much as the amount of dirt and grime in these neighborhoods. I clean all the time. I wish there weren't so many vacant lots. Maybe that would help keep everything cleaner.

- Mama, don't complain. I think Bogotá is enchanting. The climate is chilly, sometimes too much so, and there are a few too many cloudy days, but when the sun comes out my heart sings at the sight of so much beauty.

We shouldn't listen to the few who criticize life in Bogotá. They call Bogotá the city of eternal springtime, because summer never comes! They do not seem impressed by the majestic mountains that are part of the Andean cordillera. We here can look upon Montserrate and Guadalupe mountains, like protective guardians of those who dare to live in the folds of their skirts. For me these great phenomena of nature are the best thing in the world. I never tire of admiring them and would love to climb them. That would be an adventure!

As they continued to chat about this, Sarah said in a slightly mocking voice, perhaps to quell her daughter's youthful enthusiasm a bit:

- But in this city it rains for many months a years...

- I realize that. It is a problem, since it brings various difficulties that we must deal with, but on the other hand it is also a blessing, because it keeps all the greenery growing. In Europe the four seasons also have their own difficulties and challenges. Here, since we don't have the seasons, we don't have to worry about them.

- You are right. I should feel happy in this friendly country, but I still miss the old days and sometimes feel sad.

- I am sorry, mama, but you are forgetting the most important thing. In this place we have recovered our freedom, which is as important as breathing or any other basic need we have. We can go out into the street without fear of being harmed or pushed around. In fact, people appreciate us and even look up to us because of our knowledge of foreign lands.

Personally, I feel very happy among these marvelous people and I love their typical outfits: ponchos and gabardine, woolens, rope sandals, and those interesting shawls with black fringes that the women use to cover themselves. They look so distinctive in them. I have often felt tempted to ask someone to lend me one to try on and look at myself in the mirror.

- Your words cheer me and put my mind at ease. I am

pleased to see how you have adapted to this place. I see the same reaction in your brothers. Certainly, I think that the acceptance shown to you by the Bogotá people has had an important role to play in this. They have conquered our hearts with their goodness and made us love Colombia. The freedom and safety that we have found here must encourage us to go on, and the progress we have made in our work is a result of the happiness we have found here in this country. No more being afraid of the future. We are alive, together again and that is all that matters.

- Sarah, Rachel, Samuel, children, everyone come, yelled Nathan as he arrived enthusiastically bounding into the house. There is a student parade on Seventh Avenue.

- Is something wrong, Nathan, Sarah asked him alarmed, as she came out of Rachel's room.

- Nothing to worry about, quite the contrary. Get the children together. There are some wonderful carts parading through the streets, with beautiful girls dancing and a queen dressed in a gown of silver and gold. There are masks, serpentines, confetti and lights everywhere...Let us go to the party, and we can also enjoy ourselves like everyone else. They are all joining in to the general celebration: young and old, Colombians and foreigners. The important thing is to share the celebration with the others, and appreciate their ways.

They quickly got dressed and went out together to join in the excited commotion in the streets. Their hearts beat quickly with joy. They were happy, happier than they had ever been.

Chapter 30

Max and Ruth had been married a few months earlier at the Bogota Jewish Community Center, the Centro Israelita, in a lovely ceremony followed by a delicious banquet. The atmosphere that reigned in their new home was one of peace and happiness. They were living in a house purchased by the newlywed husband after a substantial increase in his income due to his successful management of the stocking factory, which he had acquired through diligent effort and sacrifice.

Max deeply loved his wife. She was beautiful and had a warm personality. As well as being a wonderful woman, she got along well with everyone in her husband's family, whom she had adopted as her own.

- Uncle Max, where are you? Samuel called out, as he ran up, panting from the effort, to the fence surrounding his uncle's house.

- Here we are, Samuel, Max answered as he opened the door quickly for his nephew.

As the boy rushed in, Max anxiously asked him the reason for the hurry.

- News, good news. Guess who arrived at our house?
- Let's see....I have no idea. Tell me.
- You will not believe it, uncle.
- It must be a very important person, judging by your mysterious behavior.
- It is Pearl!
- What did you say?
- Yes, uncle, our cousin Pearl has arrived. She is alive and she has found us. It is a miracle.
- It can't be!
- It is true, I swear it.
- Then we have been truly blessed, thank God! Only He could have brought her here to us alive after we had given her up for dead, exclaimed Max with deep emotion.

I can't wait to see her and hear first-hand all the details of what she has been through over these past few years. Maybe her parents and some of our family members have managed to survive the war. Let's hurry.

- Yes, let's go right now, added Ruth, thrilled at the thought of meeting the daughter of her husband's cousin, after having heard so much about her from the family.

The two houses were not far from each other and they soon arrived at their destination. Samuel ran in to tell Pearl about her uncle and aunt's visit.

- I cannot believe it; it really is you! shouted Max in high spirits as soon upon seeing her, and spontaneously threw his arms open as she ran to meet him.

- Uncle Max, how happy I am to see you!
- Yes, my dear. I am so happy to be able to hug you and have you here among us.
- It is a miracle that I am here alive, and sadly, I cannot say the same of papa, mama, Abel, Esther or any other of our family members, she answered, casting her gaze downward as she made an effort not to cry.

- Tell us all about what happened, he urged her, leading her by the arm to the living room sofa, where the family was already sitting, ready to listen to her recount her tale.

Pearl paused as she tried again to control her feelings, but seeing her family's faces looking at her expectantly and nervously at what they were about to hear, she tried to be brave and began to tell them her story.

- As I believe you already know, in Warsaw the Germans forced us to build and move to ghettos. They were real fortresses, or I should say, prisons, and they wouldn't let us leave for any reason, unless we had a special written permission.

At first, it didn't seem so bad. We thought that even though they had taken away our homes, businesses, and belongings, we were still alive and it would be a matter of time before we would work enough to get back what we had lost.

Then we started suffering from shortages of everything: water, food, clothing and even space to move around. The Germans brought people in continuously until there was terrible overcrowding. It was even worse when we began to notice the atrocities committed by the Nazis against everyone, no matter whether man, woman or child, who dared disobeyed any of their orders. Oh, uncle Max, it was unimaginable! she exclaimed with anguish.

- Please, don't suffer so, Sarah begged her, embracing her in an attempt to calm the girl. If you wish, you can tell us some other time. You have just arrived and been through so much emotionally...

- No, aunty, Pearl answered, drying her tears with determination. I want to continue.

Illness and fights were a daily occurrence and this did not help our situation. Finally, it reached a crucial point, as we later found out. The Germans, unable to place more people there, offered to move thousands out by train to a place where they would be more comfortable and could work for their room and board.

Many people believed this tempting offer of an opportunity to get out of the ghetto, but my parents still hung onto the hope that I would leave and be reunited with you, so they decided not to go with the first group. They thought they would have the chance to go later once I was truly safe.

My mother had carefully hidden some savings well beforehand in order to avoid having them taken away, and she was anxiously looking for a chance to negotiate my departure from Poland in exchange for this money.

This opportunity finally presented itself when the German doctor in charge of weekly rounds came to examine a critically ill person who was staying with us.

- Help us, my mother pleaded with him. We want to save our only daughter from a life of forced labor. You are an influential person. You could help her get out of here and on a ship to South America. We have family there who will take care of her. You are the only one who can help us. We have enough money to pay for the trip, and we could pay you very well for your services, for which we would be eternally grateful.

That fateful conversation bore fruit almost immediately. Two weeks later, Doctor Gerstenblutt came to us with a permit issued in my name, which would allow me to leave the ghetto. Where did he get it? We never found out and did not think it wise to ask, but from that moment forward, my whole life changed.

After having to bid a difficult farewell to my parents, I prayed fervently to God to be able to see them once again in this life. I wasn't able to even say goodbye to the rest of my family and friends, since the doctor told me not to do so, with an argument that seemed convincing at the time. If anyone were to make some comment, even innocently, both he and I would be in grave danger.

On my way out of the ghetto, I silently said goodbye to everyone I knew and asked for God's help to end that horrible nightmare and make the Nazis understand the enormity of the crime that they were committing without any reason nor justification.

I prayed all the way, not even so much for myself as for the millions of persons who were remaining behind to suffer with all those dangers, and I asked God to grant them peace.

The doctor walked hurriedly and told me to keep very close. Once in a while we would meet a member of the Gestapo and with an effort that was as great as my own, he would struggle to appear calm and greet them, and then we would continue on our way as if nothing was out of the ordinary.

From the wide avenues of Warsaw we continued to narrow streets and finally arrived at an alley that was bordered by two rows of small houses lining it on each side in parallel lines, and for the first time I noticed he hesitated as to what direction to take. He looked quickly at a notebook that he took out of his jacket vest pocket. He sighed and then we continued on again at a quick pace, looking behind us from time to time to see if anyone was following, and seeing, with relief, that the streets were empty.

Finally we arrived at our destination. It was a blue-gray two-story house, somewhat faded from the passage of time. The staircase was steep and the doctor began to climb up it, tired and perspiring, not even so much from the effort as from his nerves. He knocked at the door twice, looking nervously behind him at the street, and a woman opened the door to us.

- Come in, come in, she said anxiously, as if afraid to open the door any wider.

Once we were inside, she asked us if everything had gone according to plan, if we had been followed, and the doctor answered, almost without speaking, just nodding or shaking his head. Finally Mrs. Gluck sighed with satisfaction. The doctor spoke:

- I must be going now. Otherwise, they might suspect something from my absence. I leave Pearl with you and ask that you take special care with this case. Her parents have paid me a large sum of money and surely will be willing to pay much more to ensure that their daughter gets out of here alive. Just do the same as we have done the other times. After all, one more, one less – what is the difference?

- Don't worry, we will do our best to make sure it all goes according to plan.

- Thank you, answered Doctor Gerstenblutt and, wishing me luck for my trip, he left quickly, looking all around before he left to avoid discovery.

- For three weeks I was hidden in the basement with several other people: a family with two children and three men, one old man and two young ones who, like myself, were all relying on this family that trafficked in human beings and who were to travel on the same ship as me.

Shaken by fear, anxiety and anguish, that period of less than a month seemed to us like a year. The nervous tension was unbearable. The least little noise or movement outside our hiding place put us on guard and even when the small trapdoor opened and Mrs. Gluck appeared with a tray of food, we trembled with fear. The positive and unforgettable aspect of all this torturous time was the support I received from these people who were my companions in this sad situation, both while we were in hiding as well as during the trip.

- Dear little Pearl! Nathan exclaimed, his voice thick with emotion as he stood up from the armchair where he had been listening to the girl's painful memories. With your presence, as the only survivor of our family in Poland, you have brought happiness to this home. Sarah, myself, and the children all want you to stay with us here as a daughter and sister in our family. We would be greatly honored if you would accept our offer.

- Thank you so much for your generosity, Pearl answered gratefully.

- Your thanks are welcome but unnecessary, Sarah said, delighted at Nathan's noble gesture. This is your home and we are your family.

- Welcome home, Raquel answered, running to give her cousin a hug. One by one, each of the cousins came over to embrace her, and as they did so each one gave new hope to Pearl's life.

Chapter 31

Nathan Ratovich and Morris Liberman had been partners for four years. The latter's contribution to the company was the money they needed to purchase two knitting machines and Nathan was in charge of production. The arrangement worked out well and the partners, moreover, had become great friends.

Liberman was a natural businessman and had a distinguished bearing. He was not overly tall and rather portly, with brown eyes that were always gazing intently through his round spectacles. A small, well-groomed mustache gave him a unique look. While still in Poland, he had married Lea, a gentle, generous woman and they had produced four children: David, Simon, Benjamin and Tanya.

As soon as he had got to know Nathan's progeny, the idea had sparked in his mind to bring the two families together. One night, he went to visit Nathan and after a succulent repast prepared by Sarah, the men went into the parlor to dring their tea. After some pleasant conversation on various topics, Liberman mentioned to his host his intention to ask for Rachel's hand for his eldest son.

His guest's words took Nathan by surprise, but after thinking about it for a short time, it seemed, in principle, an acceptable proposition and he answered:

- Morris, I like your idea. But there is one problem. My niece, Pearl, arrived from Poland to live with us a few months ago and we have taken her in as a daughter to the family. She is older than Rachel and I would rather see her married first. She is not engaged yet, but I am sure I can find her a nice young man. She has many qualities and will make someone an excellent wife.

Liberman pondered this for a few minutes and looking at his companion straight in the eyes, proposed a solution.

- I think I have the answer. I have three sons, and none of them are engaged as yet. As she is your niece, it would be an honor for me to have her as a daughter-in-law, if you are in agreement.

Nathan's face lit up with joy. He had never thought of such a perfect arrangement and felt happy for both girls, who would surely have a wonderful life beside two of the sons of his good friend, both excellent young men. However, in order to keep up appearances and not seem to be too anxious, he merely answered:

- I think this double union of the members of our families would be satisfactory, but I must, in any case, consult Sarah.

- Think about it and get back to me soon, answered Liberman with a smile, as he rose to take his leave.

As soon as he had left the house, Nathan ran to the bedroom to find his wife and excitedly told her:

- My dear, I think I am the luckiest man in the world right now. We have just received a proposal of marriage for Rachel and for Pearl.

- To be married to David and Simon? asked Sarah curiously.

- Indeed. Isn't it wonderful?

- Of course, they are wonderful matches and we couldn't do better for our daughters.

They hugged each other jubilantly, thinking of how they would break the news to the girls as soon as they woke in the morning.

The next day, after breakfast, Nathan called them to one side and told them about Mr. Liberman's proposal.

Pearl sat silently as she listened to her uncle's words. Meanwhile, Rachel began to cry inconsolably.

- I am surprised by your reaction, dear. I thought I was giving you good news.

- Papa, Rachel answered through her tears and sniffles, I wanted to be married for love and not by arrangement. Times have changed and I want to decide for myself who will be my husband for the rest of my life.

- You are speaking nonsene, Nathan responded angrily at his daughter's unexpected reaction. Parents have always been the ones most suited to choose the best spouses for their daughters, and this has not changed. I suggest you accept this idea. There will be no more discussion on the matter. It has been decided. First Pearl will marry David and after three months, you will marry Simon.

- Oh no! she shrieked, running out of her parents' bedroom.

Sarah heard the cries and instinctively ran after her daughter, who immediately ran to her room and threw herself on her bed decrying her terrible fate.

- There is no reason for those tears, sweetheart, she said gently, stroking her hair.

Rachel wiped away the tears that were rolling down her cheeks and trying to calm down, looked up at her mother.

- So, you think Mr. Liberman's proposal to father is fine?

- Naturally. I don't see anything wrong with it.

- Mama! I cannot believe that you, too, really agree with all this!

- Well, yes, I think it is a wonderful opportunity. Morris Liberman's sons are good boys and come from our country, are Jewish and have been raised with the utmost moral standards. I can guarantee you all this, since I know their parents well. What more could we want?

- I feel so disappointed. My dream was to marry Jacob Lempert.

- Have you not heard what happened to that poor fellow?

- Please, tell me. I haven't heard anything more of him.

- He was the victim of a terrible fate. When he heard the Soviet army was liberating prisoners in the concentration camps and going after the Nazis, he decided, with his father's permission, to travel to Poland to help hunt down the ruthless members of the Gestapo. During one of his missions, a German gun cut short his life.

- No, no, it cannot be! exclaimed Rachel, shuddering pitifully and covering her face with her hands.

- I am very sorry to have to break this to you and cause you such pain, but you should know the truth. You cannot continue to live an illusion.

After a time, once she had managed to get herself under control, Rachel spoke to Sarah again with resignation.

- Do you think I will be able to fall in love again and be happy?

- You shall be happy, I have no doubt. And as for love, first comes attraction between two people, then with the union, their feelings become intertwined….once you have gone through these steps, you will be in love, without knowing how nor why it happened.

- Do you really think so, mama?

- I am sure of it. Your father and I were married just like that and we have always loved each other.

- I hope it will be so. I cannot fight papa's wishes…in the end, I know I will give in anyway. But I still regret not being able to choose my own future myself and face the consequences of my own decisions.

- I know, darling, but your future and Pearl's are already decided. Let us pray to God that you shall both find happiness and success.

Chapter 32

David and Pearl were wed in a simple but moving ceremony, in accordance with family traditions, which was followed by a modest celebration at Nathan and Sarah's house. They contentedly observed the exchange of affectionate glances and the couple shyly holding hands, prophetic signs of a happy life together, and prayed that Rachel and Simon's future marriage would be as successful as her cousin and her groom.

Three months later, on a typically overcast Bogota day, Rachel, dressed in her bridal gown and with a sad expression on her face, left with her family for the synagogue where she would join her life forever with that of Simon.

The hall where the ceremony was to take place was decorated with bowers of white lilies, eucalyptus leaves and floral arrangements set on pedestals and surrounded by ribbons, lining the red carpet to the altar in two long rows. The arrangements, every detail of which had been organized and supervised by Sarah, looked as beautiful as she had imagined and the setting was enchanting.

Simon, a young man of twenty-two years, had a fair

complexion, brown hair, dark eyes, an aquiline nose and was tall and handsome. He was standing beside his parents, under the chuppah, waiting for the ceremony to being.

Suddenly, the strains of the wedding march rang out and Rachel appeared on her parents' arms. She took a deep breath, finding within herself the courage she would need to face her destiny, and slowly walked down the formal entranceway delineated by the floral arrangements, which were giving off a delicious fragrance, until she arrived at the side of the man who would be her husband.

He did not dare to look at her, given his natural shyness, but he felt her presence near and a strong emotion overwhelmed him. The marriage ceremony began and absolute silence reigned, broken moments later by the Rabbi's resonating voice.

Their families, wrought with emotion, watched the couple and wished for them a life blessed with good fortune. Rachel looked secretly at her groom from time to time, and wondered anxiously if she would ever be able to love this person.

When it was all over, there were embraces and congratulations. Nathan came over to his daughter and in a barely audible voice that only she could hear, he whispered to her with intensity:

- My dear daughter! Do not worry. This will be the beginning of a life full of happiness and good fortune. Give all of yourself and this come to you.

- I will, papa, she answered, hugging him with tears in her eyes.

The newlyweds moved into a small apartment, which had been rented before the wedding. Rachel, following her father's advice, tried from the beginning to be a good wife and started by giving their home an original and cozy touch, and in certain details her mother's influence could be seen. Light cream-colored walls, flowered curtains that matched the bedspreads, dark, polished wooden night tables and a white, impeccable kitchen with a traditional round table similar to the one in Sylvia's house, where she had sat down so many times to drink her tea.

As she looked over the results of her efforts, Rachel said to herself:

If only my grandmother could have been here! I would have so many things to ask her.

Simon, on the other hand, worked tirelessly in the shops of fine men's clothing, which were owned by his father. The whole family worked in different shifts: Morris, his wife and their three sons, trying always to keep their select clientele satisfied in all aspects of their needs for suits and accessories.

In the afternoon, he would arrive back home tired and Rachel would wait expectantly to welcome him into a pleasant and tranquil home environment. Their relationship began to grow. He started to tell her about details of the business and they would chat for hours about how to improve their economic situation.

For part of each day, Rachel worked with her father in the sweater factory, trying to maximize production, and her husband would help them after work to distribute the merchandise, which he did very effectively. He showed more talent for these tasks than the persons who were usually in charge of them and Nathan observed this happily, since he could tell that his son-in-law had natural business instincts and would surely improve his situation, sooner or later.

His predictions soon became a reality. A business of buying and selling real estate grew out of Simon's meetings with other businessmen. He received a healthy commission on each transaction, and this became an incentive for him to continue to look for other properties to set up new business deals. His financial situation began to improve quickly.

One day he arrived home from work to find Rachel waiting for him with marvelous news: they were going to have a baby. Simon hugged her and tried to tell her how happy he was, but not being gifted in expressing himself he didn't know how to tell her how much he loved her and how deeply he felt this love knowing that she was carrying their first child.

The months passed and their household routine continued, interrupted at times by visits from family and friends, who were impatiently awaiting the birth of the new baby.

One morning, in her ninth month of pregnancy, Rachel woke up and restlessly got up from the bed to make her way heavily to the bathroom. She felt vaguely unwell and the night had seemed endless. She was now also suffering from lower back pain, which she had never felt before. As she made her way to the wash basin to brush her teeth, suddenly an intense pain made her double over and holding on to her belly in a protective gesture, she began to tremble and perspire profusely. She waited, bent over, for a time until the incapacitating pain began to diminish and she tried to straighten up.

Am I about to have the baby? she wondered anxiously. Was that the first contraction that will start labor? But she felt nothing more and was returning to her normal state.

Maybe it was just a passing cramp, she thought hesitantly. I will wait for a while longer and see how it goes. She began to brush her teeth and looking out the window, saw that it was still pitch black. It is still hours to sunrise. Rachel decided to return to bed and try to make up for the lost hours of sleep. After only half an hour in bed, she felt a strong twisting pain again and this time, she could not suppress a groan.

Simon, half asleep, asked her what was the matter.

She didn't answer.

- Are you ill? he asked again.

Still in pain, she answered him with an effort:

- I think it is time. Our baby is going to be born so I think we had better go.

Everything was ready at the Magdalena Hospital for their arrival. They had called the doctor on the telephone to explain the symptoms and he immediately ordered everything to be prepared for the delivery.

Simon parked the car in front of the clinic and helped Rachel carefully get out of the car. They went in slowly through the emergency door and a male nurse immediately appeared pushing a wheelchair.

- Good evening. Are you Mrs. Liberman?

- Yes, sir, she answered a little shakily.

- Please, sit down. I have instructions from your doctor to take you up to the prep room.

- But where is Doctor Hoffman? Simon asked nervously.

- He is already in the delivery room waiting for you. Let us not waste any more time...

Rachel made herself comfortable in the wheelchair. The nurse arranged the bar so she could rest her feet and efficiently pushed her up the narrow hallways of the hospital followed by her anxious husband, who was trying to stay close by his wife's side.

- You may only follow us up to this point, Mr. Liberman, said the nurse in a commanding tone as they drew up to the entrance to the "Delivery Room". No one else besides the obstetrics team is allowed in, but there is a waiting room here in front and you can wait there in comfort for the doctor.

- Good luck, Simon called out, with a look of resignation.

- She nodded while a pained look crossed her face as a new contraction made her double over again and the nurse, seeing this, began moving forward more quickly with the wheelchair, leaving behind the worried husband.

231

Chapter 33

The first rays of sunlight filtered through the window of her bedroom, gently waking Sarah, and she stayed still a few minutes before beginning to stretch, enjoying the pleasant warmth of the comforter and sheets. She turned her head. For a while she watched Nathan deep in sleep and smiled contentedly. She got up carefully so as not to wake her husband, and placing her feet into her slippers, went to the bathroom. She washed, put on her bathrobe and went out to the kitchen to prepare breakfast. As soon as it was ready, she sat down at the table to sip her first cup of coffee before starting to clean the house. She turned on the radio. It was time for the news and she never missed it.

Suddenly, she turned pale as she heard the announcer's first words:

"The war is over" he was saying. "Today there is victory in Europe. Nazi German has unconditionally surrendered. Long live freedom!"

- Blessed be God! Our nightmare is finally over, she exclaimed, feeling tears springing to her eyes and clouding her sight.

- Nathan! she called out, running straight to the bedroom

The war is over. They just announced it on the radio. God has answered our prayers. No more killing, no more suffering.

- That's good, was all he was able to say. He was speechless from emotion and large tears began to run silently down his cheeks.

Sarah came over to him. She understood how much her husband was suffering as he remembered his parents and family who had died in the war, and for whom this day of triumph had come too late. Gazing at him and seeing his silent, raw pain, she simply placed her hand on his shoulder and felt his body racked with sobs and heard raspy sounds escape from his throat coming from the depths of his being. Nathan continued thus for several minutes, allowing his emotions to flow freely and when he was finally able to contain himself, he said:

- So long waiting for a miracle and finally it is here! Who from our loved ones will have been saved from the claws of those ruthless Nazis? Will we find alive anyone who we knew from our homeland?

- We shall have to try and find out, my dear, said Sarah, drying his tears quickly. Today is a day of celebration, of happiness. With victory in Europe, our people are finally free from the yoke of those murderers. We shall call Max, Ruth and our children in case they haven't yet heard the good news. She went over to the telephone and spoke with each of them, telling them excitedly about the news, but when she tried to call her eldest daughter, no one answered. How strange, she thought. They should be at home at this time of the morning. I will call again in half an hour.

- Come here, Sarah. Sit beside me, Nathan said. I want to talk to you.

- I am listening, she answered, coming over and sitting down in a small chair in front of her husband.

He paused for a few seconds and then began, saying:

- The end of the war forces us to think about the future. We came to Colombia and stayed here because of circumstances forcing us to do so, but it has been a big sacrifice for me in terms of spirituality. I have always been dedicated to our religion and in Poland I would have the opportunity to continue my studies and obtain the materials I need to further my knowledge.

I have never been a good businessman. When I arrived in Bogota, I had to go door to door to sell merchandise and then set up a sweater factory just to be able to make ends meet and earn enough money to send for you. For these purposes I have fought for the business with all my might and given up my selfish wish to dedicate myself to studies. But now, that I see my family in quite a satisfactory situation, I think it is my duty to return to my land and make up for lost time.

She stayed quietly thinking for several minutes and in a moment of decision began to shake her head and let her ideas flow freely.

- No, Nathan, I do not want to go back to Poland and I do not want my children ever to go back there. Colombia took us in with generosity and gave us all kinds of opportunities, which we have been able to take advantage of. We are free and our children are being educated in an atmosphere of peace and tranquility and have received all kinds of social and cultural opportunities. Now, they are married and happy, and when our grandchildren are born, they will not be afraid of being rejected. On the contrary, they will share in the equality of rights that are given to us by the citizens of this country. It was very difficult for us to get the visa that we saw stamped so proudly in our passports and I don't want to lose it, just to chase after some other adventure that may turn out to be dangerous for us. Our parents, families and friends are not there anymore. I feel such a terrible pain just thinking about going back and not finding them there. Here, on the other hand, we have new friends. They can never substitute for our loved ones in Europe, but we love them equally. Please, do not ask me to go back to Poland! Our life is moving ahead here and we should continue here.

- I will think about it, Sarah, he answered her, sounding unconvinced.

Just then, the telephone rang and she, with a strange premonition, ran out to pick it up.

- Hello, who is calling? she asked anxiously.

- It is me, Simon. Rachel has been here in the hospital since last night. Everything had been going well and we thought by now we would be calling with news of the birth of the baby, but there have been some difficulties. According to the doctor, the baby is tangled in the umbilical cord and they have not been able to deliver the baby for fear of risking his life. I feel so impotent that I cannot do anything to help.

- We will be right over there, answered Sarah with a trembling voice.

She immediately hung up the phone and held on to the telephone table, while her heart raced with tachycardia brought on by her high blood pressure that took her breath away and increased her feeling of unease. She took deep breaths for several minutes, trying to recover, and then began to walk forcefully toward the living room to tell Nathan about the problem.

Chapter 34

Nathan and Sarah moved hurriedly through the heavy glass doors of Magdalena Hospital and once inside, looked for the information desk. As soon as they arrived, an employee came up to help them.

- Miss, please, Nathan asked, his face revealing his worry, could you tell us where to find Mrs. Rachel de Liberman? She was admitted to the delivery room last night.

The nurse, a redhead with a lively personality, went to the file in front of her and taking up her eyeglasses that were hanging from a cord on her ample breast, put them on and took out the corresponding admission file, then turned back to the anxiously waiting couple.

- What is your relationship to the patient?

- She is our daughter, Sarah answered nervously.

- This lady is still in the delivery room and her family members are in the waiting room. If you wish, you may meet them in room 2B, which you will find taking the elevator to the second floor. From there, turn left. It is the second door on the right.

- Can you tell us anything about her condition? asked Nathan.

- No, sir. Since six a.m. I haven't received any reports, but perhaps your family will have seen the doctor and can tell you more.

- Thank you very much, they answered in unison and went in the direction the nurse had indicated, through the narrow hallways with very white walls, saturated with a penetrating odor of disinfectant. They hurried along until they reached the elevators. Nathan arrived first and pressed the call button. The elevator took a few minutes to arrive. Finally the arrow lit up and the doors opened. The people waiting there, among them Nathan and Sarah, hurried inside. When the stopped at the second floor, they followed the instructions and entered the waiting room.

Simon stood up as soon as he saw them come in and went over to them.

- How is Rachel? Nathan asked him with concern lining his face.

- A few minutes ago the doctor gave me some information. It seems that besides the umbilical cord, the cervix is not sufficiently dilated and he wants to give Rachel more time before deciding to perform a caesarian surgery, taking into account her young age and the fact that it is her first child, since it would mean she may have problems having more children. He told me to be patient, and that his team are doing all they can.

-Oh, dear God! exclaimed Sarah, overcome, please don't let anything happen to my daughter and her baby.

Lea, who had been listening attentively to Simon's explanation, came over to Sarah and put her arm around her to try and console this woman, who had always been so brave through years of difficulties and suffering to raise her family and whispered to her:

- My dear, have faith. She will be all right. She is young and will overcome any obstacles.

- Sit down with us, Morris said. Surely the doctor will be out soon to give us some good news.

While his parents and in-laws talked, Simon paced anxiously while dark thoughts ran through his mind.

I cannot stand so much uncertainty, he said and suddenly, without thinking, ran toward the delivery room. He knocked on the door until it opened and a nurse dressed in green surgical garb came out and asked him:

- Sir, can I help you with something?

- I need to speak to doctor Hoffman. It is very important, he added, his nervousness evident.

- One moment, please.

He waited a few more minutes, becoming more and more impatient, and finally the doctor appeared.

- What is the matter, young man ? the doctor asked, noting his pallor.

- Can you please let me see my wife? This waiting is unbearable.

The doctor hesitated for a few seconds, but then, nodding his head, he opened the door to let Simon come in. They walked in silence and entered the room.

- My assistant will give you a sterile gown and mask, said the gentleman.

He obeyed the nurse's instructions and once he was dressed in the green gown and mask, went into the room where he saw Rachel. Suddenly, Simon heard a scream so piercing and haunting that he would not forget it for the rest of his life and as he backed into a corner of the delivery room, he watched the doctor and nurses rush over to the delivery table.

- It is time, said the doctor.

The doctor pulled over a bench with wheels and sat

down in front of Rachel's legs, which had been placed in the gynecological position. He moved his large gloved hands inside the dilated opening of the woman in labor and with all his skill, tried to rotate the baby's head, which was already crowning, in order to free the umbilical cord.

An assistant was standing behind Rachel and she dried the perspiration from her brow, as the labor nurse continually massaged the abdomen, trying to speed up the process.

Another scream pierced the air and Simon, unable to bear the terrible scene a moment longer, fell to the ground in a dead faint on the hard floor, where he lay like a rag doll thrown away on a trash heap.

Her labor pains continued. Rachel shook from the effort and her eyes seemed about to roll out of their sockets at times.

- No more, please God, she cried in desperation. I can't take any more!

The doctor continued to gently move the head, trying to untangle it from the stranglehold.

Moments later the baby came out, covered in blood and finally freed from the umbilical cord, and the doctor let out a relieved sigh.

Rachel felt as if her body were breaking in two. As the baby was delivered, the whole room began to go dark before her eyes. The doctor took the newborn's two tiny legs between his fingers and suspended the baby upside down to coax out the first breath. Immediately a high-pitched cry filled the room and provoked an immediate reaction from all those present.

Rachel was silent as she heard the cries and tears of joy rolled down her cheeks. The nurse, noticing her state, placed the newborn on the sheet covering the mother's breast and announced triumphantly:

- It is a girl, beautiful and healthy. Everything is fine.

- Oh dear God! she cried out with joy. I have a daughter!

Simon, who was meanwhile recovering from having fainted, heard these words and felt a wave of joy engulf him. He hurried over to his wife and lovingly kissed her and held her hand, saying:

- Mazal tov! My brave, brave wife. I knew you could do it.

- We have a daughter! she answered him with delight.

- I know, my love. Now, try to just rest and recover your strength. This has been so terribly hard on you.

- Do you have a name for the child? The assistant asked curiously.

- Not yet, answered Simon.

- You should call her "Victoria", the assistant suggested. Victory has been declared today in Europe and this girl has been sent by God into the world just as we are celebrating this happy day.

Simon and Rachel looked into each other's eyes and smiles of happiness appeared on their faces on hearing this news.

Another of the nursing assistants interrupted just then to speak to her colleague.

- Did you already tell them about the doctor's instructions ?

- Oh, yes, I had forgotten, said the other, turning to speak to Simon. Although it turned out to be a normal delivery, since the mother had such a strong labor and it was her first baby, and because of the complications that occurred, the doctor thinks that she should rest now and asked that she not receive visitors until tomorrow.

As soon as the nurses began cleaning up the mother and baby, the proud father went out to the scrub room, and quickly took off the gown, cap, and mask in order to go out and share the good news of the birth with the family. On entering the waiting room, the whole family came over to hug him and give their best wishes for the new baby's happiness and health.

Morris and Lea looked lovingly at their son. Meanwhile, Nathan and Sarah were overjoyed to have seen their daughter through these difficult moments and to have their first grandchild, healthy and safe.

Finally, Simon, grinning ear to ear, began to speak:

- As you all know, thank God, everything is fine now. I was there with her, he said pointedly, and the doctor says that Rachel must rest. She cannot have visitors until tomorrow.

The news was received with a few grumbles by the family, but they had no choice and so they all left for Simon's apartment to visit for a while and exchange their impressions.

As they made themselves comfortable in the parlor, Morris asked that they turn on the radio to hear the news of Europe. Simon tuned into the station and they heard a loud noise fill the room – the sound of multitudes shouting joyfully and the announcer saying:

"Throughout Europe and America, with the exception of Germany, people have spontaneously come out to express their joy and to celebrate the victory in Europe. Paris is celebrating as never before. General Charles de Gaulle has announced the end of the war and the Marseillaise is being played everywhere. The crowds are growing and have taken over the streets with singing and dancing as the Allied soldiers parade through. In London, first in the House of Commons and then, from one of the balconies of Whitehall, Prime Minister Winston Churchill proclaimed before an attentive and hushed crowd: "In all our long history we have never seen a greater day than this. Everyone, man or woman, has done their best. God bless you all. Our gratitude to our splendid Allies goes forth from all our hearts in this Island and throughout the British Empire. Advance, Britannia! Long live the cause of freedom!" The British Royal family, the announcer continued, has gone out to greet the crowds from their balconies and the cheers of their people have called them out again eight times before they finally retired to continue the celebration.

In Switzerland the bells are chiming out the good news and the Swiss and Allied flags have been raised in a salute to the great day.

In Zurich and Stockholm, the inhabitants are flooding out from their homes into the streets of the cities to dance traditional folk dances until the wee hours. The consulates have raised their flags and are playing the national anthems in a sign of respect.

Dutch and Danish towns are lit up with the festivities, the announcer added, and the townspeople are spontaneously dancing in the street according to their local traditions. The Nazi reign has ended!! is heard over and over as the townspeople shout their triumph and are answered jubilantly by their neighbors.

In Moscow, the inhabitants are observing in amazement at the thousand cannon salute ordered by Joseph Stalin. And in Portugal, the celebration is breathtaking. Children are running through the streets with their parents, who have left their daily tasks to celebrate the end of the war with their European brethren.

In every corner of Europe, collections have begun to undertake the reconstruction of the countries that have been attacked. The sky is lit up with fireworks that shine on the happy faces of thousands of people who can now leave behind the years of pain and look toward the future with optimism, hope to rebuild and to erase from the memories the tragic times that the Nazis inflicted on their lives.

The celebration continues and it seems it will go on for quite a while." With these words, the announcer finished his description and Simon turned off the radio.

- Poland wasn't mentioned, Nathan exclaimed, somewhat disturbed.

- I noticed that, too, answered Morris. But, just imagine how happy our people must be to know that the war is finally over.

- Oh, yes, they all exclaimed fervently.

- President Roosevelt should have been alive to see this triumphant day, said Simon. He would have loved to have seen all his efforts end in this successful day.

-You are right, Morris added, sadly. In the end, he was the one who convinced the Americans to help Europe. At first, the United States didn't feel they were threatened by the war and thought it had nothing to do with them and they shouldn't get involved. But their contribution of soldiers, the air force and other units and their military expertise was a decisive factor in the Allied victory.

For both Nathan and Sarah's family and Morris and Lea's family, it had been a day of enormous joy for two major reasons: the arrival of Simon and Rachel's daughter and the end to the cruel and bloodthirsty war waged by Adolph Hitler and his legions of savage henchmen.

Chapter 35

The Liberman household rejoiced over the birth of little Annie, who her maternal grandmother always called Hannale. She was a charming little girl with almond-shaped eyes and light brown hair and her face was usually lit up with a captivating smile. The child became the center of attention for her parents, grandparents, aunts and uncles, and not a day went by that one of them didn't come to visit her or bring her a small gift. Her presence in the house contributed greatly to Rachel's contentment and she now felt useful and needed, which also gave a boost to her self-esteem and a feeling of self-assurance and respect.

Every day after work, Simon ran home to try and arrive when his daughter was still awake and whenever he had the chance, he would spend as much time as possible with her, growing every closer to his offspring. His wife was amazed to see him so enthusiastic, since from early in their marriage he had always seemed shy and introverted. The child had seemingly brought about a miracle by waking in him feelings that had been hidden for many years and that he now was able to express easily.

Time passed effortlessly within that warm glow of family peace and understanding. In no time at all, Rachel was pregnant again and soon a second daughter was born into the family, who they named Karen. Although they received her in love and acceptance as any good parents would, they were still missing a son in the family. Simon's dream was to see a son born to carry on the family name and take over the business when he grew up.

The little girl, with her pale, porcelain complexion, huge blue eyes and curly hair, reminded all of them of the famous child actress of the time, Shirley Temple. However, unlike her sister, she was not a tranquil baby. She was awake most of the time and would cry at the slightest noise or disturbance.

- She is a very sensitive little girl! Sarah would say proudly. She is just like me, not only her looks but also her personality and feelings. Rachel, you will see what I mean as she grows up.

The Liberman home's happiness was made complete when, two years later, the long-awaited boy was born into the family and given the name, Charles. The newborn wailed constantly in his bassinet and the doctor diagnosed a difficult ear infection that did not respond to treatment. For three long months his parents took turns carrying him and walking with him, trying to relieve his discomfort, which seemed to get worse at night and would not allow him or them to rest.

Annie and Karen, five years old and two years old respectively, looked on happily at the tiny bundle who was cared for so sweetly by their mother, but as soon as the infant began to wail inconsolably, the two girls would back away from the crib in confusion and go off to play with their dolls who they felt were much quieter and easier to manage. As time went on, the infant's distress became less frequent and he began to smile. His sisters waited impatiently for the day they could start to play games with him.

David and Pearl had also brought three children into the world: a girl and two boys. Their lives went on relatively smoothly. They would all meet regularly at the grandparents' home and while the adults would spend some pleasant time in conversation, the cousins would play happily together. Occasionally, Rachel and Pearl would have a small falling-out, however, these minor discords would separate the sisters and their children for a short time and then they would make up again. "It happens in all families" Leah used to say sadly, trying to convince herself of this, as she could never get used to the idea that her daughters-in-law would be on anything but the best of terms. Her greatest happiness lay in being able to watch her whole extended family together around the table, tasting all the delicacies that she had prepared for them with her with such pleasure and anticipation.

- You have such a way with a meal, my darling wife, Morris would say to her after these dinners when, as the head of the family, he would honor her with the compliments that made her glow with delight.

Leah would outdo herself in her preparation of the Friday night Shabbat dinner. Her greatest satisfaction on these occasions, besides presenting her best recipes and enjoying the well-deserved congratulations that went along with this, was to look at the whole family all together, no one missing from the picture. She hated to see rivalries or spats between her daughters-in-law and always wished that these wonderful times that she and her husband spent with her sons and grandchildren could be enjoyed peaceably after so many years of hard work and effort.

- Mama, the gefilte fish[1] is absolutely delicious! exclaimed David, taking a mouthful.

- And the challah[2] as well, added Pearl with a delighted smile. It is incredible how the bread rises for you. I am sure many bakers would love to know your secret. You should publish a recipe book. You would be famous.

- It is not such a big deal, she would answer blushing. My only secret is preparing the food with love. This is what makes the difference.

- Thank you, mama, Simon responded with affection. We all appreciate your effort to bring the family together on Friday nights and we notice you and papa's limitless patience with our little ones, also.

Leah smiled and answered sweetly:

- With the help of my daughters-in-law it is never a burden to care for the children, and I think it is so important to always teach them the traditions we have kept for so many generations. If they do not grow up with these traditions, they will never really learn them properly, but by living them from the time they are small, they will become part of their lives and once they are grown up, this will set them on the right path to live their lives well.

After she had finished, Leah fell into silent contemplation and the meal went on with each one concentrated on his plate. As dessert arrived at the table, Pearl asked with interest:

- Rachel, how is Nathan's health?

---

[1] *Gefilte Fish.* Ground fish prepared with spices and vegetables and shaped into an oval ball. It is eaten traditionally in Ashkenazi homes: the Jewish communities originating in Germany, and Eastern, Western or Central Europe (Author's note)

[2] *Challah.* Braided loaves of bread that are traditionally eaten on the Sabbath. Also the part of the bread traditionally reserved for the priesthood (Author's note)

- Papa continues to have quite bad headaches, she answered sadly. We have noticed that as time goes on, they are occurring more often and are getting worse. For the past few years he has not wanted to go for rides in the car and it seemed that this movement was affecting him, but now it seems that the pain comes spontaneously for no apparent reason.

- What does the doctor say about it? Leah asked gently.

- They have done all kinds of tests on him, mama, Simon answered, following the conversation with interest, but the doctor has not been able to find any cause for his suffering.

- I am so worried about papa! Rachel added, as if talking to herself. Lately he has been so tired out that the slightest effort exhausts him and he seems to have aged so quickly. I truly hope they can find the reason for his problems.

Morris nodded silently and reflected with concern about Nathan's health. He remembered for a moment Nathan's struggle over so many years to bring his family from Poland. He should now be enjoying the fruits of his labor of all those years, he thought. Instead, this continual pain does not even let him rest. Life is so ironic. What would the future bring to this good man?

Coffee was served and they all sipped it in silence, each lost in his own thoughts. Ovaldina, the maid who had worked for Leah for so many years, led the children away from the dining room and an atmosphere of peace and tranquility reigned.

Following the traditional prayers of thanksgiving at the end of the meal, Morris stood up and invited his sons to accompany him into the parlor. The ladies were about to clear the table and he did not want to get in the way of this task.

Benjamin, the youngest of the brothers, was the first to fol-low him out. He was a lively and intelligent young man. He had not yet married, but he followed closely the conversa-tions between his father and brothers on business and oth-er current events. David and Simon glanced at their wives wordlessly and followed Benjamin into the parlor.

- We can never be fully happy, Leah commented with a sigh. Sarah is worried about Nathan's health and I, on the other hand, miss my daughter, Tanya, at times like this. Since she got married and went to live in Canada, I miss her so much. I wish she could visit us more often. Then, my happiness would be complete.

Pearl and Rachel looked over at Leah sympathetically and began to clear the table.

It grew late and the children began to fall asleep. The time had come to say goodnight and with yawns, hugs and kisses they returned to their homes.

Saturday was a quiet day and the families rested, as was their custom. A typically rainy Bogota morning greeted them on Sunday, with the accompanying chill that was usual at that time of the year. Rachel arose early. She had slept poorly, without knowing why and went into the kitchen to serve herself a cup of hot coffee with milk as usual in the morning, but before she could finish, she heard the tele-phone ring.

- Hello, she answered, wondering who could be calling so early on a Sunday.

She waited impatiently on her end of the receiver and suddenly heard a sob and in that instant recognized Sa-rah's trembling voice trying to speak to her.

- Mama, why are you crying? she asked, alarmed.

- Sarah, regaining control of her voice, exclaimed:

- Your father lost consciousness. The neighbors helped me take him to Palermo hospital. I am so afraid. Please, come now. I am all alone and so worried.

- I am going over there right now, Rachel answered, struggling against her own desire to burst into tears.

Nathan remained in serious condition for several days. His doctors did not dare venture any prognosis regarding his recovery, and his family grew impatient and began to try and seek better options of treatment to help the gravely ill man.

One day while Max was visiting the hospital, they finally decided to move him to the Mayo Clinic in Rochester, in the United States, which had an excellent reputation, especially in terms of the specialists who could deal with difficult diagnostic problems. They decided to go ahead with this plan, despite the financial sacrifice involved, since it seemed to be the only way to save Nathan's life, and he had done so very much for all of them over the years.

However, it was not until two weeks later that the doctors finally deemed the patient fit to travel. They finalized the complicated preparations and paperwork for the trip and Nathan, Sarah, and Rachel left for Rochester. Such a long and difficult trip could be fatal, however they had to try. It was their only hope.

Several days later, Max phoned Sarah to find out about Nathan's condition. Sadly, she had to tell him the bad news. The doctors had discovered a malignant brain tumor and the specialists were recommending that surgery be performed as soon as possible.

As soon as Sarah had finished, Max answered her with resignation:

- Do not waste any more time. Nathan must have the surgery. When we decided to take him there, we were prepared to accept the professional opinion of the doctors at the Mayo Clinic. Now, we should do as they recommend. Otherwise, all our efforts to help him will have been in vain.

- You are right, Max. May God help him to come out of the operation safely.

The surgery lasted eleven hours. During the interminable wait, Sarah and Rachel were besieged by a sea of doubts.

- Oh, almighty God, Rachel prayed aloud, help my father in his time of need. Save his life and help him to recover.

Sarah kept glancing at the clock on the wall of the waiting room. Finally one of the doctors appeared at the door.

- Mrs. Ratovich? he asked, coming over to them.

- Yes, doctor, that is me. How is my husband?

- The operation was a success, he answered, looking straight at her. We will keep your husband under observation for several days. As soon as he is out of danger, we can move him into a hospital room.

- Thank you so much, Sarah exclaimed with heartfelt emotion, shaking his hand gratefully.

The doctor nodded his head, pleased to be able to give her the good news because of his knowledge of Spanish, and added:

- We hope that he will continue to improve. He still has some difficult times to face.

The days flew by between their daily trips during visiting hours at the intensive care unit. Nathan slowly began to recover, but Sarah and Rachel felt terribly pained whenever they would see him in that state, his head covered by extensive bandages, connected to a multitude of mysterious machines that they did not quite understand, and mostly sleeping through their visits.

Finally he was moved to a semi-private room, due to their budget restrictions.

- Now, papa will start to get better, exclaimed Rachel as they looked at him lying in the bed. We can stay with him all day and he won't feel so lonely.

- Yes, darling, Sarah answered, but there is a problem. We cannot stay here at night. The room is small and there is no space for another bed. The nurse explained this to me a little while ago. I would have liked to stay with him all the time, she added worriedly.

- They will take good care of him, mama. Remember, we are in the United States.

After three days, Nathan began to gain back some of his strength, but that evening, the night nurse heard a loud noise and ran to see what had happened. She found Nathan lying unconscious on the floor. The assistant had by mistake forgotten to raise the bars on the side of the bed after giving Nathan his sleeping pills and had left the patient unattended to take care of some other matters.

Nathan was taken to surgery again, but the consequences of his fall from the bed were unavoidable. Half of his face was left paralyzed, with one eyelid permanently half-closed and he was only able to receive liquid sustenance through a straw.

- I told you, Rachel, her mother wailed inconsolably. I should never have left his side, with or without a bed. We have lost almost all the progress he had made.

On their return to Bogota, the situation became more and more difficult. Sarah tried to care for Nathan herself day and night, since she could not afford to hire the services of a nurse. However, despite his physical condition, Nathan's personality continued to be the same as ever and his family would often see him smiling. It was his way of showing his acceptance of God's will and the fate that had been set for him. He lasted in this same condition for five long years, until a bout with thrombosis ended his life.

Chapter 36

Morris Liberman woke up early on the morning of April ninth, nineteen hundred forty-eight. He moved silently through the marital bedroom to avoid waking Leah and as soon as he was ready, went down to the kitchen where Ovaldina was waiting with his breakfast. Leafing through the newspaper, he paid special attention to the political news in the country, since he had lately been aware of disturbing rumors about differences between the Conservative and Liberal parties and finally, called on the phone for a taxi cab to take him to the store.

Pulling on his dark gray suit jacket, he reached for his walking stick that he had left leaning on the edge of the dining room table the day before. He still had a limp. Despite the passage of so much time, his left foot had never fully recovered its range of functions. Most people thought he limped due to a bullet wound suffered during the war, but he knew the true circumstances so many years ago in Poland when he had been called up to serve in the army. He had been afraid then, as a husband, father and provider for his family, to be sent to the front lines with his country's troops. He couldn't let himself take the risk of leaving his loved ones unprotected, especially in the looming shadow of the anti-Semitic threat. Feeling absolutely desperate, one day he took the pistol that he always kept in his night table and screwing up his courage, shot himself in the baby toe of his left foot. He was seen at the emergency room in the hospital and then immediately disqualified for military service. For years he suffered doubts about the decision he had made. But whenever these doubts plagued him, he quelled them with a powerful argument; since he was not in the army when war broke out, he had been able to save himself and his family from the Nazis.

Morris heard the horn of the hired cab honking outside and grabbing his hat off the hat stand, he left the house, closed the door behind him and got into the car. After instructing the driver to take him to Eighth Avenue, where he had his shops of fine men's garments, he settled himself into the seat and gazing out the window, began to think back over all he had managed to achieve in Colombia since his arrival from Poland.

As soon as he had managed to adapt somewhat to the new environment, he began to work tirelessly to sell textiles, despite the difficulty posed by his lack of proficiency in Spanish. Later, using his best business abilities, he progressed quickly until the point that he had managed to become the owner of three shops, the earnings of which allowed him, his wife, and their children to live comfortably without having to deal with the financial difficulties faced by so many of the European immigrants. Their three sons also had contributed to their success, since as soon as they arrived in Bogotá, despite their youth, they had begun to work by their father's side, even sacrificing their studies to do so. At her mother's request, Tanya continued to study as she was considered still too young to go to work. Leah also helped out. It was her idea to rent out three of the rooms in the spacious house that they had bought with the money they brought from Poland. Their tenants were new immigrants from Poland who were provided food, cleaning and laundry services for a modest sum and his wife was in charge of the management of the whole arrangement.

His two eldest sons had married well. Benjamin was still single, but the time was soon coming to have him married and Morris would be in charge of choosing the appropriate match.

He looked again out the car window and saw that he had arrived at his destination. Taking his wallet out of his pocket, he paid the taxi driver and got out of the car.

He then pulled up the security gate over the shop entrance and closed it behind him as he entered. It was still too early to open the doors to customers and he wanted to check a few of the account statements from several days earlier.

After an hour and a half, one of his employees, Robert, arrived. He had been with the shop for four years. Morris opened the doors fully and they began the work day. The morning was long and dreary due to the lack of customers. A little after two in the afternoon, after they had taken their lunch break, Benjamin came in. He appeared to be perspiring and was agitated, in disarray, and had a frightened look on his face.

- Mr. Liberman, Robert called to him, taken aback by the appearance of the boy in this condition.

- What seems to be the problem? he asked, coming over.

- Please come quickly, your son does not look well.

- Benjamin, but what has happened?

- Papa, he answered, still looking shaken, as he sat down weakly on a stool near the front entrance. I left home and took a bus as usual to Seventh Avenue. When I got there, I started walking to come to the shop. Suddenly, I saw a group of people armed with machetes and carrying red flags, and they were moving in my direction. I started running as fast as I could and when I got to the corner of the street, I ducked into a shop to ask what was happening.

An older man, I think he was the manager, said to me:

"Mr. Gaitan has been killed. Every since they heard, his supporters have gone crazy. They are throwing stones, looting stores and they have already killed many people. They are insane, completely out of control. They stop at nothing. I myself am waiting for the shop owner to close the doors and go home. You had better run, my boy, because it is getting very ugly!"

- I didn't wait for him to tell me twice and left immediately and ran all the way here.

Upon hearing Benjamin's words, Robert went to turn on the radio and came back right away to tell them:

- They are saying on the radio that people are arming themselves with guns, knives, machetes and molotov cocktails. They are looting everything in their wake.

- We had better hurry up! exclaimed Benjamin. We have to close the shop. It is too dangerous to stay in this part of town.

- You are right, son, Morris answered nervously. While Robert and I lower the security gate here, you run and tell your brothers to close the other shops. I will wait here for them so we can leave together. Please, don't delay another second.

As soon as Simon and David arrived, they sent off all the employees and left hurriedly. It was impossible to get a taxi by then, and the streetcars had all been burned by the protesters, so they were forced to walk as quickly as they were able. They heard shots ringing out and people shouting. Suddenly, a shot sounded nearby and Benjamin stopped short.

Morris noticed this and rushed over, fearing the worst, but when his son lifted the hem of his trouser leg, they saw a bullet hole, but the bullet had only grazed the boy's leg.

- Thank God! he exclaimed and they continued to rush home.

Leah, who had heard of the uprising on the radio, was wringing her hands with worry as she stared out the window, awaiting their arrival. It was pouring rain and with each minute that passed, her concern grew. Finally, she spotted them running down the street toward the house and she heaved a sigh of relief.

The terrible events that occurred that day in Colombia's capital city, from which Morris and his sons managed to escape unscathed, was known as "El Bogotazo". It began with the shots from three hit men that killed the renowned criminal lawyer and Liberal party leader, Jorge Eliecer Gaitan, a populist leader who had apparently become a threat to his own party and to the opposition Conservative party, due to his radical platform. The assassination occurred at one-thirty in the afternoon and as the news was spread by radio broadcasters, Gaitan's supporters took to the streets brandishing any weapon they could lay their hands on, including homemade firebombs, and incited a huge populist uprising among the poorer classes, for whom Gaitan was considered to be a great defender.

The rioting moved on to general sacking and looting of all commercial establishments located in the downtown area, and faced with the efforts of the police forces and the military to put down the uprising and restore order, a veritable battle ensued. The end result was thousands of dead and wounded and whole neighborhoods left in ruins. The riots spread throughout the whole country and forced Conservative President Mariano Ospina Pérez to dissolve Congress and declare a state of siege throughout the nation. The epilogue of these tragic times was the defeat of the Liberal party in the 1950 elections. Another Conservative, Laureano Gomez, was elected President.

"El Bogotazo" had two main consequences. The city was never the same again. The peace that had reigned in the capital until that moment was over. Henceforth, the inhabitants felt they might have to protect themselves against any eventuality. Alarm systems were installed in the homes of the wealthy families and they hired bodyguards and night watchmen. The dangers in Bogotá and in the rest of the country continued to grow with the ever-increasing appearance of such urban evils as thieves, prostitutes, and beggars.

Chapter 37

- Mama! Karen cried out with fear from her bedroom.

After waiting a few moments and hearing no answer, the child cried out again.

- Annie, from her bed, asked anxiously:

- Why are you calling mama?

- I am afraid. I heard footsteps downstairs and everyone should be asleep at this time.

- You silly baby! You are just excited because it is your birthday party tomorrow. Now, try and go back to sleep and forget about the noises.

- But, what if there is a stranger downstairs?

- You have such an overactive imagination. Now, just go to sleep. I am very tired.

- No, I am not making it up, Karen insisted.

- Here we go again! Annie answered with disgust, sitting up on the edge of her Louis XV bed, parallel to her sister's matching bed. I am going to tell mama not to let you watch any more scary shows on TV. A few months ago, you thought you heard someone climbing up to our bedroom from a ladder outside the window. You were so sure about it you managed to convince me to get up and we ran out of the room screaming for mama and papa. When papa opened the window to face the supposed burglar he saw that the ladder that was "really there" was only the wind blowing some papers about and the footsteps were only raindrops falling on a tin can and making noise. The burglar was, of course, a creation of your brilliant imagination.

- That time it happened just like you say, but now it is different. I really do hear footsteps, I swear!

- You are keeping me awake with your silliness, Annie answered, lying back down again.

- Mama! Karen yelled out again. Come, I am afraid.

- Rachel, used to these nighttime calls from her daughters, got up slowly from her bed and went into the girls' room.

- What is the matter, child? Why are you yelling? You are going to wake the whole house.

- There are burglars downstairs, really. A little while ago, I heard them moving around.

- There is nobody there. I checked all the doors myself before coming up to bed. There is no way for anyone to get in the house. Please, go to sleep now so you can enjoy your party tomorrow. Everything is going to be wonderful. You saw all the cakes, cookies and gelatine that your grandmother and I made. And you will have soft drinks and candies. If you don't sleep well tonight, you won't be able to enjoy your day tomorrow with your friends and school-mates. It would really be a pity. So let's tuck you in and you go back to sleep. Goodnight!

The next day, Rachel woke up early and going downstairs, noticed a bit of a mess on the floor. She didn't remember the maids having left it that way the night before.

That is odd, she thought, and went into the dining room feeling slightly uneasy. A moment later, her eyes widened in astonishment. There were pieces of cake broken up and strewn all over the floor. The beautifully arranged table that had been left ready for all the party guests was a complete disaster, with gelatine and soft drinks spilled all over the tablecloth and the cookies broken and scatttered over the upturned plates.

- Maria! Come here quickly.

- What has happened, ma'am?

- I was just going to ask you the same question.

- I don't know anything about this. I woke up early and have been in the kitchen getting breakfast ready. I haven't left the kitchen to clean anywhere else.

- Please wake up my husband and tell him I need to see him.

- Yes, ma'am. Right away.

Meanwhile, Rachel took a good look at the mess. It definitely seemed to be a robbery. The silver goblets and platters that she had received as wedding gifts had been taken out of the glass cabinet where they were always kept. The drawers of the buffet were open and had been ransacked. It seemed that nothing had escaped those thieving hands.

- What is this mess? Simon asked with dismay as soon as he entered the room.

- We have been robbed and they have taken our silver and valuables, answered Rachel, beginning to cry.

- I am going to call the police immediately, Simon said in a serious tone, going over the telephone in the parlor.

- Oh, no mama! It can't be, Karen cried out. Look at the cakes, the gelatine, the cookies. Now I have nothing to give my friends, she added plaintively.

Hearing the child's words, her mother came over and spoke to her gently.

- Now, don't you worry. I will call everyone and we will just postpone the party for later.

- I told you last night that I heard footsteps and nobody believed me.

- I am so sorry, Rachel said, contrite.

When the police arrived, they found the burglars' entry point into the house had been through the gardens at the back of the house. They found several of the stolen objects lying about the grounds and Simon's overcoat hanging from the brick fence dividing their yard from the neighbor's yard.

After finishing their inspection of the premises, there was no doubt that Rachel's footsteps upstairs when she had gone into the girls' room had scared off the thief, who was inside the house at that moment and perhaps fearful of discovery, had run outside and dropped various objects in his hurry. Thanks to his rush to escape, the losses were less than they would have otherwise been.

Nonetheless, Rachel was deeply affected by the thought of the burglar entering the house and eventually suggested to Simon that they should move to an apartment for the sake of security.

- I understand your concern, but it is better for our children to be raised in a house, he answered. They have lots of space to play and a feeling of freedom that is so important for their development. There is space for everything and besides, we have Yonnie, the white Pekinese, and the children are so happy with their dog.

She would not be convinced by his arguments and soon the family moved into a spacious apartment. Despite the luxury and charm of their new home, they still felt sad at having to leave the magnificent house surrounded by the verdant, pleasant gardens and their beloved Yonnie, who they had to give away, since their mother said the dog could not live with them inside their new apartment.

Despite this, the children continued to grow to be

strong and beautiful. They now played their games in a small park near the building, where they would go with the maid to keep an eye on them and meet their friends after school.

Life continued its inexorable course. The siblings' relationship grew ever stronger, supported by the love, understanding, and help they gave to each other despite the difference in their ages.

Karen continued to have a wild imagination. For her, even more than games or any other activity, she loved to read for hours on end about all kinds of fantastical adventures. People would often say she was a dreamer or even that she told tall tales, but she paid no attention to these comments and continued to live in her charming and fascinating fantasy world.

Chapter 38

Karen loved hearing the applause of the audience, who was moved by the eloquent speech she had just finished delivering. She held back the stinging tears of emotion that were threatening to spring forth, because she did not want to miss a single moment of her high school graduation with her friends and schoolmates. With a quick bow of thanks, she moved back to her chair on the stage. Smiling at the affectionate pats that her classmates gave her as she moved in front of them, she sat down to wait her turn to receive her diploma from Mr. Meckler, the school principal. Meanwhile, she continued to look for her parents, grandmother, and the rest of her family seated in the auditorium, and as she found them, thought back on her years as a primary and high school student with her brother and sister, waiting for the school bus every morning.

It was a small, private, exclusive school, with wonderful teachers and a strict but friendly environment. Thanks to her father's dedicated efforts at his job, they were able to afford the costly tuition and this had allowed them to study with the upper crust of the society. The academic requirements were tough but this was fine with Karen and her siblings, since they were good students and wanted to continue on to university and so it was important that they have a good grounding. Karen, staring off into the distance, thought about her choices for the future. She had decided to enter university to study to be a writer. At various times, since she was a child, she would feel an overwhelming urge to sit down and write about all the feelings and thoughts that were bubbling up from inside her, and leave a testimony of them. Yes, this was her field, no doubt about it!

- "Karen Liberman", a clear voice with perfect diction called out.

Coming out of her reverie, she stood up and walked over to the school principal, who, moments later placed the long-awaited diploma into her hands with a smile, congratulating her as he did so. The rest of the morning was a blur of hugs and more congratulations.

When they returned home, Simon, Rachel, and her brother and sister had prepared a wonderful surprise party with the rest of her family and friends. She thought to herself during the celebration that it was so wonderful to be able to share these moments of pure happiness with all the people who mean so much in her life.

A new stage began in Karen's life: university studies. At first it seemed so complicated, but after a few short months she had adapted to the new and rigorous study regime and was able to produce the professor's assignments skillfully. She was in her element and felt privileged to be able to find the time to dedicate to her favorite activity: writing. She was busy with her studies and everything seemed fine, but one day as she reflected on her life, she felt perturbed. As a student, she had outstanding grades and would probably graduate with honors, but what had happened to her other goal: to meet the man of her dreams, get married and have children? She noticed more and more how her classmates would wait happily for their boyfriends and then see them holding hands and gazing into each other's eyes. She wanted to experience that, too, she thought broodingly. I am already nineteen years old, and even though I have dated several fellows, I haven't met the man with whom I want to share my life. Will there be a man for me? she asked herself. When Karen mentioned these worries to her sister, she always answered: "Don't worry, you will find him. Everyone has his soul mate in life and you will meet yours one day, too".

Annie married her lifelong boyfriend, Alan Mitrani, and they seemed happy together. Karen was delighted to see them so in love and wished all the best for her sister, and thought Alan was the right person for her.

A few months later, out of the blue, Philip Abadi called her on the phone. He was a fellow who had seen her at the university and wanted to meet her.

- I am very sorry, she answered honestly, but I have a very tough exam on Monday and since today is Friday, I have very little time to go over a huge pile of readings to prepare.

- Please, let's go out tonight, even for a short time. I want to get to know you better. I promise to bring you back home early, so you aren't too tired out, as long as you don't refuse my invitation.

- All right, she answered, still not very convinced. But, truly, I only have two days to study and I need all the time I have.

- It is a date, then, he answered happily.

That evening, Karen put on a simple black dress that set off her slim figure, a pearl necklace and earrings that her grandmother had given her, and chose from her well-stocked closet a matching pair of black snakeskin shoes and purse to set off the ensemble. Her silky blond hair cascaded down her shoulders. She looked gorgeous, and Philip told her so as soon as he arrived at her house to pick her up. He greeted Rachel and Simon and thanked them for allowed him to go out with their daughter, then saying goodbye, left the house with Karen. This girl is so beautiful, he thought.

Karen, sitting inside Philip's luxury car, asked him curiously:

- Where are we going?

- Would you like to have dinner at the La Carreta restaurant? It is nice and quiet and we could talk.

- Yes, I would love to, she answered, admiring his manly bearing. There is something about him that I can't quite put my finger on, she thought, intrigued.

Philip started the motor. As soon as they arrived, he helped her out of the car. The polite maitre d' showed them to a semi-private table, as Philip had requested when they entered. Once they sat down at the table, they started chatting comfortably.

He talked about his life, which had been very interesting. He was the son of wealthy parents and after finishing his law studies, he had specialized in criminal law and was teaching at the university. Although successful in this endeavor, he pushed on to make a name for himself professionally, in a field with strong competition. He worked very hard but enjoyed what he was doing, especially now that he was becoming well-known after having won several difficult court cases.

Karen spoke to him of her fervent desire to become a writer, of her success at her studies and her enormous gratitude to her father for all his efforts so that she and her siblings could pursue their studies at the Javeriana University, which was private and therefore, expensive, and of her wish to repay in some way her parents for all they had done.

- You shouldn't feel that way. I am sure they feel rewarded by the fact that they have been able to provide you with a good education.

- I do agree with you, but you don't know my family history. The fact that I am able to enjoy the wonderful things I have today is, after all, the result of so many tears and tribulations in previous generations. I only hope that my future accomplishments can somehow compensate all those sacrifices.

Philip listened to her with admiration. It was unusual to find young people today who thought that way. He had dated many flighty and frivolous girls, who only cared about material possessions or who were vain and convinced that they deserved to get everything on a silver platter.

As time went on, they began to feel an attraction to each other that grew as the evening progressed. At about two am, a waiter came over to tell them the restaurant would soon be closing. Astonished at the lateness of the hour, they paid the check and left.

As soon as Karen arrived home, she ran to Sarah's room and opening the door carefully, checking to see if she was asleep.

- I have to tell you all about my evening. I am so happy you aren't asleep – I am so excited.

- Tell me all about, my dear, I am all ears.

- Philip is incredible, grandma. He is a gentleman. He is intelligent, refined, charming and he is very manly. I listened to him talk for hours and I could have kept talking to him forever. I hope he calls again. I felt so safe by his side, such a sense of well-being and happiness that I had never felt before.

She did not have to wait long for another invitation and they soon were out dancing at a well-known discotheque called La Morocota. And so they got to know each other better, with mutual friendship and admiration until true love blossomed in their hearts. The days apart seemed to be endless to them and when nightfall came, they ran to be together. Life is certainly strange, thought Karen, it is as if we were meant for each other. I wonder if reincarnation really exists? Maybe I shared one of my past lives with Philip....I feel so close to him...it is as if I had known him forever.

The families were happy with the match, despite the fact that everything seemed to be moving so quickly.

- Don't forget about your studies, Rachel admonished her. If you have too many late nights it will affect your grades.

- Don't worry, mama. I have always been a responsible student and I have no intention of changing now.

- I am glad to hear that, my dear.

Finally the day arrived that Karen had so longed for; Phillip asked for her hand in marriage. They were in a small restaurant and he had asked for a bottle of Dom Perignon champagne. She looked at him, hardly able to contain her joy, and without thinking jumped up and hugged him, saying:

- Of course, my love, I will marry you. I love you with all my heart.

They kissed passionately and were surprised when suddenly they heard applause from the people seated at the nearby tables. Blushing, they pulled apart, but could not stop staring into each other's eyes, shining with the enormous depth of love they both felt.

Annie hugged her sister long and hard upon being told of the news of the upcoming marriage.

- I told you so. Everyone finds his soul mate. If you ask me, you are too young to get married, but that needn't be an obstacle. I am sure he will make you very happy.

- Thank you, Annie. Philips fills me up with happiness, every speck of my being. I want to be with him forever.

The wedding was a major social event. Twelve hundred people were invited to the Red Room at the Tequendama Hotel to toast the couple's happiness and the elegant reception that followed was a sparkling success. As the last guest left the party, Karen took her husband by the hand and went over to her parents, who were speaking animatedly to the new in-laws.

- Come, sit down with us for a while, said Simon.

- We would love to stay with you, Philip answered, but we are exhausted. We have had so much excitement in one night and our plane leaves tomorrow for Brazil. We just came to say goodbye. I want to thank you with all my heart for all you have done for us. With these words, he began to hug each one and bid them farewell. The presidential suite of the hotel had been reserved for their wedding night and they went upstairs to the room.

- Karen, you look like a princess, Philip whispered in her ear.

Arriving at the door of the room, he lifted her in his strong arms and after a long, deep kiss, he placed her on the sofa in the living room of the suite and sighing, said to her:

- Now that you are my wife, I feel I am the happiest man on earth.

- Me, too, she answered, holding out her arms to embrace him. They stayed that way for some time, feeling how lucky they were to have found each other. They talked about the magical first night they met and then, exhausted, decided to change their clothes. Philip helped Karen undo the tiny buttons of the bridal dress and when he finished with the last one, she let the sumptuous gown slide off and placed it carefully on the sofa, then went into the bathroom. Once inside the spacious and luxurious bathroom, she started feeling for the first time how shy she felt being alone with her husband. She loved him, but could not shake from her mind the thought that this would be the first night she would spend with a man. She changed out of her clothing and removed her makeup, but her heart was pounding. Finally she was ready, and she went into the bedroom.

- Come, my love, he said sweetly from the bed.

Trembling slightly, she lifted the cover and laid down by his side. Philip began to kiss her fervently and she, responding instinctively, forgot her fear and let herself drift into the intense feeling of passion that began to carry her away.

The next day, they arrived early at the airport. The airplane was leaving at eleven am and they were surprised to find not only their families, but also a large group of friends waiting to see them off. The time came to leave and embracing each one warmly and with tears of happiness, the newlyweds departed to board the plane under showers of rice and wishes for marital bliss.

Chapter 39

The airplane, cutting through the crisp, luminous Brazilian skies, began to circle over the huge city and finally set its shining silver wings down at the Santos Dumont international airport in Rio de Janeiro. Karen and Philip were perhaps the happiest passengers, but also the most exhausted, from the wedding itself, the first ecstatic night of love-making and the bustle of the long air journey.

After going through customs and immigration, they went outside the building to find a taxi. It was a Volkswagen and the hugely fat driver chatted to them about his prowess as a beer drinker, to which he owed his large belly. His stories, recounted in a barely understandable mixture of Portuguese and Spanish, created a friendly atmosphere inside the uncomfortably small car. Finally they arrived at the Copacabana Palace Hotel, where Philip had made reservations, and they got out of the cab, thanking the driver for the trip and his agreeable company.

Once inside the room, they decided to take a rest, despite the fact it was eleven o'clock in the morning. They were worn out. At five in the afternoon, they awoke and ordered room service. They didn't feel like going out any-where and wanted to be alone. Once they had revived somewhat from the light meal accompanied by Dom Perignon, which brought back happy memories, they hun-grily began to exchange kisses and embraces and rekin-dled the ardent passion of the previous wedding night. The next day, they decided to visit the legendary beaches of Rio. Leaving the hotel, they were startled by an extraordi-nary panorama, almost surreal.

The sky was clear and transparent, with not a cloud to mar it. The calm waters were a crystal blue color. Golden sand caressed by the sun extended as far as the eye could see. The newlyweds looked down the beach and saw the rows of hotels facing the beach, in every size and shape, looking like so many soldiers guarding the sea, and behind them., the impressive, tall mountains.

- I never thought I would see such a beautiful sight! Ka-ren exclaimed happily. It is like a dream. She and Philip, holding hands, crossed the busy street that separated them from the beach. They lay their towels down on the sand and settled down to enjoy the penetrating rays of the sun. After some time, they were perspiring from the heat and needed a break, so they went back to the hotel. On the el-evator, they met a tourist who was also on his way back from the beach, fleeing the hot mid-day temperatures of the summer season. He told them that Brazil had not seen such heat for thirty years as they were experiencing that December of nineteen sixty-eight.

As soon as Karen and Philip changed their clothes, they went out to walk around the city. They arrived at a res-taurant specialized in seafood and ordered a meal. Catchy samba music filled the ample space and people at the neighboring tables were tapping on their glasses in time to the rhythm with forks and spoons.

- These Brazilians have music in their blood and know how to enjoy life, Philip commented with a grin as he sipped his aperitif.

- The food was delicious, Karen commented with satisfaction as she left the restaurant. And all the different kinds of skewers: shrimp with cheese, and vegetables.

- Delicious! Philip agreed, coming close to kiss her on the lips.

- Oh, my love, you make me so happy.

- Come, my sweet one, let's find a car and take a tour of the rest of the city.

Unfortunately, the only vehicle available was a pink jeep with brown stripes and a roof of the same color edged in a ruffle.

- Now we really look like newlyweds, said Karen, with an irrepressible giggle.

- We don't seem to have a choice, so, let's just take what we can get, was Philip's reluctant answer.

He skillfully drove the jeep as if he were a native of Rio. They visited many galleries and spent a good deal of time at the Museum of Modern Art, where they admired dozens of the latest avant-garde works and styles.

On December thirty-first they visited the city. They went to the Pan de Azucar landmark and Cristo del Corcovado Mountain. They bought beautiful jewelry set with semiprecious stones and Philip, asking his wife to close her eyes, placed around her neck a necklace made from a large piece of amber as a souvenir of his love, which she would always treasure. Later they went to Petropolis and Terezopolis. There they visited a museum that contained incredible and priceless gems. Ignoring the prohibition against taking pictures, Karen, with a small camera hidden under her hat, took a number of shots while the guard wasn't looking. This naughty gesture only made them enjoy the visit even more and they would laugh about it many times through the years. That night, Karen suddenly developed a fever. Since she was feeling poorly, she didn't feel like going out and since it was New Year's Eve, she urged Philip to at least go and take a walk around hotel and enjoy the festivities on the busy streets and the crowded bars and restaurants. At eleven pm he came back in high spirits, looking for his wife.

- Wake up, he called out. You are missing something absolutely amazing.

- What is it? she asked sleepily.

- Just get dressed. If I tell you, you won't believe it.

She put on an olive green cotton ensemble, simple but perfectly suited to bring out her beauty. Without any makeup and leaving her purse behind in the room, she followed him out. When they crossed the street and arrived on the beach, they saw a lot of people moving as if they were hypnotized, to the beat of music they were making themselves. The dance began to move faster and faster and both men and women appeared to be in a trance. The dancers moved tirelessly as if under the spell of a strange power. They were wearing white robes and carrying lit candles in their hands, and as far as Karen and Philip could see, they seemed to be from the slums that clung to the Rio mountainsides, known as *favelas*, where the inhabitants were known to practice voodoo rituals and worship the saints and deities of those rites. This particular rite took place every year on this date.

It is so interesting, thought Philip. He had never seen anything like this before nor did he ever expect to see something similar. They continued watching the strange spectacle until the early hours of the morning. They had heard that the dancers would continue their trance-like movements until they fell from exhaustion.

On January second they left for Punta del Este, in Uruguay, and from there went on to Buenos Aires, where they visited the city and bought gifts for their families.

One afternoon, while Philip was trying on a leather jacket in a shop, his wife began to feel unwell. So as not to alarm her husband, she sat down on a bench, but the dizzy spell did not abate and she was afraid she would fall.

- My dear, I am feeling faint.

- I am nearly ready to go. It won't be much longer.

Just then, Karen fell down in a faint and as she lost consciousness, slipped from the bench.

- What happened? she asked as she came to her senses.

The owner of the shop told her what had just occurred and added with a smile:

Will you both do me a big favor? Let me know in nine months if it is a girl or a boy!

Chapter 40

The return of the newlyweds was like a wave of joy washing over the whole family. Karen and Philip moved into a comfortable, modern apartment. The main area consisted of a large living room, decorated in earth tones with paintings by a great Uruguayan artist, Carlos Pérez Franco. They had clearly favored chrome and glass as was evident in the coffee tables, lamps, and other accessories placed around the room. The sunken dining room was adjacent to the living room and had an oval table in the center of the room with a matching long and elegant buffet on the left hand wall. An elegant silver tea set was placed on the buffet as a permanent decoration. Indirect lighting illuminated the whole space in a pleasant and relaxing fashion. The kitchen was done in a light cream color and the three bedrooms, each with its own bathroom, in various pastel tones.

- This is all so wonderful! exclaimed Karen as she walked around the apartment. But who did the interior decoration? I would like to congratulate that person for the fantastic job.

Philip had been watching with a smile as he showed

his wife around their brand-new home. It made him happy just to see the expression of delight on his young wife's face.

- I have a friend who is an interior decorator. He and I spent a lot of time on the place. I couldn't wait to see your reaction. All during our honeymoon, I imagined you coming into our new home and I am so pleased that you like it. It is our little love nest. Here, with God's help we will be happy together.

- I have no doubt about it, she answered, wrapping her arms around him, and he in answer, lifting her up and carrying her into the bedroom.

The Argentinean shop owner's prediction was right on the money. Nine months after the wedding a sweet baby girl was born, and her parents gave her the name, Danielle. Her lively dark eyes stood out against the rosy paleness of her lovely face and seemed to be forever discovering the world around her. Long, graceful fingers moved quickly to reach out for her rattles and toys and her mind was constantly active. She was a delight to her mother, who loved to spend all the time possible with this adorable child. Two years later, Aaron was born and everyone called him "Ari". He was a handsome child who looked like his sister and was a great companion to her. From his first day in the world, she accepted his arrival with endless affection, and cared for him with tenderness, attentive to his slightest gurgle or cry. It was fascinating to watch them grow together, bound by the strong ties of love and sharing everything. A few years after Aaron, Kevin came along, who was a living doll and the apple of his grandparents' eye.

Karen and Philip were contented with their children and felt as if God had given them a wonderful prize. Life was also kind to them in terms of their personal ambitions. Philip, who was a tireless worker, became known in his field as an outstanding criminal lawyer. Despite his youth, he was very responsible and had a depth of knowledge beyond his years. These two qualities gave him credibility and as he acquired even more experience, his client base grew. As for Karen, she shared her time between her husband, children and the home. But, she still tried to write whenever she could find a free moment. She would have liked to have spent more time writing, but the days seemed to fly by and though she was young, she tried to prove to everyone as well as to herself, her worth.

One day Annie came to visit with her children. They played for a while with the children and when the maid came to take them out to the garden, Karen offered Annie a cup of tea and some delicious pastries that she had baked herself.

- Annie, my in-laws are really great. Ada has already shared all her cooking secrets with me. She calls me all the time to invite me to try out a new recipe and I always jump at the chance to learn. You know how Philip enjoys a good meal. Besides, it gives me an excuse to invite our family and friends and show off with tasty new dishes. And I have been so lucky with my father-in-law, Akiva. He is not only a well-known figure in the city but he is also extremely generous with us and with everyone around him. I feel honored to belong to their family.

- I know, and I am happy to see that you are settled and content with your husband, children and in-laws. Annie continued, hesitating:

- I do not want to spoil your happy mood now, but I have to share a worry of mine. For some time, I have been noticing that papa is not the same man he used to be. He was always so strong and now I notice that he seems listless and lacks energy.

On Saturday I was visiting mama and papa and I really

noticed that his color was not good and he seemed so different than usual. His face looked exhausted. I was about to call you, but I have been so busy these days and also, I didn't want to worry you in case it was just my imagination.

- We should speak to a doctor as soon as possible, Karen replied with determination.

A few days later, Simon and his wife went to visit Doctor Parejo, who after performing a complete check-up, sent him to a specialist, Doctor Schuster, an oncologist. Simon had to undergo various tests prescribed by the oncologist, including a biopsy.

- My secretary will phone you to set up an appointment so I can explain the results to you, Doctor Schuster said in a professional manner.

On receiving the call from the doctor, Rachel, Annie and Karen went to his office. Simon was too tired to attend the appointment.

When the three were settled in their chairs that the doctor's assistant had brought in, the doctor said to them perfunctorily:

- I hate to have to give you bad news, but the results of the biopsy indicate the presence of a cancerous tumor in the bladder.

He paused and then continued:

- If my own father were facing this problem, I would go immediately to the best hospital in the United States. They may be able to do something with this case there, since a large hospital would have the latest equipment and techniques.

- They prepared their trip right away and a week later were departing for the M.D. Anderson Hospital in Houston, Texas. The trip was difficult because of Simon's poor health. After they had explained his condition to him, he told them that he had been suffering a lot of pain. Papa is so brave, Karen thought. Despite these terrible pains over the past months, I never heard him complain.

Immediately upon landing, they went straight to the hospital. There was no time to waste. After delivering Simon to the emergency room, they waited impatiently. A few hours later, a young doctor appeared in the waiting room and introduced himself as Doctor Francisco Vidal and proceeded to explain the treatment to them. First he would take steps to reduce the swelling in the legs that was due to chronic phlebitis, and then apply chemotherapy to try and kill the tumor. His next words gave them some hope:

- In my opinion, the patient is in time for treatment. Because of this, I think his chances of recovery are good, but it will be a hard struggle. You must all be prepared to follow my instructions faithfully.

- Naturally we will. We all want him to get better, answered Annie.

Simon spent that night in the emergency room and the next day was moved to a private room.

- There you go, papa, said Karen, plumping his pillow. You will be more comfortable here, especially after your long trip. You should try and sleep a bit. Soon you will be better.

- I truly hope so, he answered with fatigue and yawning, fell asleep.

She watched his father and a deep sadness welled up. Cancer! Could he really get better? Now the only thing we can do is help him fight for his life. Papa has always been such a healthy man and if anything can help him now, it is his strong constitution.

Dear God, protect him, she prayed silently. Carry him through this test and help him to recover and come back to us safe and sound.

An exhausting routine began, with treatments and hospital visits. His wife and two daughters took turns staying with the patient and even so, they were long and tiring days.

- It is all the stress! the sisters agreed.

- I would like to see him well again and he is still so weak.

- It is part of the treatment, Annie. The doctor explained this to us in detail. The chemotherapy is not selective and it kills the cancerous tissue but also damages many healthy areas. I hope to God that the tumor will be eradicated soon and papa can get better.

One day, when Karen was watching TV with Simon in the hospital room, he suddenly turned to her and began to speak.

- My dear, I am so thankful for your company and for taking the time to care for me. I am sorry that you have had to be bothered by my illness, but I need to ask you another favor.

- Tell me what it is. I will do whatever I can.

- As you know, some years ago, I left retail sales and concentrated on wholesale and with this, I was able to achieve good earnings and provide the family with an excellent lifestyle.

- You were always so hard working and dedicated.

- Thank you, but allow me to go on. After having amassed a veritable fortune, I began to suspect that someone was stealing from me. This person is causing a lot of damage to the business and I know that business is going down constantly and I am very worried about it. Your mother does not understand these things, as she has always stayed out of the business, and therefore, I cannot count on her to help me. But, you and your husband could do it. Please, I am desperate. Help me! And saying this, he began to cry.

- Papa, please don't cry, exclaimed Karen and moved over closer to him. Of course, we will help you. I can't take care of it right now at such a crucial time in your recovery, but I will speak to Philip and when you tell me all the details of the matter, we will know exactly what to do. But you must promise me that you will not upset yourself any more. This is not helping you to get better.

- I promise, my dear.

Karen caller her husband that very night and after telling him a bit about Simon's treatment and hearing how the family was doing, she laid out the problem.

- Not to worry, my love, he answered. I will put all my efforts in finding out if something is really wrong, even though I have never been involved in your parents´ business. But you must hurry back home. We are missing you terribly.

She hung up the phone and dried her tears. How she missed them and wanted to be with them. The hospital had an excellent reputation for treating patients with cancer, but it was so awfully depressing! Every patient had his own sad story, especially the children, whose suffering faces reflected the daily torture they were living.

- Oh, dear God, help those poor suffering souls, she prayed, and give them some hope.

Crying quietly, she left the hospital and went to the van that would take her to the hotel. It was her free night and she wanted to lose herself in sleep.

Time passed and Rachel felt a wave of worry sweep over her. Her husband, despite the doctor's favorable prognosis, was not getting better. Her daughters, worried about her, asked her not to stay overnight anymore and to rest up. They would manage on their own. But their mother's emotional condition worsened with each passing day and they decided to seek professional help.

- Try to understand the situation, they explained to the psychiatrist. She has been married to our father for more than forty-five years and his life is in danger now.

- Can we do anything? Annie asked, with concern.

- I am going to speak to her. Meanwhile, be patient. It is my only advice to you, given the serious nature of her husband's condition.

It was all in vain. After five long months, the doctor called them into his office to give them the tragic news. The chemotherapy had failed and the cancer continued unabated. In other words, Simon was dying.

- No, I cannot believe it! Karen cried, sobbing inconsolably and hugging her sister, who was also beside herself. We are going to lose papa and there is no way to stop it. I was not expecting this.

- Neither was I, Annie answered, trying to control her emotions, but it is the bitter truth. Everything has an end. We must try to be strong and help him, and make his last months on earth as happy as possible.

- You are right. The hardest part is still ahead. We must do our duty and make it more bearable.

- Goodbye, Doctor Vidal, added Karen, taking notice of the doctor's presence. It is time for us to go home. There is nothing more to be done here.

Chapter 41

Simon's return home to his family was accompanied by mixed emotions. On the one hand, Karen and Annie's return to their respective spouses and children was the cause of great rejoicing; on the other hand, the fact that the head of the family had come back even more worn down by his illness caused them all a great deal of sadness. He suffered piercing pains, which were not relieved even by the morphine that had been prescribed in the American hospital as a last recourse.

One day, Karen went to her parents' house.

- Papa, are you awake? I have come to visit you.

- Yes, he answered, trying to move over to the edge of the bed.

- Would it help you to sit in the reclining chair?

- Thank you. I have been lying down for too many hours and my back is sore.

He got up with effort, helped by Karen, and sat slowly in the chair, saying:

- Oh, my dear! I didn't think there would be so much pain...I wish I could understand God's message to me through this trial.

- Just recently I have read a few books that tell about some doctors who report on life after death experiences and near-death experiences, she said with meaning.

- And do you think you have learned something from these books?

- Yes, I do. These experts have proven that a person can live various lives. When we leave this life, through death we enter into a spiritual state and there we study and prepare for the next earthly existence, to avoid or repair the errors committed in the previous one. So, just as a painter preps the canvas before he starts painting, the individual must plan for his passage to the next lifetime. When he is ready, he is born again under conditions that he chooses for himself during this preparation time. But there is something surprising. In his new stage, he surrounds himself by his loved ones again, even though the roles they are assigned in the next lifetime may be different.

- I don't understand. Are you telling me there is a chance, after dying, that I can be with you again?

- Yes, papa. This is what I have learned from the new scientific studies that are being carried out by prestigious doctors, who have proven their theories through hypnosis.

- That would be of great comfort to me. I hope it is so.

- Believe it. There is convincing evidence about the truth of the conclusions of these studies.

-You don't know how it hurts me to have to leave behind my wife, children and grandchildren. I love them all so much.

- We love you, too, exclaimed Karen, giving him a hug. We will always carry you in our hearts, no matter where you are.

- Thank you, my dear. Your words bring me comfort.

- Now I want to tell you about your concerns about your

business, which you mentioned to me when you were in the hospital.

- There is money missing, right?

- Yes. After fully studying the situation and talking with a few people, we have found the truth. The financial losses you noticed are due to Carlos' lack of business experience. I am sorry to have to tell you this, because he is your son and my brother, but that is the truth. After graduation from university, you thought he was ready to face all these responsibilities but he did not have the preparation. He took them on in good faith, but as we have discovered, he did not have the ability to make important decisions or deal with difficulties successfully. The result of this is that there have been no earnings over the past few years and in fact, there have been large losses. However, there has in no way been any deliberate theft, and this should be of some consolation.

Simon looked at her sadly and nodded sadly.

- Thank you, Karen. I feel better now. I will die with a clear conscience. But, my only regret is that I will not have been able to leave the family with economic security, as was my wish.

- Papa, you always gave us a life filled with love, education and all that we needed. Could we have asked for anything more?

- Forgive me if I have failed you in any way. I always tried my best.

- I know, she answered, with tears in her eyes. Now, please, just rest.

Simon died a few days later and his family felt a tremendous painful void with his passing, but was consoled in their belief that God's mercy would give him rest and that he would suffer no more. One long year had gone by since the fateful day when his illness had been diagnosed.

Chapter 42

It was a rainy morning on December fourteenth nineteen ninety. Karen was sitting on a hassock, with her feet tucked under her, beside the living room window in her house, watching a torrential rainstorn fall and hit the window with deafening gusts. She gazed unseeing into the white, impenetrable fog outside and the only perceptible movement of her body was the rise and fall of her chest as she breathed.

- My love, where are you? her husband asked from the other room, his voice muffled by the constant noise.

- In the living room, Philip.

- What a storm out there…and it doesn't show any sign of letting up, he commented as he entered the room.

- Yes, she answered gloomily.

- You seem sad. It seems that this horrible weather has affected you.

- No, no that's not it. Four months have gone by since my father's death and I still haven't got used to the fact that he is gone for good. I feel as if part of me left when he died and I keep reliving the terrible time he had in the hospital.

Sometimes these memories come to me in my dreams, and sometimes during the day in the middle of any normal activity. It hurts so much to have lost him! she exclaimed with a heavy heart and burst into tears.

- Please, don't cry, he begged her as he embraced her firmly. All human lives come to an end one day. You father's destiny was to die on that day, at the age of sixty-eight. We cannot understand the workings of divine providence, but we have to accept it. Anyway, your belief in multiple lives must be of some help to overcome your grief, which is shared by me and the rest of the fmaily. Of course, it is too recent for your heart to have mended after this loss, but you will see, my dear, that time heals all wounds. Soon enough, you will only remember the happy times with him and you will feel closer to him.

- Thank you for your kind words. You have made me feel better. Meanwhile, until this future arrives, I will spend my time on other activities so I don't think so much about it. Our children, even though they are grown up and becoming more independent, making their own lives, still need my affection and guidance, but less every day. As for you, you are a brilliant man who spends nearly all his time and energy on the law firm. I think the time has come for me to become productive and start doing something.

- That's the way, he answered enthusiastically, since over the past few months he had noticed with concern his wife's growing depression.

The rain finally let up and they both decided to put on their coats and go for a walk. After their conversation, Karen enrolled in a gym. But, despite the fact she enjoyed the classes and company, she couldn't fill the void she still felt. Finally, like a ray of light, a brilliant idea penetrated her mind. I should start writing again, and use my talent to create different worlds and lives from my imagination. Between raising children, taking care of home and family, she had lost sight of something important. Enthused by this new challenge, one day, as soon as Philip had left for work, she sat in front of the computer, turned it on and put a diskette in the slot and when the monitor lit up, she began to write as if she had never stopped. Suddenly, thousands of ideas crowded her mind. All her mental and spiritual energy came together in rush of creative energy that spilled her feelings onto the screen. Yes, this definitely was her field and she should have started doing it a long time ago. The hours flew by as she kept her eyes on the illuminated screen and her agile fingers moved effortlessly over the keyboard to jot the ideas that her mind created and created, filling her with a sense of heady euphoria. Her husband pulled her from this wonderful fantasy world when he spoke tenderly to her:

- Hello! How is my favorite writer?

She got up quickly and after kissing him hello, told him about the wonderful transformation she was undergoing.

- Imagine, I have been writing all morning and haven't stood up from the keyboard for even a moment. I feel so happy!…

Philip watched her with a sense of relief. Thank God, he said to himself. His wife was coming out of her depression. She was once again the same enthusiastic and animated woman he knew. He put his coat on a chairback beside Karen's desk and pulling her toward him, kissed her passionately.

- Careful, the maid is in the next room and she might see us.

But he continued to kiss her, ignoring her warning, until his excitement could no longer be contained. They went into the bedroom and Philip took her in his arms and lifted her onto the bed.

- I am so crazy about you, my love, he said.

- And I love you, my dearest lawyer.

He undressed her gently and then removed his own clothing. Between hugs and kisses they melted into one being, feeling themselves transported to another world that was exclusively reserved for them and their love.

Chapter 43

Karen heard a knock at her office door.

- Come in! she called out.

Her daughter came in. She is so beautiful, Karen thought with maternal pride as she watched her walk across the room. When had she become a young woman? She hadn't seen it happen, although it had happened right before her eyes, slowly, day by day. Danielle, with her statuesque bearing and her slim figure, which was the result of her willpower, had long, silky hair, a sensual air about her and huge, sweet eyes that were lit up with goodness from within.

- Hi, mom!

- I am so happy to see you. You couldn't have come at a better time. I am so excited!

- And why are you so excited?

- I just finished my book. Finally, it is done!

- That is the best news I have heard all day. Now I can share your happiness with you. You have worked so hard; it was time for you to enjoy the fruits of your labor. Now, all you have to do is publish it…

- You are not going to believe it, but I never even gave it a thought.

- Why not? She asked curiously. Did you put all that hard work in just to let your masterpiece gather dust on a shelf?

- No, Danielle. I started writing three years ago, after my father's death, to be able to let go of the pain and frustration I was experiencing at the time. The idea was to keep me busy and get over my depression.

- Well, I look at it another way. Your purpose may have been to get over depression, but now that the book is finished, this is the reality. You were able to get over your problems and now, she added with an impish grin, I would like to be the daughter of a famous author.

- That sounds like a pipe dream, her mother answered, bemused.

- No, not at all. You deserve to give it a shot after all the effort you put in. Besides, I have read a few chapters and it looks great to me. Why don't we take your book to an established publishing company and see what they say?

Karen looked at her daughter with doubt, but inside, she could feel butterflies of emotion swirling about. What if I could publish my book? she thought.

- We should check all the possibilities, Danielle continued. Maybe papa has a friend who is an editor.

- Excuse me, I didn't hear what you just said. I was thinking about something else. Could you repeat that?

- I was saying that we could see if any of papa's friends works in publication, or even, maybe one of them can tell us the best way to go about getting your book published.

- Not so fast, young lady. Let me get used to the idea and then if I decide to publish, we can talk to your father.

- All right, mom, she answered, somewhat disappointed. But please, don't take too long to decide.

- Come give me a hug, Karen said tenderly. I must have done something right in this life to be so lucky to have children like you and your brothers.

- And for us to have parents like you, Danielle answered, putting her arms around her mother.

After a short time, Karen asked:

- By the way, when you came up to my office, did you want to tell me something?

- I got so excited that I had already forgotten. Dad called on the phone to tell you that he would be late getting home tonight and so he won't be able to have dinner with us. He explained to me that some clients have come in from the United States. Since your husband has abandoned you tonight, she added, grinning mischievously, Aaron, Kevin and I have decided to invited you to the movies. How do you like that plan?

- It sounds delightful, she answered, taking her hand. Find your brothers and let's leave right away. Otherwise, we will never make it, she said, glancing at her watch.

- All right, let's go then. Danielle added with her characteristic decisiveness.

The movie was "War Horse", but during the movie, Karen paid almost no attention to the images flickering across the screen, since a recurring thought had taken over her mind: Should I publish my novel or not?

- Mom, Aaron said to her curiously. You don't seem to be enjoying the movie. It is almost as if you were on another planet.

- I am sorry. I will try not to let my mind wander so much and pay more attention.

When they left the theater, they commented on the ingenious and impressive special effects used in the movie. They were really something special.

- Steven Spielberg is my favorite director, said Danielle.

- I love him, too, Kevin chimed in.

- What I most enjoy is to be here with my three children, Karen said.

- Sure, mom, answered Aaron in a mocking tone. You enjoy it so much that you wrap yourself up in your thoughts and don't pay any attention to what is happening in the here and now.

- You are right, son.

- It is not her fault, Danielle commented, glancing at her brother. Maybe I am the one to blame, for suggesting that she publish her book.

- So, you finished it? Kevin asked with interest.

- Yes, she answered. But I am not sure whether I should publish it.

- You should, mom, Danielle insisted.

- Of course, you should, Aaron added.

- I agree with my brother and sister, Kevin said, putting in his two cents.

Karen looked from one to the other and with a smile on her lips, asked them:

- Are you ganging up on me?

- Quite the opposite, mom, we are on your side, Aaron answered immediately. Your book will be very interesting to everyone, especially because of the subject, which is such an important one.

- I will think about it. Count on that.

The next day, the family was gathered at the breakfast table and Danielle decided to mention the idea of publishing the novel to her father.

- I think it is a marvelous idea.

- But you also think it is the right thing to do? his wife asked, perplexed.

- Of course. Three years of your time and effort shouldn't be relegated to a shelf. I will start today to find out the options available for the publication of the book.

- She looked at him without a word and decided not to answer. She seemed outwardly calm but her heart was beating wildly. Two days later, Philip called her on the telephone from his office.

- Hi, honey, how are you?

- Fine, thanks.

- I am calling to give you some good news about your book. I just made an appointment with a first-class editor, who will be able to represent you in the undertaking to publish the book. His name is David Paulton and he has a great deal of experience in the field. The meeting will take place in my office, next Wednesday at four-thirty in the afternoon. Can you make it?

- Of course, answered Karen, barely believing her ears.

- Then I will confirm the meeting. I must go now as I am very busy. See you tonight, darling.

On Wednesday afternoon, as agreed, Karen met with the agent. He did not promise anything as he first wanted to read the book, but he assured her that if he liked what he saw, he would do everything possible to help her.

A few weeks went by. Karen, although she did not show her preoccupation, was very anxious to have an answer back. One Monday morning, when she was alone at home, she heard the telephone and after two rings, picked it up.

- Mrs. Abadi? a woman inquired.

- Yes, this is she.

- This is Carol. I am a secretary at Century publishers. How are you?

- Very well, thank you, she responded nervously.

- Mr. Paulton would like to speak with you. Please hold on the line.

- Good day, Karen. I am calling to tell you that your

book has been accepted. We had three of our best critics read it and they all came to the same conclusion independently. Your book has the potential to be a success. It will be necessary to make a few changes in a couple of chapters and do the editing work, but in general, we like the idea of publication and will work with you to make it happen.

He paused, then continued:

- Now, you must be prepared to work with us. Since it is your first novel, you are perhaps not familiar with the steps needed to bring a book to publication.

- Of course, I will cooperate fully.

- In that case, congratulations! My secretary will be in touch with you to advise you of our next meeting.

- I will see you soon, he said, saying goodbye and she hung up the phone.

With a pleasant feeling of utter satisfaction, she plunked herself down on the chair beside the telephone and exclaimed aloud:

- Can it be true or am I dreaming? They have really accepted my book!

After a few moments, when she had recovered from the surprise, she called Philip at the office to tell him the good news.

- Congratulations from the bottom of my heart, darling. Wonderful! My wife is going to be famous!

- Don't make fun of me, she answered, a bit hurt.

- Make fun of you? Nonsense! David Paulton is one of the best publishers today. If he has decided to publish your book it is because he thinks it is excellent.

- I cannot believe it. It all seems too wonderful for words.

- Believe it! I am very proud of you.

The next day, Carol called her to set up an appointment at the publisher's offices. After the call, Karen suddenly found herself in an endless round of meetings, contracts, negotiations, and agreements.

One morning, when she was in the waiting room of Mr. Paulton's office, she noticed the secretary looking sad.

- I don't want to butt in, she said cautiously, but you look so sad and you have always seemed so happy and full of life. Can I do anything to help?

Carol, hearing Karen's words, broke down in tears.

- Please, don't cry, she begged. Have I said anything to upset you?

- No ma'am, quite the contrary. To tell you the truth, it is that my family has been suffering because of recent events in the world.

- What do you mean? Karen asked compassionately.

- Because of what happened at the twin towers in New York, on September eleventh.

My husband was working in the first tower at the time and although he did not die, he was left permanently disabled. Eighty percent of his body was covered with third degree burns and despite all the scientific progress and his deep desire to live, he has been confined to a wheelchair for life; and now, I have to support all of us by myself. We have three small children and sometimes I despair just trying to take care of our basic needs.

- I understand your pain, Karen answered inmediately. This tragedy that you just mentioned has set off a series of events that have changed the world, filling us all with pain, uncertainty and mistrust.

Al-Qaeda and other radical Islamic groups are destroying the world peace and if we don't stop them in time we will all be lost.

Just then, they heard a buzz from the adjoining office.

- Mr. Paulton will see you now, Carol told her, her voice still shaky with emotion.

- We should talk some more later, but I want to promise you something. I will pray for you and your family. Only God in his goodness and justice has the ability to remove from the human race that evil desire to destroy others.

- Thank you for your words. You are a good person.

She reached over to give the secretary a hug and then went into the office.

- I am sorry for the delay, Mr. Paulton said to her, shaking hands.

- Not to worry.

- I wanted to meet with you today to tell you of our decision to translate your novel into English for publication in the United States simultaneouly with that in Central and South America. He paused, then continued:

- The main reason is the current situation of tension in the world with its similarity to the Second World War and the consequences this entails for all humanity. This has awakened a new interest in learning about the past and it is an excellent opportunity for us to distribute your novel. I have already received several calls from North American publishing companies that want to distribute your work in the United States.

- That is amazing, Karen gasped.

- Well, believe it, my dear lady. We have something very good here.

Chapter 44

The book, "Inhuman Conspiracy", was already on display in bookstores in the major cities throughout North and South America. The first reviews appearing in newspapers and literary journals seemed to be generally favorable and this augured well. It was a moving and genuine story, written simply and from the heart, and was quickly becoming a bestseller. Given the successful publication of this book and the fact that the market was looking very positive for a future publication, the Abadi family had decided to hold a party at home to thank all those who had participated in the efforts to see the book through to publication.

At seven-thirty pm, Philip opened the front door to his house and quickly entered and strode upstairs, where one of the maids greeted him.

- Good evening, sir. Your wife is waiting for you in the den.

- Please, tell her that I am going to change and will be there in a moment.

- Yes, sir, the girl answered.

Karen had nodded off. Petra, despite the fact she was

the housekeeper who had been with the family the longest, did not dare to wake her mistress and decided to leave the task to the master. Half an hour later, he came into the den and giving her a soft caress, woke her.

- Hello, my dear, he said softly. Are you planning on coming to our party?

- Oh, I must have nodded off. Are our guests here already?

- Not yet. They should arrive at nine pm.

She sighed with relief and taking her husband's hand in hers, pulled him gently to sit beside her.

- I have been thinking about everything that has happened to my family from their life in Poland until arriving at where we are today. It all inspires me so. This chain of events has marked my life.

- Let us toast the past generations of your family, Philip proposed, getting up and moving over to the bar. He took out a bottle of his favorite champagne, Dom Perignon, that had been chilling for the occasion, and opened it with a familiar twist, filled two goblets and put the bottle on ice in a silver bucket, then raised a toast with his life companion.

Karen held the crystal goblet by the slim base and raised it near her face, then pronounced these words with heartfelt emotion:

- Thanks to the perseverance of my ancestors, who survived and arrived in South America, there will be no more tears in our family – only happiness from now on, and wherever they are, I know they are sharing our joy today. I pray that humanity can somehow eradicate war and that peace will reign over our earth.

Philip clinked his glass with hers and after a sip of the bubbly golden liquid, added somewhat gloomily:

- I share your noble desire, but history has to show us otherwise. Human cruelty seems to return like weeds in the garden and if you do not pull them up by the roots, they will grow back, with a legacy of hatred and destruction. Faith can move people to reach unimaginable spiritual heights or inspire them to destroy the world; it is unfortunate, that the latter is the choice of most.

God has endowed humans with a great capacity to love their neighbors, which develops qualities of compassion, kindness, peace and spirituality, and likewise, "He" instilled the love for ourselves, providing us with a defense mechanism and preservation. However, for genetic, economic or social reasons, many individuals develop excessive self-love, which generates among other things, envy, greed, egotism, and consequently hatred and cruelty.

The basic problem lies in the case of these unscrupulous people, which has been proven through history, to justify their selfish and Machiavellian ends and to convince their followers that their cause is just and reasonable, they usually act on behalf of God and religion. Hidden behind these flags, they have committed and continue to commit the greatest crimes and atrocities against humanity.

As you know Karen, I am more spiritual than religious, however it continues to amaze me that religions such as Judaism, Christianity and Islam, despite having the same father: the patriarch Abraham, and the same origin of their religion, instead of seeking spiritual growth to bring us closer to God, fight among each other to defend the religious differences that divide us, and have generated unusual events in history and today.

During the time of the Crusades and the Inquisition, Christians in Spain in the name of God and the Catholic Church, and for purposes of "purification" expelled and exterminated Muslims and Jews. Hitler, inspired by the Crusades and with the excuse of "purifying the Aryan race", wiped out millions of Jews and non-Aryans.

At this time, Islamic Radicalism with the same "precepts of purification" has proposed to vanish off the face of the earth, all those people considered infidels because they do not profess the same beliefs. Based on the hatred in the concept of God and religion, has declared war on the Jewish people, Western society, Protestants and Christians alike.

Despite everything, the moral code of Jews and Christians is based on God's word and the Ten Commandments, and over the past sixty years a friendlier relationship has been created with mutual respect for the differing beliefs.

"The Passion" is a representation of the religious divide that exists between Jews and Catholics. The death of Jesus was interpreted eighty years later by unscrupulous people seeking to increase their influence and become powerful religious leaders. The story of Jesus was passed along orally from generation to generation, with a tendency to become exaggerated and embellished. The one certain thing is that the Romans dominated the land at that time and those who tried to oppose their will faced the death penalty. Thousand of people were crucified at that time, without concern for beliefs or origin, and the purpose for the Romans was to dominate the country and the people at any cost.

The birth of a Jewish child and his ties to his religion and beliefs, were the foundation for the history of the events that followed.

Jesus, with his goodness, faith in God, and love for his fellow man, was a great scholar and wished to show people the way back to God through the teaching that his ancestors had given him. He was able to attract multitudes, which at those times of suffering sought refuge in the Supreme Being to face the unbearable difficulty of their lives.

The Romans, seeing the danger that Jesus represented for their plans of domination, decided to crucify him and created the story that he represented the king of the Jews. They wanted to make a mockery of him but did not take into account the pain they caused to his family and all those who loved him and for whom he had represented a haven of peace and love to give them strength to face the misery in their lives.

This story was recorded and finally, someone decided to benefit from it and tell it in a way that served his purposes while gaining converts. Thus, the religious intolerance was born that divides us today and has caused many wars and so much pain.

Karen, motivated by the explanations and views of Phillip asked:

- Tell me my love, what do you think the future holds?

- Phillip, pursing his lips and clenched his chin, nodded in sad acceptance and continued saying:

- Today, the Jewish people are facing a new attempt on their life and safety, similar to that experienced in 1930.

The anti-Semitism had been declining around the world, since the end of World War II, but in recent years, is returning armed with the powers of global terrorism.

I hope, Phillip said vehemently, that the atrocities of the Holocaust will never happen again, but I see coming with concern, uncertain times, as the anti-Semitism continues to be a form of religious and ethical intolerance that neither the lessons of the past could erase, with tragic consequences for all those who yearn for a just and peaceful world.

A knock at the door interrupted their conversation.

- The guests are arriving, Petra announced.

- Thank you, he answered, we are on our way.

The band started playing classical music. Philip and Karen, leaving the den, gave a last look around the living room, which was sumptuous with its tables covered in gold lame, with tulle tablecloths in the same color. The tall floral centerpieces were set in transparent Murano glass and crowned by white, cascading flowers, with a mixture of roses, tulips, eucalyptus, small orchids, and four lit candles in the very center. The carefully chosen buffet table, laden with platters of succulent food, was equally elaborate. The colors and mixture of flavors looked very appetizing. The chef was a veritable artist and had carved a beautiful ice sculpture in the shape of a swan to set off the rest of the table. The meats were fine and abundant. From the caviar and salmon to the pheasant, turkey and veal. The multi-colored salads delighted the eye and the sweet table, with mirrored and beribboned platters, gave a feeling of elegance to the guests choosing their dessert from the large variety of pastries and small cakes.

- Here comes Mr. Paulton and his wife, Karen whispered to her husband. Let's go and say hello.

The guests continued to arrive. The Abadis, holding hands, greeted each one with a smile, and received from each one good wishes for the success of the book. They could see the admiration of their friends reflected in their eyes. As everyone settled in, the band began to play the Blue Danube waltz. Philip held out his hand to his wife and she, with the majesty and grace of a great lady, accepted his invitation. They arose and went together to the dance floor.

- You look radiant. I am so proud of you, he whispered in her ear.

- And I love you, she answered tenderly. I owe to you this moment of supreme happiness, because you have been my mentor and help through it all.

The strains of the waltz continued to reverberate, reminiscent of the Viennese empire, as they felt themselves transported in the swirling dance to a lovely paradise.